Once a
LAIRD

ROGUES REDEEMED

MARY JO
PUTNEY

CANELO

First published in the USA in 2021 by ZEBRA BOOKS, an imprint of
Kensington Publishing Corp.

This edition published in the United Kingdom in 2021 by

Canelo
Unit 9, 5th Floor
Cargo Works, 1-2 Hatfields
London, SE1 9PG
United Kingdom

A CIP catalogue record for this book is available from the British Library.

Print ISBN 978 1 80032 582 1
Ebook ISBN 978 1 80032 581 4

This book is a work of fiction. Names, characters, businesses, organizations,
places and events are either the product of the author's imagination or are
used fictitiously. Any resemblance to actual persons, living or dead, events
or locales is entirely coincidental.

Look for more great books at www.canelo.co

Printed and bound in Great Britain by Clays Ltd, Elcograf S.p.A.

1

Once a Laird

Mary Jo Putney is the *New York Times* and *USA Today* bestselling author of more than sixty novels and novellas. A ten-time finalist for the Romance Writers of America RITA® award, she has won the honor twice and is on the RWA Honor Roll for bestselling authors. In 2013 she was awarded the RWA Nora Roberts Lifetime Achievement Award. Though most of her books have been historical romance, she has also published contemporary romances, historical fantasy, and young adult paranormal historicals. She lives in Maryland with her nearest and dearest, both two- and four-footed. Visit her at MaryJoPutney.com.

Also by Mary Jo Putney

Rogues Redeemed

For all the frontline workers who have kept the wheels of civilization turning in these very difficult times.

Thank you.

Chapter 1

The letter was dirty and folded, not surprising considering how far it had come. Ramsay was reluctant to break the seal because he had a strong suspicion what it would say. He was right.

The letter was addressed to Kai Douglas Ramsay and said tersely:

> Kai,
>
>   Time to stop playing around and come home, laddie boy. Your grandfather is dying. He may be swilling ale in Valhalla by the time you get this. You know the price you promised to pay for your footloose wandering. Now the bill has come due.
>
>   Signy Matheson
>   Skellig House
>   Mainland, Thorsay
>   Scotland

Of course it would be Signy who was writing him. Only islanders he'd known as a boy would call him Kai. Signy had become his grandfather's deputy as well as being the head schoolmistress in the islands. Ramsay smiled a little, remembering her as a knobby-kneed girl with a tongue that could flay a whale when she was in a critical mood. She was the younger sister of Gisela, his first and only love.

His smile faded. After laying the letter on his desk, he moved to the window and gazed out at the domes and minarets of Constantinople, which were visible above the walls that surrounded the British embassy compound. He'd spent five years here, the longest time he'd lingered anywhere in his wandering years.

His official position was Under Secretary for Special Projects, a vague enough title to cover his various nefarious activities. With all the layers of history in Constantinople, he could spend a lifetime here and barely scratch the wonders of this city and this land.

It was hard to imagine a place more different from the far northern islands of his homeland. But Ramsay had always known his time here was limited. He might have stayed in Thorsay if Gisela hadn't died suddenly of a fever when he was finishing his studies at the University of Edinburgh. The pain was so numbing that he'd been unable to bear the thought of returning to the islands.

His grandfather, the wily old devil, had known how Ramsay would feel. After giving the news of Gisela's death, the laird had said that Ramsay could feed his wanderlust until his grandfather died or was near death. Then he must come home to assume his responsibilities as Laird of Thorsay.

Ramsay had seized on the proffered bargain, both because he couldn't imagine returning to Thorsay with Gisela gone and because he'd yearned to visit distant lands and study ancient ruins. He'd had a dozen years of that freedom and had managed not to get himself killed, though it had been a near-run thing more than once.

That led him to thoughts of a certain cellar in Portugal where he'd been held captive with four other men as they drank bad brandy and waited to be executed at dawn. But the five of them had worked together to escape and made a pact to meet up again after the war if they survived. Now Napoleon was gone for good, exiled to a bleak rock in the South Atlantic to rule over the seabirds, and perhaps that reunion would be possible.

How many of the men who had been in that cellar were still among the living? They'd all been leading risky lives. When Ramsay traveled through London on his way home, he could check for letters at Hatchard's Bookshop, which had been their chosen venue to exchange information.

Ramsay forced his wandering mind back to practical matters. Though he'd wished this day would never come, he'd been mentally preparing. It was time to make the long journey through the Mediterranean, west around the Iberian Peninsula, then north through the English Channel and North Sea to Thorsay.

The three island groups north of Scotland were due west of Norway, closer to Oslo than London. Orkney was visible, barely, from the northernmost coast of mainland Scotland. Thorsay lay beyond, and far-flung Shetland was most northerly. All three archipelagos were inhabited by tough, stubborn islanders whose first language was Norn, a Scandinavian dialect. Over the centuries, Gaelic-speaking Celts had also settled on the islands, and even a few English. No wonder the Thorseach, the people of his islands, were good with languages.

Ramsay turned to his painting of the Egyptian pyramids set against a blazing sunset sky. The picture was hinged on one side, and he swung it away from the wall to reveal the mirror mounted on the back.

He concealed the mirror to avoid being accused of vanity. Its real purpose was so he could check his appearance when he was dressing up in local clothing in order to travel through the teeming city without being recognized as a foreigner.

He studied his face. Years spent in the sun had tanned and weathered his complexion so he looked much like a native of this part of the world. He had also dyed his hair dark brown so he wouldn't stand out as a Northern European. He'd stop the dyeing, so by the time he reached the British Isles, his natural light brown hair would have grown in.

He turned to gaze around his office and over the scattered mementoes of his travels. They'd have to be carefully packed for the journey home.

He lifted a richly decorated silver mirror from Italy. Gisela would have loved it. If she'd lived, the shape of his life would be completely different, yet he could barely remember her face. She'd been sweet and funny and very, very pretty. He would have returned from Edinburgh and married her, and they'd likely have had children by now.

Ramsay would never have seen the sun set behind the pyramids, but he wouldn't have known the loneliness of his solitary years. Would his life have been better or worse if she had lived? Impossible to say. Certainly it would have been significantly different.

Face set, he left his office and headed down a floor to see the ambassador. There was no reason to delay handing in his resignation. Once he did that, his life here would be officially over.

He thought he'd have to make an appointment, but the secretary said, "Sir Robert is available, so you can go right in."

No reprieve here. Ramsay knocked on the door, then entered. Sir Robert Liston glanced up from his desk. A Scot, he'd studied languages at the University of Edinburgh as Ramsay had done several decades later. Ramsay had used their common history to persuade the ambassador to create this unusual position for him as part of the British delegation.

Sir Robert started to rise, then settled back into his chair with a frown. "The evil day has arrived?"

Sir Robert was a perceptive fellow. Ramsay replied, "I've just received a message summoning me back to Thorsay."

The ambassador's frown deepened. "Have you considered refusing the summons? Surely there are others who would leap at the chance to become the next laird, but there is no one else who can do the work you do here. Your skills are unique."

"My deviousness and affinity for disreputable rogues, you mean," Ramsay said dryly.

Sir Robert smiled. "Exactly. Most of the young gentlemen who join Britain's diplomatic corps are entirely too conventional. Good for many things, but not for what you do so well."

For a moment Ramsay allowed himself to consider the older man's suggestion. If he refused the call, another laird would be found and he'd be free to continue learning and exploring and quite possibly dying in some violent way.

No. He'd promised to return and take up his responsibilities not once but twice. The first vow had been made to his grandfather, the second seven years ago in that damp cellar in Portugal. He and his fellow captives had spent a long night drinking and discussing what they would do with their lives if by some miracle they survived.

All had spoken of becoming better men and redeeming past sins. Ramsay had privately renewed his vow to answer the call to Thorsay when the time came. Though he'd make no more wondrous discoveries, he'd gathered enough notes to spend the rest of his life writing scholarly articles about what he'd observed in his wandering years.

The thought was not exciting, but at least his conscience would be clear. "This is one call I can't refuse, Sir Robert."

The ambassador nodded regretfully. "The trouble with honorable men is that they're honorable. When will you be leaving?"

"As soon as possible. The letter I received was written when my grandfather was still alive. Perhaps he still is." Ramsay would like to say good-bye if possible. He and the old laird had fought like two cats in a sack, but there had been real affection under the fireworks.

"You islanders are a tough lot. I hope he'll be there to swear at you one last time." Sir Robert unlocked a lower desk drawer and produced a bottle of good Scots whisky and two glass tumblers. "A toast to the old laird, and thanks to you for all the nefarious and useful things you've done for Britain."

He poured a couple of fingers of whisky in the glasses, handed one to Ramsay, and lifted his in a toast. "To auld lang syne."

"To auld lang syne," Ramsay repeated before downing the whisky in one long burning swallow. "Next Hogmanay I'll be in Scotland."

"I envy you." The ambassador leaned forward and poured more whisky into Ramsay's glass. "Lift a glass for me, lad."

"I will," Ramsay promised. But by God, he'd miss this part of the world!

Chapter 2

Ramsay's voyage home benefited from fair winds and was swifter than expected. The light became bluer and the winds more chill as he traveled north. By the time he reached London, Constantinople was only a distant sunburned memory.

He spent several days in London attending to business and staying at Thorsay House, which was owned by the laird of Thorsay. The Browns, the couple who maintained the house, hadn't heard that the old laird was dead, so perhaps Ramsay's grandfather was still holding on.

Thorsay House served as a way station for traveling Thorsayians. Ramsay found that he'd just missed a favorite cousin, Kendra Douglas, who had taken refuge in the house after a disastrous scandal. As a girl, she'd been a lively little thing. He'd taught her and Signy Matheson and several other younger children the basics of fencing.

He stopped at Hatchard's and found a trove of letters from the Rogues Redeemed of the Portuguese cellar. Impressively, they all had survived the wars, and while he was in London, he managed to dine with one of the men, named Hawkins, and his intrepid wife, Lady Rory. Then he set sail again, first to Edinburgh and finally, on a small coastal trading vessel, the last stretch to Thorsay.

Ramsay spent much of this last leg of his long journey in the bow of the boat, feeling an unnerving sense of homecoming. The silvery seas and austere scattered islands seemed to be bred into his bones despite his reluctance to return.

When the vessel finally moored at the pier below Skellig House, Ramsay left the deckhands to unload his luggage. Personal possessions were few, but there were a fair number of the best ancient artifacts he'd found.

Impatiently he climbed the hill to the Ramsay family home. Skellig House was a low, sprawling stone structure designed to stand against the fiercest winds off the North Sea. In the distance beyond, he could just see one of the circle of towering stone monoliths erected by the ancient inhabitants of these islands.

Nothing seemed to have changed in the dozen years since he'd left. His pace quickened as he wondered whether his grandfather still lived.

As he approached the entrance to the house, the door swung open and someone stepped out, his gaze turned toward Ramsay. No, not a man but a tall woman—that was clear from the way the wind shaped her gray gown around an undeniably female figure. The same wind rippled her blazing red-gold hair like a banner of war.

She brushed her wind-whipped hair from her face and said in a voice colder than an Arctic gale, "What took you so long, Kai?"

He stopped dead in his tracks and stared. In the years he'd been gone, bony little Signy Matheson had become a damned Nordic goddess!

As the sweetheart of her older sister, he'd seen a great deal of Signy. She'd been a delightful little girl, full of energy and curiosity and with a quick, clever tongue. He guessed that her grimness now was because of the laird's impending death. The old man had taken her into Skellig

House after Gisela died and had been like a father to her. She'd been mentioned often in his grandfather's letters. Now Signy was about to lose him as she'd lost the rest of her family.

Speaking English, Ramsay said, "Well met, Signy Matheson. Is the laird still among the living?"

Her eyes narrowed. "He's still alive, though barely. Fortunate that you made good time. He's been hoping his unreliable grandson would return for a last scolding."

Signy replied in Norn, the traditional dialect of Thorsay, and from the malicious glint in her eyes, she wanted to see if he could still speak it. Years had passed since he'd heard the ancient tongue. It took a moment of mental adjustment for her words to make sense, but he'd always had a gift for languages. Ramsay relaxed a little. "I'm glad to hear he's still with us," he replied in Norn. "Can I see him?"

"I think he's awake now, but he's very weak. He'll not last much longer."

"Then I mustn't waste any time." Ramsay turned to the stairs that led up to his grandfather's rooms, but Signy stopped him with a gesture. "We made up a bed in the library for him."

In other words, his grandfather was unable to climb the stairs and it was easier to tend him on the ground floor of the house. "That was always his favorite room, I think."

"Where should I have your things put?" she asked in a flat tone.

Ramsay realized she was asking if he wanted to take over the laird's rooms upstairs. *No.* Not while his grandfather still lived. Maybe never. "If my old room is available, that will be fine. If not, any room will do."

"Your old room, then. It's been empty since the last time you left for university."

Expression grim, Ramsay gave a short nod and headed through the house. The library was spacious and in a corner of the house, so there were windows on two sides. Bookcases rose to the ceiling; the size and quality of the library had always been a point of pride for the lairds of Thorsay.

But the long oak worktable was gone, replaced by a bed and a new bedside table that held medicines, books, a lamp, and a huge gray cat with one eye and ragged ears. As the cat glared at him, Ramsay tried to conceal his flinching from the sickroom smells of medicine and a deteriorating body. Duncan Ramsay had been a tall, powerfully built man, and the bony, painfully thin shape under the covers on the massive bed was shocking. For a horrific moment Ramsay feared the old laird was already dead.

Then his grandfather turned his head, the pale blue eyes flickering open. "So you made it home, Kai," he said in a labored whisper. "You look like something a dolphin coughed up."

"It's a long journey from Constantinople, and the last sail up from Dundee was one squall after another." Smiling a little, Ramsay pulled a chair over to the bedside and sat where he could see his grandfather's face. "I'm glad you're still here. It would be a pity to come so far and not be greeted by any insults."

The laird laughed, then began to cough as if his lungs were failing. Ramsay froze, wondering if he should call for help, but the coughing stopped and his grandfather said in a rasping voice, "Pour me some of that whisky."

"Is that allowed?" Ramsay asked as he stood and moved to the table to obey.

"Why the hell would I stop? Fear that it will kill me?"

"Hard to argue with that." Ramsay moved to the table to get the whisky, and the gray cat swatted him with an annoyed paw. He pulled his hand back, smiling. His grandfather had always liked cats. "Who's your one-eyed friend?"

"Odin, of course. The one-eyed chief god of the Norsemen." The laird stretched out a thin hand and scratched the cat's neck, receiving a thunderous purr in return. "This Odin isn't a god, but he does rule all the cats in the area."

Ramsay used the distraction to collect the whisky bottle and a pair of tumblers. "Does he get whisky as well?"

"Only if it's splashed into cream."

"I'm glad to learn that Skellig House is maintaining its reputation for splendid eccentricity." Ramsay poured two fingers of whisky into one tumbler and the same for himself in the other.

His grandfather received the drink with a shaking hand but didn't spill any as he drank half the whisky in one long swallow. "Didn't think you'd come back. Thought you'd choose Constantinople and your damned old stones."

Ramsay felt a tangle of emotions: annoyance, amusement, and relief that the old devil was still himself despite his failing body. "When have you known me to break my word?"

"Never, but you must have been tempted."

"Very briefly." Ramsay sipped his drink cautiously; some forms of the local spirits could etch iron. But this was Callan's, the islands' best—a smooth, well-aged whisky with the taste of Thorsay smoke and peat. The taste of home. He took a larger sip. "But I knew Grandmother would haunt me if I didn't return."

"Aye, she would," Duncan said with a snort of laughter. "Caitlin is waiting for me on the other side, tapping her foot with impatience because I haven't joined her yet."

Ramsay smiled wistfully at the image. After the deaths of his parents, he'd been raised by his grandparents. His grandmother Caitlin had been a true Thorsayian woman—strong, beautiful, and fiercely independent. "I'm sure you're right, and that you're equally anxious to see her."

His grandfather made a gruff sound that was neither assent nor disagreement. Thinking it was time for a change of subject, Ramsay said, "I brought you a present." He pulled an ancient coin from an inside coat pocket. Gold glinted in the thin sunshine as he put it into his grandfather's gnarled hand.

Duncan squinted at the coin. "Is it Greek or Roman?"

"No, it's much older than that. It comes from an ancient civilization we don't know much about. A people that originated in the Eastern Mediterranean and were called the Canaanites or Phoenicians."

"Like in the Bible?"

"Yes, though no one is sure exactly what the name covered. It seems to be a general term for different peoples of the Eastern Mediterranean. The Greeks called them Phoenicians. They were great seafarers. Their trade routes covered the whole of the Mediterranean and somewhat beyond. If you look closely at the coin, you'll see that one side depicts a ship with armed warriors and some kind of sea beast."

"Huh," Duncan said, interested. "Like our Viking ancestors."

"Exactly. And like the Vikings, they established towns and settlements that became trading ports."

"A thalassocracy then." Seeing Ramsay's expression, his grandfather gave a hoarse laugh. "Didn't expect me to remember my Greek, did you? Thalassocrats. People who settled along the shores but weren't interested in conquering inland." He turned the coin over and squinted at the embossed head on the other side. "Who's the curly-haired fellow?"

"I have no idea," Ramsay said cheerfully. "A king, presumably, but it will take a lot more study before we know things like that. There are so many ancient civilizations we know almost nothing about. I've spent much time in my traveling years looking for traces of these Phoenicians. That almost got me killed in Portugal. I don't suppose I told you the whole story."

His grandfather's ferocious brows drew together in a frown equal to his best. "It was some years back. You wrote that you'd visited Porto to look at some nearby ruins but the French decided to invade and you left in a hurry."

"That was true as far as it went, but it was a much more exciting visit than that." Ramsay thought dryly that *exciting* meant damned near lethal. "Porto is on the north bank of the estuary of the Douro River, with the smaller city of Gaia on the south bank. The bridges over the river were destroyed to stop the French advance, but the residents of Porto were desperate to escape, so a temporary bridge was cobbled up out of small boats lashed together."

"I read about that," Duncan said, his voice thready but his interest obvious. "The bridge of boats broke apart. Many of those trying to cross drowned, including a number of women and children."

Ramsay nodded grimly. "They'll never know the true death toll, but it was chaos as people on the shores tried to rescue as many victims as possible. I was part of a group pulling out nuns and their little girl students. We were successful, but by chance, several of the other men were also British. A French colonel captured everyone suspicious and threw us into a cellar so we could be shot in the morning as British spies. There were four Britons and one Royalist Frenchman unlucky enough to be caught in the net."

The bushy brows rose. "Obviously you didn't die."

"One of the group figured out an escape route. Working together, we managed to get out before dawn," Ramsay explained. "It was a memorable night. Having shared bad brandy and danger, the five of us have kept in touch in a haphazard sort of way. We all seem to have survived the wars, amazingly."

"For which I'm grateful," Duncan said in a rasping voice. "The living people here need you more than the dead stones do. There is much work to be done in Thorsay."

"Is it me that's needed? The fact that I'm your grandson doesn't necessarily make me the best choice to be the next laird," Ramsay said bluntly. "I grew up here, but I've been away for almost half my life."

"Thorsay needs new ideas and new energy. You're a natural leader and are Thorsay's best hope for the future." Duncan's voice was barely audible. "The day-to-day business you can learn from Signy. She's been a godsend these last years."

"You should name her the laird," Ramsay said half seriously.

The faintest of smiles showed on Duncan's face. "I considered it. But she's not close blood kin. She was born in Norway. And she's a woman."

"All true, but she'd still make a better laird than I will."

"Probably." Duncan sighed and his eyes drifted shut. "You should marry her."

Ramsay stared, wondering if that was a serious suggestion. Surely not! But the conversation was over, as his grandfather had fallen asleep. With the animation gone from the old man's face, he looked next door to death. As Ramsay rose wearily, Odin leaped from the table to the bed and curled up next to the laird's right side. After one last glare at Ramsay, he closed his eye, tucked his nose under his tail, and fell asleep.

Ramsay left the sickroom, feeling the fatigue of his long journey and of the expectations laid on him. He was grateful that no one else was about. With a sudden desperate need for fresh air, he left the house and headed south on the path that led along the bluffs edging the sea. The brisk wind cleared his head, and his legs appreciated the chance to stretch.

The path led to Clanwick, the capital and most sizable town on Mainland, Thorsay's largest island. Clanwick was built on the best harbor in the islands, so it had become the center of commerce.

Thorsay consisted of a multitude of islands, some no more than wave-splashed rocks. Most of the larger islands had residents, usually a few families that farmed and fished. All of the inhabited islands had been as familiar as the back of Ramsay's hand when he was a boy. Growing up, he'd always seen Thorsay as his destiny. Now he wondered what the devil he'd do with himself for all the years that lay ahead.

The path led past a shallow cove on his left that was edged by a pleasant little beach where Ramsay and the other children used to swim. The beach was a favorite sunning spot of local seals. He smiled down at the half dozen that basked on the sand like dark furry teardrops. Traditionally seals and swimmers left each other alone. Humans had to be in harmony with nature to survive on these far northern islands.

The coastline rose as he walked along, turning from a gentle bluff into a cliff that loomed over the North Sea as waves broke fiercely on the rocks below. At the highest point a couple of weathered benches had been placed for walkers who wanted to rest and enjoy the view.

Ignoring the benches, he paused to survey the landscape. To the right, he could see Clanwick in the distance, ship masts visible in the harbor and the tower of the sturdy little cathedral of St. Magnus rising above the houses and shops.

Directly ahead of him was a massive islet with a half-dozen rocky outcroppings scattered around it. The grouping was called the whale and her daughters.

He was a long, long way from the deserts and mountains of Asia Minor. His gaze dropped to the waves crashing at the foot of the cliff. Despairing people had been known to jump here if they were seeking a quick end to their misery.

"Why don't you jump?" a harsh female voice said from behind him. "It would save everyone a great deal of trouble."

Startled to discover he wasn't alone, he pivoted and found Signy Matheson watching him with ice in her eyes, her red-gold hair and golden shawl snapping in the wind.

"Sorry, I'm not the suicidal sort," he said mildly. "Are you angry because I'll inherit even though you're the one who has been here doing the work of running Thorsay? I suggested to my grandfather that he designate you as the new laird, but he cited several reasons why that wasn't possible. A pity, because you would do a better job than I."

"Very likely," she said, her gaze smoldering. "But that isn't the reason I want you gone."

"Envy that I've been able to travel and you haven't?" he said softly. As a gangly young girl, she'd been fascinated by his books and maps of distant places.

Her eyes narrowed as she spat out, "I can't bear the sight of you because you murdered my sister!"

Chapter 3

Signy hadn't meant to say that, but years of pent-up anger had hurled the words from her mouth without her conscious will. She wanted him to suffer as she had suffered. And if he showed no grief or guilt, she might push him off the cliff herself.

Shocked, Ramsay exclaimed, "I was hundreds of miles away in Edinburgh and planning to return home to marry Gisela! I had nothing to do with her death."

"Wrong!" Signy said with bitter intensity. "She didn't die of a fever. She died of a miscarriage and bled to death in my arms."

He stared at her, aghast, his usual calm shattered. "That's impossible!"

"Are you saying you never lay with her? You'll not call my sister a liar!" Signy said furiously.

"Only once! We didn't mean to, but I was leaving for months and we both... lost all good judgment." He stopped, his face ashen. "It never occurred to me that there had been... consequences, because she wrote when I was back in Edinburgh and said I had nothing to worry about."

"She was protecting you, more fool she! As she lay dying, she made me promise to conceal what had happened." Signy closed her eyes, memories of that terrible night more real than this island afternoon. "I promised and never said a word to anyone. Until now."

She and her sister had been constant companions, coming with their mother to Thorsay after their Norwegian father died, helping their mother teach in the Skellig schoolhouse. Growing up to become teachers themselves.

Nothing—*nothing*—had ever hurt as much as losing Gisela. The grief and rage she'd bottled up for all these years erupted with shattering force. She buried her face in her hands as she began to sob uncontrollably.

She swung around, desperate to hide her humiliating tears from the man who was the cause of her anguish. She stumbled and nearly fell, wondering if she was going to tumble from the cliff herself. Perhaps that would be for the best...

Strong arms came around her with crushing force. Ramsay held her, his anguished voice whispering raggedly, "I didn't know. *I didn't know!*"

Signy wanted to fight him off, but bleakly she recognized that his grief matched hers. She and Ramsay had been the ones who loved Gisela best, but because of her promise, Signy had mourned alone.

In the midst of her grief, she felt tendrils of relief, as if an infected wound had been lanced. Until now her sister's death had been buried in secrets and Signy's anger with Ramsay had festered for years. As she clung to him, her anger began to fade away, leaving only deep sadness. If he and Signy could have mourned together, there would have been less anger.

He held her for long minutes until all her tears were exhausted. Despite her years of hating him, there was a strange but welcome comfort in the warmth of his arms. Reluctantly she stepped back, pushing her straggling hair from her face as she studied his expression. He looked as unnerved by that unexpected embrace as she was.

Since she'd be seeing a great deal of him, she needed to sort out her feelings. As a little girl, she'd adored her sister's suitor. He'd always been Kai then, and he'd been a good-natured big brother to Signy. She'd loved that he would become a member of her family. Losing Gisela had meant also losing him.

"I'm sorry for exploding at you," she said quietly. "Gisela's death wasn't your fault. Her health was always delicate. She wasn't a great healthy horse like me. You couldn't have done anything even if you'd been here."

He shook his head, his expression raw with grief. "Perhaps, but if she'd told me she was with child, I would have returned immediately. Please believe that!"

"I do believe you. I told Gisela she should write you her news, but she was determined to let you finish at university." Signy sighed. "She calculated that you'd be back in Thorsay before her pregnancy became obvious."

"I could and should have been with her," he said tightly. "You and I could have shared the burden rather than leaving you to manage all alone. You were what, fifteen? Hardly more than a child yourself. Too young to carry so much."

"Perhaps, but I had no choice." Signy hadn't felt young since her sister had died. "I never should have promised her that I'd keep silent, but I felt I had to. My promise was the only thing I could give her as she lay dying."

"I understand, but I'm glad you broke that promise today, because it gives us a chance to clear the air," Ramsay said quietly. "If we're going to be working together for the near future, it's better not to have any great dark secrets between us."

She nodded agreement. "That's part of the reason I broke down and told you. Ever since I wrote to say it was time to come home, the laird has been telling me that I will have to train you in all that must be done. I couldn't face that when I was so angry."

"You're lucky that all he suggested was that you tutor me in the job," Ramsay retorted. "He just told me that I should marry you."

She laughed with astonishment. "I'm glad to hear that the old devil's sense of humor hasn't left him yet!"

Ramsay gave her a wry smile. "It's rather disturbing that you find the thought so laughable."

She scanned his expression. His brief flare of emotion over Gisela's death had disappeared, and his gray eyes were again as cool and enigmatic as when he'd arrived at Skellig House. He'd been a good-looking youth, and years and experience had shaped him into a handsome man with a compelling aura of command. That would serve him well as the laird, though she doubted he was as likable now as he'd been when he was Gisela's sweetheart.

In theory he was good husband material, but she'd thought of him first as a brother, then as a brother she despised. She couldn't imagine having romantic feelings for him no matter how attractive he was. "There will be no shortage of Thorsayian girls applying for the position of your wife, and most of them are better tempered than I am."

"So you're going to be a terrifying teacher. Not the first such I've had." He gestured toward the benches. "It's time for my first lesson. Where do I even begin learning how to be a good laird?"

Surprised, she said, "Don't you want to go into Clan-wick?"

"Not today. I only took this path because I wanted some fresh air." He settled on one end of the bench, frowning as he gazed down the coast toward Skellig House. "Is it my imagination, or has the coastline changed shape?"

"It's not your imagination," she replied as she sat on the far end of his bench and pulled her shawl more tightly against the wind. It was always windy here. "Thorsay has storms of all sizes but very rarely any of the great hurricanes. But one of those struck two summers ago. Chunks of the shore were torn away. In South Cronsay, a cottage with four people in it was dragged into the sea."

"Did they survive?" he asked softly.

She shook her head. "No one could have survived the power of the waves. Livestock was lost as well, and because it was near the harvest, most of the barley crop was destroyed. Not long after the storm came a vicious fever that swept across Thorsay and killed far too many people. It was a bad year, and the islands haven't recovered yet."

He frowned. "I knew none of this."

"It will all be on your shoulders soon enough." She studied Ramsay, thinking that there hadn't been a man in Thorsay so well dressed since the old laird had stopped visiting London. She supposed that embassy officials needed to look impressive. "But I doubt you'll need as much tutoring as the old laird thinks. You grew up here, after all, and you're reasonably clever. You've had a long journey home to think about this. You tell me what you think your duties will be when you become laird."

"You really do want to make me work." He stretched his long legs out and crossed them at the ankles as he thought. "I believe the first and least interesting responsibility is administrative. Dealing with the Scottish government in Edinburgh and sometimes the central government in London. Maintaining the official connections that make Thorsay part of a larger nation."

She hadn't thought of the governmental tasks in quite that way. "I should think you'd be good at bureaucracy since you've worked in an embassy. What else?"

"Looking out for all islanders," he said slowly. "Thorsay is not rich, but there should be enough resources to ensure that no one goes hungry or homeless."

"That includes caring for orphans as Duncan and Caitlin did for both you and me," she commented. "Islanders are good at looking out for our neighbors, but there are always some who will need extra help. What else will you need to learn?"

"How to oversee the family properties. Sheep. Cattle. The peat cuttings. The fishing boats. I'm neither farmer nor sailor. I'm sure my grandfather has competent managers, but I should understand what needs to be done and why."

"An admirable ambition." She tried to imagine him cutting peat and failed. "Don't forget that one of the laird's chief duties is administering justice. You're the only magistrate on Thorsay."

His brow furrowed. "I recall that in the library there was a large book of the laws of the land, and a smaller volume that listed Thorsayian customs and particularly interesting cases. I need to study it to get a better sense of how justice is administered."

"Surely you sat in on some of the court sessions when you were a boy?" Signy had done that, and had always been fascinated by the cases and how they were handled.

"Yes, but it's been a lot of years. As I recall, the laird was usually lenient with crimes that didn't involve injury or serious destruction of property."

Signy nodded. "Grandmother Caitlin once said to me that the island population is small and poor, so we need to deal gently with each other."

"That's a good philosophy." Ramsay frowned. "I wonder if there should be a couple more magistrates. One on Cronsay and one on Stromburgh since they're the largest islands after Mainland."

"That would break with tradition, but it's an interesting idea," she said thoughtfully. "It would reduce the work-load for the laird and be safer in winter when the seas are rough and it's hard to travel from the outer islands to Mainland."

"Could you suggest some men who might make good magistrates?"

"Ian Maclean on Stromburgh and Jean Olson on Cronsay." She gave him a challenging glance. "Unless you're too old-fashioned to appoint a woman to such an important post."

"If we're going to break with tradition, we might as well be thorough," he said imperturbably. "Magistrates are usually chosen because they are mature, wise, and respected members of the community. I assume that's true of the two people you're suggesting."

"Yes, though of course you'll want to draw your own conclusions," she said absently, distracted by the way the wind was playfully blowing his hair about. "Why is your hair dark at the ends?"

"In Constantinople I dyed it dark brown so I looked less European when I went into the streets," he explained. "I couldn't change the color of my eyes, but with dark hair, tanned complexion, and local clothing, I didn't attract much notice."

Her brows arched. "Do most embassy officials try so hard to fit in? Or does this have something to do with you being a special projects secretary to the ambassador?"

"The latter."

"That suggests that you were a spy for the embassy," she said thoughtfully. "Will you miss the excitement of that work?"

"Some interesting projects walked through my door. I don't expect the same here," he admitted.

"It must be difficult to give up your travel and passion for antiquities."

He frowned. "I was rather hoping that my grand-father would live another twenty or thirty years so I could continue exploring and studying. I keep telling myself that I should just be grateful I had as much time as I did."

"I've read your published articles. They were inter-esting and well written. Will you write more?"

"I'm glad you enjoyed them," he replied, looking surprised that she'd read his work. "I plan to do more writing in the long winter nights. I have enough material for a number of articles and perhaps a whole book about the Phoenicians."

"If you run out of material from the Mediterranean, there is no shortage of old stones in Thorsay," she pointed out.

His eyes sharpened. "Very true. That's how I first developed interest in ancient builders and what they left behind." He rose from the bench. "I think I'll pay a cour-tesy call on the Ring of Skellig. Care to join me?"

She also stood. "I shall. It's cold sitting in the wind. Just beyond that boulder there's a path to the circle. It's a pleasant walk over common land and has an abundance of sheep."

"Of course there are sheep. What would Thorsay be without sheep?" he asked rhetorically as they walked side by side along the cliff path, then turned left on the faint track that headed inland.

"Poorer and emptier," she said pragmatically. "Thorsay wool is the best available, even better than Shetland wool, though saying that in Shetland could start a fight."

"Saying we're more Viking than Shetland or Orkney could also start a fight in either place."

She chuckled. "I see you haven't forgotten everything about the islands!"

Chapter 4

Ramsay found himself stealing glances at his companion as they headed toward the hilltop crowned with the Ring of Skellig. Trying to read Signy Matheson was like trying to translate an ancient text in which words had multiple meanings. With the long swinging strides of a Viking shield maiden and that glorious mane of red-gold hair, her fierce beauty was enough to catch any man's attention, and to intimidate most men as well.

But her emotions were harder to read. Her revelation about Gisela's death had been shattering for them both, though it seemed to have cleared long-suppressed rage and perhaps some of her grief even as it had reawakened his own deep sorrow. He would survive that as he'd survived the original anguish.

Yet Signy was still a mystery to him. He saw glimpses of the eager, energetic child she'd been, loving the world and loving to learn about it. He suspected that she resented the opportunities he'd had because he was male and heir to Thorsay.

He couldn't blame her for her resentment. She had a keen, questing mind and had taken full advantage of the laird's library. She'd sometimes written him when he was at university, asking questions about his classes and what foreign places he was studying. She had wanted desperately to travel and knew she wouldn't have the chance.

"I gather that much of your time recently has been spent helping the laird. Do you still teach, or have you not had the opportunity for that?"

"I do some teaching of the most advanced students, but for years I worked with Mrs. Wilson. Remember her? She's the most senior teacher in Thorsay, and we've developed several teacher training programs. Every hamlet and village in Thorsay now has a free school to teach all children the basics of reading and writing and figuring. There are also two teachers for older students who want more advanced education, and the best go on to the grammar school in Clanwick. A few lads have even gone to university."

She smiled with genuine pleasure. "I give thanks that Scots and Islanders have always revered education. It wasn't hard to persuade the laird to support expanding the schools after Mrs. Wilson and I convinced him that a better educated population would enrich the islands, which has proved to be true."

"Well done! I'd like to call on her."

"She lives in the cottage that Gisela and I shared. She doesn't get around easily these days, so I'm sure she'd appreciate a visit."

"I need to take a grand tour of the islands to meet people and listen to what they have to say," he said thoughtfully.

"Most will be inclined to accept the laird's grandson, but they'll want to meet you to assure themselves that you haven't been ruined by your travels."

Given how much of his life had been lived away from Thorsay, that made sense. He set the thought aside as they reached the Ring of Skellig. Fifteen roughly rectangular stones stood endwise, with the tallest close to twenty feet high. Several other stones had fallen over, leaving gaps in the circle. Maybe someday he'd see that they were erected again. It would be a good winter project for farmers who needed work in the cold season.

He stopped at the closest stone and flattened his palms on the cool rough surface, feeling the pulse of ancient times as well as a sense of homecoming stronger than when he'd entered Skellig House. "I've always been impressed with how similar the stones are to one another given the makers' primitive tools."

"Do you know what sorts of tools they had, or are you guessing?" Signy asked.

"Guessing," he admitted. "Though if I was writing an academic paper, I'd say I was theorizing. That sounds better."

That comment surprised an unexpected and rather lovely smile out of her. "So learned articles are as much about vocabulary as actual knowledge?"

"That's often the case." His hands dropped away from the stone and he began pacing around the outside of the circle.

Signy fell into step beside him. "How old is this circle and who built it?"

"I don't know," he said. "Two thousand years old? Four thousand? We know nothing about the builders." He circled a pair of sheep that were placidly cropping the grass short. "There's no shortage of mysteries in our northern islands."

"Perhaps you should do an inventory of all the ancient structures in Thorsay," she suggested. "It will keep you from becoming too restless as you yearn for Phoenician ruins. Stone circles and monoliths and brochs and ruined forts, and no one knows how many there are."

He caught his breath, then turned to her. "That's a brilliant idea. I can do an overview survey as I travel around meeting people." He felt a stirring of excitement at the prospect. As a boy he'd been fascinated by these ancient mysteries. Now it was time to learn more about them.

"Start with a map of Thorsay upon which you can mark the locations of ancient structures," she said. "There are interesting sites scattered over all the islands."

"You're right. I hope you'll help me."

"It could be an intriguing project." She turned away from the Ring and headed toward Skellig House, which was visible at the edge of the sea. "I need to get back."

"So do I." He fell into step with her. "I should make a courtesy call on Cousin Roald soon, since I assume he's the heir after me." He'd never liked Roald, who was a dozen years older than Ramsay. His father's cousin and something of a bully. Maybe he'd improved in recent years, but Ramsay doubted it. "Will he be disappointed that I've returned?"

Signy snorted. "I doubt he wants to be laird. Having to look after lesser people would interfere with making money. He owns the largest kelp-burning works in Thorsay and has made a fortune. Now he has a grand house in Clanwick and attends all the fashionable balls and entertainments."

Kelp burning had been an important industry on Thorsay for many years and employed both adults and children. The burned kelp produced soda ash, a necessary ingredient in soap and glass. It was a rather profitable business. Even so, his brows arched. "Clanwick has fashionable entertainments?"

"The last two years have been difficult, but overall the town has become more prosperous. It's a convenient provisioning port for ships heading to Canada, especially those of the Hudson's Bay Company, so Clanwick is grander than you remember."

"Much has changed since I left," he observed.

She shrugged. "Much has changed, more has not."

The land and sea and ancient monuments hadn't changed. The people were another matter. He glanced at her elegant, determined profile, wondering how long it would take for her to warm up to him, and if it was even possible. If they worked together regularly, surely she'd become more relaxed with him in time.

His gaze moved back to Skellig House. "Has Odin appointed himself my grandfather's guardian? He was not welcoming."

Signy smiled. "That cat has had the run of the property for years and was most often found in the stables or the kitchen. Since the laird became bedridden, Odin spends most of his time in the library. Your grandfather enjoys his company."

"He has cats and whisky to see himself out." Ramsay's voice because serious. "How long do you think he has?"

She glanced at him, her eyes sad. "Not long. He's been failing for some time. I think he was waiting for you to come home. Now that you're here, he may just let go. It could be days or maybe only hours. Soon."

Half seriously, he said, "When he's gone, should we launch his body in a burning boat to give him a Viking funeral?"

"He'd probably like that," she said, amused. "But I doubt the local kirk would. He'll receive a grand funeral in

32

St. Magnus Cathedral with half the population of Thorsay in attendance."

"He'd like that also," Ramsay agreed. "And it will surely be followed by a grand funeral feast for family and mourners."

"That's underway," Signy said. "You remember Mrs. Donovan, the housekeeper? She's made plans and has already chosen the ox that will be roasted."

"I'm glad my grandfather has always insisted on having capable people around him. That simplifies my life. Otherwise, I'm not sure I'd be able to live up to his standards." He hadn't felt that he could when he was a boy.

"The laird had no doubts about you. He was proud of your accomplishments. He said that times were changing and it was good that the next laird would have broad experience of the world." Signy gave him a sidelong glance. "He wasn't wrong. It may be difficult for you to settle down here again, but you'll bring Thorsay new possibilities."

"I hope you're right. The settling down part will take time." Ramsay's gaze moved across the hills to a familiar sight, and he remembered digging out blocks of turf, drying them in stacks, and eventually carrying off the fuel in two-wheeled carts. "The harvesting of peat doesn't seem to have changed."

"It's backbreaking work, but peat has provided warmth for islanders for centuries. Though if you can come up with a fuel that's less work, I'm sure no one would object," she said.

"I can't think of a more affordable or available fuel source. The peat may turn the local water brown, but there's nothing like the scent of a peat fire."

"To an islander, it's the scent of home." She drew a deep breath. "But what I sense on the wind now is a storm coming. A normal storm, not a huge one."

"You always were good at predicting the weather," he observed, remembering. "Even though it will be a normal storm, I'm glad I won't be on the sea tonight."

They'd reached the front steps of Skellig House. Ramsay noted that railings had been added to both sides, probably to help the laird up and down. A good idea for anyone, really.

He hadn't been very observant when he'd arrived at Skellig House earlier, but as he stepped inside the entry hall this time, he noticed that the wall to the right had a collection of pictures that were new to him.

Attention caught, he moved to the wall and studied the watercolor images. They were rather abstract landscapes and nature studies rendered in the blues and tans and grays of Thorsay. Images of waves rolling onto a beach, sunsets splashing color across wet sand, a lightly sketched and haunting view of sailing ships in Clanwick harbor. Silhouettes of a mother and child gathering shells were only small shapes in a larger seascape, yet there was tenderness in the way the figures turned to each other.

The pictures were framed in silvery weathered wood, and most drawings included images of seabirds arcing into the sky or swooping low over the sea. They were scarcely more than V shapes, yet so skillfully done that he could identify different species of seabird.

"These pictures are remarkable," he said in a soft voice. "I wish I'd had one in Constantinople to remind me where I came from."

"Thank you."

"This is your work?" he asked, startled.

She shrugged. "It's just a hobby, but the laird likes them. You'll find them all over Skellig House since there isn't much space to hang them in my cottage. If you wish, I can hang a couple in your bedroom."

"I'd like that," he said sincerely. "But this is more than a hobby. You're a true artist. Have you considered having pictures engraved so you could sell prints?"

"Who would be interested?" she scoffed.

"Galleries in London," he said promptly. "There's a particular gallery that belongs to a friend of mine. The owner, Richard Maxwell, is the grandson of a Thorsayian and we went to school together. He exhibits and sells interesting original artwork and loves discovering new talent. I think he'd love your work."

"You really think so?" She tried to sound casual, but in her eyes he saw the hope of a creative person yearning for appreciation of her art.

"I really do." He barely managed a reply as he gazed at Signy with a shock of unexpected emotion. He had seen her strength and beauty, but now he also saw her vulnerability. She moved him in ways he hadn't known since Gisela's death. He wanted to know her complexities, her heart and soul. He wanted her to look at him with caring rather than cool reserve.

He took a deep, unsteady breath. Perhaps his grandfather was right that he should marry her.

Chapter 5

Ramsay focused a gaze on Signy so intense that she looked away. He seemed to *see* her as no one else had, and it was unnerving. But also flattering that a worldly gentleman such as he genuinely liked her work.

Dismissing the subject, she said, "I'll look in on the laird, then go home."

"I'd assumed you lived in Skellig House, but I gather not?"

"I live in Sea Cottage. Remember it? It's only a few minutes away. I wanted more privacy, so I asked the laird to let me live there."

"I'll walk you back after I look in on my grandfather."

Her brows arched. "That's hardly necessary."

He disarmed her with a smile. "True, but I might as well start familiarizing myself with everything on the island. I'd like to see more of your work as well."

"You can come if you like, but most of my pictures are here in Skellig House. I've been too busy lately to spend much time drawing."

He nodded as they walked to the laird's sickroom. When Signy opened the door partway, she saw Robby Burnes, the laird's chief shepherd, sitting by the bed. Burnes saw her and got to his feet. "Time I was going, sir. I don't want to tire you out so much that you can't see anyone else."

"If that's my grandson lurking by the door, send him in," a thin voice replied.

Burnes came out and greeted Ramsay with a pleased nod. "Good to see you, lad. You've grown."

Ramsay smiled and offered his hand. "So have you."

Burnes laughed and patted his rotund figure with the left hand while he used the right to return Ramsay's clasp. "A wife who's a good cook will do that. Now that you're home, time you took a wife. Unless you found one in some foreign land?"

Ramsay glanced at Signy, and she gave him an *I told you everyone would be interested in marrying you off* look. There was a flicker of amusement in his eyes before he turned his full attention to Burnes. "No foreign wives acquired. It takes a Scottish woman to handle a Scottish man."

"Aye, that's right." With a nod to Signy, Burnes left.

She said quietly, "A number of the laird's old friends have been stopping by to see him. To bid him farewell."

"They're also saying good-bye to a long era and way of life," Ramsay said. "The old laird will soon be gone, they'll be stuck with a near stranger of dubious character, and the world as a whole is changing. I'm sure there are Thorsayians who served in the Royal Navy or Army against Napoleon, and some have come back with new ideas."

"Yes, you'll meet a number of veterans when we travel about the islands." She gestured at the door. "You go on in. Scratch Odin's head for me. I have a few things to do before I head home."

He nodded agreement and entered the laird's room. Signy did need to talk to Mrs. Donovan, the house-keeper, but first she wanted to hang one of her pictures in Ramsay's room. Which would be most suitable? She

37

thought about the things he'd revealed during their talk today. Ah, she knew exactly which one to choose.

—

Ramsay walked soft-footed to the bed, not sure if his grandfather had drifted off again. Odin shared the laird's pillow, his tail giving a slow warning twitch. But the old man's pale blue eyes opened and regarded him steadily as he approached and settled into the bedside chair. "How are you feeling, Old Duncan?"

"Tired, Young Kai." The laird sighed. "It won't be long."

"Don't be in a hurry to leave," Ramsay said lightly. "I still have a lot to learn."

"Don't worry. Signy can tell you what needs to be done, and if you make mistakes, there will be no shortage of people willing to point out your errors."

Ramsay laughed at that. "I'm sure you're right."

"You look so much like your father. Uncanny," Duncan said abruptly. "I wish you'd had a chance to know Alastair better."

Ramsay felt an unexpected stab of pain. He barely remembered his parents, and they were seldom mentioned in his presence. His father had died at about the age Ramsay was now. His mother had been an Edinburgh girl a couple of years younger. They'd met when his father was studying at university.

He had only brief fragmentary memories of them. Young Kai squealing with pleasure as he rode on his father's shoulders. His mother's warm hug and a scent of lavender. Gone too soon. How had it been for Duncan and Caitlin to lose their only son? Surely it was a devastation beyond what Ramsay could imagine. "I wish that too."

"Alastair would have been proud of you. Both for your going out to adventure and for your coming home." Duncan exhaled roughly. "I expect I'll see him soon enough."

"I hope so," Ramsay said. He had no strong opinions about what happened when one died, but the idea of being met by departed loved ones was appealing.

Preferring to talk of more practical matters, he said, "Signy is going to accompany me on visits across the islands. Hamlets, villages, churches. So I can see and be seen."

"That's a good plan. You'll inherit my horse, Thor the Fifth. Best horse I ever had."

All of the laird's horses had been named Thor. "I look forward to meeting him. Our Thorsayian horses are a rare breed."

"It's their Icelandic heritage," the laird said in a tired voice. "Off with you now. I need my rest."

Ramsay rose. "I'll stop by again later tonight. Till then."

How much longer would his grandfather last? he wondered again.

The door opened and Signy entered quietly. After walking to the bed, she scratched Odin's head and got a rumbling purr in return, then she kissed the laird's bristly cheek. "I'll see you tomorrow. Rest well."

The laird gave her a slight, fond smile before his eyes closed. She turned and collected Ramsay with a glance, and they left the sickroom. Outside, she said, "I'm heading for home now. You might want to raid the kitchen for some food to hold you over until dinner. You've had a long day."

"I'd still like to visit to see where you live, if you don't mind."

She shrugged as she wrapped her shawl around her shoulders. "As you wish."

He did wish. People's homes often showed a great deal about them, and he wanted to know more about Signy.

—

Signy led the way outside and turned left along the cliff path that ran the opposite direction from Clanwick. Sea Cottage was only a ten-minute walk. Skellig House and its outbuildings were on a solid bluff well above the water, but the cottage was lower, on a small rise halfway down to the waterline.

She'd had a railing built along the path that angled down the bluff to her cottage. When storm winds were blowing off the North Sea, she needed a secure grip when she was coming and going. As she led the way down the path, she breathed the air and knew there would be a storm tonight—she could feel it. Not one of the fiercest, but fierce enough.

The beach stretched in both directions below the cottage. Ramsay observed, "I see you have material for your work literally on your doorstep." He glanced up at terns flying overhead, obvious inspiration for the V shapes in her artwork. "Do you ever get flooded during storms?"

"I don't, but in the past it happened occasionally. The chance of flooding is one reason I give most of my work away. It's safer on higher ground."

The path led to the cottage's back door. It was unlocked, as was true of most island residences, and there was a dog door cut at the bottom. Signy opened the door into the kitchen and was greeted by a happy woof. She bent to scratch the neck of her dog, a smallish sheep-herding dog who was mostly black with white trim and shaggy fur. "How's Fiona doing?" she cooed. "Your fur is warm, so you've been sleeping in the sun, yes?"

Fiona replied with a lavish lick of Signy's hand. Then she turned her attention to Ramsay, regarding him thoughtfully as if unsure whether to welcome or bite.

Ramsay held out his hand for her to sniff. "Hello, Fiona. Are you willing to let me into your mistress's house?"

She licked his hand, then moved her head in a way that suggested that ruffling her ears would be welcome. He obliged, attending to both ears. She responded with a lolling tongue. "Are you a former sheepdog, old girl?"

"Fiona the Fluffy was retired early because she hurt her foot and acquired a limp that would make it hard for her to work." Signy smiled as she placed a dish of food next to a water bowl. "I'm not quite sure how she did it, but one day I realized that she'd moved in and expected me to feed her."

He chuckled. "She knew who to target."

Straightening, he saw that the cottage layout was simple, with the kitchen and single bedroom on this back side of the building. The bedroom was the only private space, since the kitchen was open to the wide front room that was a combination sitting room and studio.

The curving coast meant that the cottage faced south and the wide windows provided both light and a stunning view of the waves rolling onto the beach below. The south-facing windows didn't provide the even northern light considered ideal for artists, but it made her home bright and welcoming, a pleasure this far north. A vase of wildflowers on the kitchen table accented the peaceful loveliness of her home.

"I only visited this cottage a couple of times, but I've always felt that it was a happy place," Ramsay observed. "Sun and sand and sea. Beauty and peace all around you, and no shortage of subjects for painting."

"That's why I wanted to live here." Signy gazed pensively at the rolling waves. "The sound of the sea is soothing. I always sleep well. Would you like a cup of tea?"

"Thank you, that would be welcome." He stepped into the front room, then froze when he saw the furniture. Hooded chairs with tops that curved over the occupant were common in Thorsay and Orkney, but the one facing the windows and waves was a rare double chair that allowed two people to sit side by side.

Ramsay had built that double chair for Gisela's birthday, and Gisela and Signy had together woven the sea grass hood that was anchored to the chair's frame. They'd used light and dark grasses in a simple pattern. Below the seats was a wide drawer that held a folded knee rug that could be draped over the laps of the two occupants. It was cozy on even the coldest nights.

In the old days, Signy would burrow into another hooded chair so she could watch Ramsay and Gisela as they talked and laughed together. They'd been good times.

Ramsay swallowed hard and looked away. "I didn't expect to see these chairs, but it makes sense that you'd use the furnishings from the old house. The drop leaf table you use for your art supplies was in the kitchen there, wasn't it?"

She nodded as she stoked the fire, then moved the water-filled kettle over the flames. "We're a frugal lot in Thorsay. It would be foolish to throw away good furniture, especially since there isn't a lot of wood to spare here."

He glanced down at the muted colors of the time-mellowed rag rug, then to the small loom in the corner. Seeing the direction of his glance, Signy said, "I'm not a brilliant weaver, but I sometimes work the loom on long winter nights. Simple things like this wrap. It's soothing."

His gaze moved around the room again, studying both old furniture and new paintings hung on the whitewashed walls. "Do you ever feel your furnishings are haunted by those you've loved?"

"If my sister and mother are haunting me, they're friendly presences. I find them comforting." She scooped tea leaves from the canister and shook them into her china teapot. "This kitchen table came from the attic of Skellig House and has no particular memories. It's just a good solid table."

As she spoke, Fiona finished her meal and ambled into the living area to flop in the widest area of sunshine. She was a dog who appreciated the good things of life.

The water rose to a boil quickly and Signy poured it into the teapot. While the leaves steeped, she opened a tin box containing shortbread and transferred the irregular squares to a small plate. "You'll have to get used to the presence of past residents if you're living in Skellig House. Did you feel them when you were a boy?"

He hesitated, a little shy of telling the truth. But this was the wild north of Scotland, where people believed in the second sight and long-legged things that go bump in the night. "As a boy I took everything about the house for

43

granted. But visiting ancient ruins put me in the habit of being still and opening up to whatever might be present. I need to do that here as well."

"Yes, but slowly. Since this is your home, the spirits and memories might have more power than the ancient ruins of another race." Signy poured two cups of tea and set them out with a cream pitcher and a small pot of honey.

Ramsay studied the mugs and round teapot with interest. They were stoneware, made of red clay that must have been baked at a high temperature. The pitcher and the small plates matched them in material and style. "As a student of ancient artifacts, I've studied my share of old pottery. These pieces aren't old, but they're a lovely example of redware. Where are they from?"

"They're quite new and made locally, on Eastray, so they carry no associations with times past."

He dug into his memory. "If I recall correctly, Eastray is the island inhabited by a tribe of Jansens. I didn't know there was a pottery."

"Jansen Pottery is fairly new," she explained. "One of the younger members of the clan, Hakon, had worked for a pottery in the English Midlands and he learned a great deal about the trade. When he returned home, he found there was a large deposit of high-quality red clay on his grandmother's farm, so he built a kiln and started to experiment. Since there aren't any other potteries in Thorsay, he thought there would be a good market locally, and he was right. Jansen ware is very good quality, and the prices are reasonable because the pieces aren't imported."

Ramsay lifted the cream pitcher, admiring the simple, elegant shape. "I definitely want to meet Hakon. He's the kind of businessman Thorsay needs."

"Actually, Hakon's talent is for making pottery. His wife, Inga, is the one who runs the business, and she does it very well. She's a friend of mine. I trained her as a teacher, but she left teaching after she married Hakon and started to work with him in the business. He was happy to turn the accounts, sales, and shipments over to her." Signy lifted one of the tall redware mugs. "I had these made specially for me because I like a drinking vessel that holds a serious amount of tea. Dainty little teacups don't hold much, and they cool off too quickly."

"I agree." Ramsay poured milk into his mug, then stirred in a spoonful of honey. "I'll have to order mugs like these when I visit the Jansens."

"This style has proved so popular that Inga added it to their regular product line." Signy chuckled. "Thorsayians are serious about tea."

"All Britons are." Ramsay took a bite of shortbread, then washed it down with a swallow of nearly scalding tea. "Ambrosia!"

She chuckled. "You must be very hungry to be that impressed with simple shortbread."

"I am. All I've eaten today was a piece of bread and butter on the boat, and that was hours ago." He finished the first piece of shortbread and took another, then several slices of the bread and cheese that appeared on the table. "It's been a long, strange day."

"And it's not over yet." Signy set a pair of sketchbooks on the table between them before she sat down. "Since we were talking about an inventory of the ancient sites of Thorsay, these might interest you."

He flipped the sketchbook open and found a pencil drawing of an old broch tower, the circular shape half collapsed. Flowers bloomed around the base, and behind was the sea. The drawing was made with swift, sure strokes, not very detailed but vividly evocative. "This is the broch on the northernmost tip of Stromburgh, isn't it?"

She nodded. "I don't know how many brochs there are altogether, but this is one of the better-preserved towers."

He thumbed through, seeing sketches of ancient fishermen's huts and nousts, the scooped-out trenches along beaches that were used to shelter fishing boats in destructive weather. Castle ruins, the remains of old farmsteads, a small click mill. "You're a very talented artist. Perhaps we should work together to produce a book of Thorsay's ancient places. I could do the research and writing, and you could do the illustrations."

Her brows arched. "Who would be interested in old Thorsay stones?"

"Not a lot of people," he admitted. "But that doesn't mean it's not worth doing. If you're introducing me around the islands, it will be a good time to map all the ruins and for you to do sketches."

Her gaze dropped. "I don't know that I'd have enough time for that."

"It will be a long-term project," he said peaceably. He turned the page and found what looked like a brand-new broch. "This is a Martello tower, isn't it? Built to repel Napoleon's troops if they tried to invade?"

"Yes, it's only five years old. Clanwick needed to be protected since the harbor is important to British shipping, but luckily it was never used."

"One can see how this tower is a direct descendant of the old brochs. They're all round coastal fortresses, which makes them ideal for resisting attacks."

"Basic building of defenses doesn't change." Signy consumed a piece of shortbread in two bites. "I wonder how many of the old brochs were put to use in the old days? And if they were attacked, which side our ancestors were on?"

"Probably both. There has always been a lot of traffic between Norway and the northern isles." Ramsay finished his tea and rose from the table. "Time I was getting back. Will you come over to Skellig House this evening?"

"Tomorrow is soon enough for your next lesson in becoming a laird."

He smiled. "I look forward to it."

As he set off along the seaside path, he was surprised at just how much he looked forward to spending time with her.

–

After Ramsay left, Signy poured the last of the tea into her cup and then sipped it as she gazed at the waves rolling in. She was going to be seeing a lot of Ramsay, and she needed to sort out how she felt about him. He was so confident and knowledgeable about the world. Very annoying.

But she'd been deeply grateful for his understanding when she fell apart after talking about Gisela's death. He'd been surprisingly sympathetic and even vulnerable.

The years had almost made him too blasted attractive for a woman's peace of mind. Now that he was back, he'd be surrounded by young women interested in applying for the position of wife, and Signy hated crowds.

She pulled her sketchbook over and took a pencil from the china cup that held pencils, pens, and a pen knife. With a few quick strokes, she drew his face but frowned at the result. His features were too regular to be distinctive, and it was hard to capture the intelligence and humor in his eyes.

She ripped out the page and tossed it on the peat fire. It disappeared in a swift burst of flames. Apparently she'd have decades ahead to draw him again and again. She wasn't sure whether to be annoyed or pleased.

Chapter 6

When Ramsay entered Skellig House, he was met by Mrs. Donovan, the housekeeper. "There you are, lad. We're having a welcome home dinner party for you tonight, and I was afraid we'd have to start without you."

He blinked, realizing he should have expected this. "Not too large a one, I hope? It's been a long day."

"Just members of the household and those who live nearby," she assured him. "But people want to see that you're finally home. Make sure you're really you."

"Will there be bagpipes?"

"No, we don't want to disturb the laird," she said regretfully. "The dinner won't run too late either. But we couldn't let your return go unnoticed."

"I'm glad it won't be late. I want to sit with my grandfather. When will dinner begin? I haven't even been to my room yet."

"You have about an hour to prepare yourself," she assured him.

As she turned and headed to the kitchen, he made his way back to his grandfather's sickroom. He tapped lightly on the door, then entered to find a fishing boat captain sitting by the bed, sharing a laugh with the laird. The captain had a weathered face and looked familiar, but Ramsay couldn't place him. Fortunately Duncan said,

"Eh, lad, you remember Alan Innes, don't you? The best fishing boat captain in Thorsay."

"He says that to all the captains," Innes said as he rose and offered his hand. "Just like a sailor says such things to all the lasses."

Ramsay laughed as he took the captain's hand. "Flattery generally works even when we know it's flattery."

"Aye, and your grandfather knows when to flatter and when to give a kick in the arse."

"Both useful skills," Ramsay agreed. His gaze went to Duncan, who looked exhausted, but he'd obviously been enjoying his visitor.

Innes extended a hand to Odin, who licked the captain's fingers with interest. "He likes the hint of fish on my fingers," Innes said with a chuckle. "I'll be off now."

Innes gave the laird one last long gaze, as if he knew they wouldn't meet again. His expression was somber as he left the room.

When the captain was gone, Ramsay settled into the chair. "This is quite a salon you're operating here, with honored guests dropping by to say hello and perhaps share a dram of whisky." His gaze flicked to the bottle sitting on the bedside table. It had been almost full earlier, and now it was half empty. "More of Callan's best?"

"Aye. I'm too old to drink rotgut." His grandfather smothered a yawn. "Go off to Jenny Donovan's welcome home dinner. People will want to see what you've turned into."

"Would you like to join the gathering? I can get the wheelchair and take you in for a few minutes," Ramsay offered.

"I'm tired enough without being surrounded by mad chatterers," the laird said tartly. "But come back after dinner is over and tell me all about it."

Ramsay stood and lightly touched his grandfather's age-spotted hand, feeling the bones under the thin skin, and he gave thanks that his journey home had gone quickly. He could so easily have been too late. He extended his hand to Odin and was given a swat for his effort. "I must not smell fishy enough."

"Odin is a cat of strong opinions," the laird said as his eyes closed. "But he'll accept you eventually."

Weary to his bones, Ramsay left the library and headed up to his old room. It was much as he'd left it all those years ago, though freshly cleaned and with a vase of wildflowers on the desk. The flowers looked much like the ones in Signy's kitchen, which was probably not a coincidence.

His personal luggage was neatly stacked beside the wardrobe. He turned slowly, scanning the familiar surroundings. The small bookcase was spilling over with books, just as he'd left it—but dusted. On the windowsills, he'd lined up particularly interesting stones and shells, and they were still there, also dusted.

The carpet, the bedspread, the upholstered chair by the fireplace were all the same. Familiar and welcoming.

Then his gaze was caught by the one thing that was different: the watercolor painting that hung over the desk. Unmistakably Signy's work, it was a rather abstract depiction of the sun setting across the sea, low in the sky so that it cast a long, long shadow behind the small dark shape of a man who stood on the shore and gazed toward the light.

Ramsay stepped closer to study the painting. The sea was shades of blue and subtly sun-touched waves, while the shore under the man's feet was done in soft tones of tan and umber. He wasn't sure if the picture depicted peace or loneliness. Perhaps both. Like Signy's other work, it had the uncanny ability to get under his skin.

He began unpacking his clothing, automatically organizing garments in the same way as when he was a boy. He briefly wondered what it would be like to move into the laird's spacious suite someday, then buried the thought. He wasn't ready.

The ringing of the dinner bell was another familiar sound. Since the gathering was in his honor, he changed into fresh clothing. Given a choice, he'd have preferred a quieter evening, but it would be good to see old friends.

He was watched with a certain wariness at first, but his friendly greetings to old acquaintances thawed the atmosphere quickly. There were Stewarts and Inneses, Johannsons and Olsons, Browns and Fieldings. These same familiar names were found on all the islands, and they reflected the mixed heritage of Thorsay: Vikings, Celts, English, and a scattering of other nationalities. Ramsay had grown up assuming Thorsay's diversity was normal but had since learned that it was unusual for such a remote place. He liked that unique mix.

He also noticed speculative glances from the women, particularly those unmarried. Signy was right that everyone was interested in marrying him off. He carried the inheritance of the lairdship on his back, and it was already chafing.

As they ate fresh fish and drank toasts to the prodigal's return, the storm Signy had predicted began to herald itself with rising winds and a feeling of rain in the air. Thorsayians were keenly aware of the weather, so guests excused themselves and headed for their homes before the storm hit full force.

After seeing off the last guests and thanking Jenny Donovan and the rest of the staff, Ramsay returned to his grandfather's room. He expected the old man to be asleep, but when he moved to the side of the bed, Duncan murmured without opening his eyes, "Tell me more of your adventures. I'm sure you have enough to see me out."

Smiling wryly, Ramsay seated himself beside the bed. "Years' worth. I hope you stay around long enough to hear them all."

"Prop me up with some pillows and pour me some of that whisky."

Ramsay helped his grandfather sit up, then stacked two extra pillows behind his back. "I hope you have another bottle stashed somewhere, since this one is getting close to empty."

"When it's empty, there's another bottle on the shelf of travel memoirs. I'll have enough to last the night. Pour yourself some. Callan's whisky is the best drink for the dark hours of the night."

Ramsay found two tumblers and splashed whisky into each. His grandfather took his glass in a surprisingly strong grip. He raised it in a toast. "To going out and coming in!"

Ramsay clinked his glass against the laird's. "And may both be blessed!" He took a sip, welcoming the smooth, smoky taste. He needed it after this endless day.

As the laird settled back against the pillow, his glass in one hand and his other hand resting on Odin's warm gray flank, Ramsay began to talk of the countries he'd visited around the Mediterranean and his travels into deserts in search of cities long buried in the sands. He spoke of the night in Constantinople when he'd helped an English sea captain make an impossible rescue from an impregnable palace. He compared the wines of Portugal, Spain, Italy, and Greece. He spoke until his voice was growing hoarse and the storm had intensified to howling wind, soaking rain, and occasional flashes of lightning and cracks of thunder.

"Pull back the curtains so I can see the lightning," his grandfather ordered.

The old man had always loved a good storm. So did Ramsay, preferably from inside a warm, dry house. After pulling the curtains open, he set a couple more chunks of peat on the fire. The sweet vegetal smokiness was the scent of his childhood.

Abruptly the laird said, "Take me outside."

Ramsay stared at him. "It's cold and wet and the wind is making merry with the rain and the sea. Why do you want to go out?"

"I never wanted to die in my bed. Help me up, dammit!" Duncan swung his legs over the side of the bed, swaying but not falling over.

His request was insane, but why not? When death is imminent, risk fades away. Ramsay moved to his grandfather's side and steadied him on the edge of the bed. The old man wore nothing but a long nightshirt, so Ramsay said, "I'll get some rain gear from the hall."

The house was silent, and the entry hall was lit only by a dim lamp. A door tucked in a corner opened to reveal a variety of oilcloth coats and capes along with hats and scarves hung on pegs. Below were boots and shoes and a couple of umbrellas that would never stand up to a serious Thorsayian wind.

He donned a caped and hooded coat himself and decided a long cape would be easiest for his grandfather to wear. After adding a pair of boots that looked as if they belonged to the laird, he returned to the bedroom and gently slid the old man's feet into the boots. "You're mad, you know," he said conversationally as he draped the cape around the thin figure and buttoned it shut.

"Thank you," his grandfather returned politely. "Bring the whisky bottle."

Again, why not? Ramsay shoved the bottle into the large left pocket of his coat, then wrapped an arm around the laird's thin waist. With surprise, he realized that he was taller than his grandfather. When had that happened?

"Where to?"

"Out the side door, then left to the bench," Duncan ordered.

Silently Ramsay followed the orders, half carrying his grandfather. Odin pattered along behind. As soon as the outside door opened, a blast of wind caught it and slammed it against the wall, but the sound was drowned out by the roaring of the wind and waves. The bench was only a few feet away, set into a partially sheltered recess in the wall.

Ramsay closed the door, settled his grandfather on the bench, and sat next to him, his right arm steadying the old man. Odin leaped up on the laird's other side and leaned against his thigh. The cat was nothing if not loyal.

Duncan raised his face into the wind and gave a nearly inaudible sigh of pleasure. "Nothing like a good storm to get the blood moving!"

"Then your blood must be racing." Ramsay had to admit that the wind and waves were splendidly invigorating for a man who had had a very long and tiring day.

"Give me that whisky," Duncan demanded.

Silently Ramsay uncorked the bottle and handed it over. His grandfather tilted his head back and took a long swallow, followed by a sigh of satisfaction.

"It was a night much like this when your mother brought you to Caitlin and me in a rain-drenched pony cart." He sighed. "Your parents had taken you to Edinburgh to visit her family. They contracted some wicked fever there, though it didn't appear until they were back in Thorsay. Alastair was dead or dying when Jeannie made her way through the storm to bring you here. She collapsed after handing you over to your grandmother and died a few hours later."

Shocked, Ramsay said, "Why didn't I know this?"

Duncan shrugged. "You never asked. You were ill also, but not so seriously. You didn't seem to remember what happened that night, and I guess no one felt like talking about it. It was a bad, bad night for us all. Your mother was a game lass for all that she was a city girl." He sighed again. "Gone too soon. Both gone too soon." He took another swig from the whisky bottle. "But at least we had you."

Ramsay appropriated the whisky bottle and took a deep swallow before handing it back. His grandfather was right—it was a good drink for a dark night. "With all the grief I gave you, I'm surprised you didn't drop me into the North Sea."

His grandfather chuckled. "I won't say I wasn't tempted, but you were just a high-spirited lad like your father had been. Like I was. There was no meanness in you."

He began to cough horribly, bending over as he fought for breath. Alarmed, Ramsay supported him. "Time we went inside."

"No, damn you!" his grandfather growled when he regained his breath. His voice faded to a whisper. "I always wanted to die like a Viking, facing into the storm."

"I wish you'd stop talking about dying!" Ramsay snapped. "I've only just returned."

"No need for me to linger, now you're here," the laird said in a thin voice. "I'm tired, Kai. So tired. And I'm leaving you a parcel of troubles to sort out."

Wanting to lighten the mood, Ramsay said, "Signy and I discussed whether you'd like a Viking funeral, sent off to sea in a burning boat."

Duncan gave a husk of laughter. "I would like that, but best do it the Christian way in St. Magnus Cathedral so everyone can come and say what a grand old man I was and Thorsay won't see my like again."

"True, and thank God for that," Ramsay said tartly. "For heaven's sake, let me take you back inside!"

Duncan shook his head stubbornly and took another gulp of whisky. "You really should marry Signy. She's a grand girl and can run things if you take off for your foreign lands again."

"I won't be leaving," Ramsay said, his words a solemn vow. "And I doubt I could persuade Signy to marry me even if I wanted to ask her."

"Use some of that damned charm of yours, lad. That will change her mind." Duncan began coughing again, paroxysms shaking his thin body. "A grand girl," he repeated in a soft murmur. "The daughter I wished we had."

After a long silence, a fierce tremor went through the laird and he whispered, "*Caitlin?*" in a voice of wonder. "*Alistair!*"

The whisky bottle tumbled to the ground as he slowly folded into himself with one last rattling breath.

Horrified, Ramsay felt for a pulse but could find nothing. *Nothing.* Odin rose, put his paws on the old laird's arm, and gave a soul searing feline howl of despair. Then he leaped from the bench and disappeared into the stormy night.

Swamped with grief, Ramsay stood and gathered his grandfather into his arms. The old laird was so light, a shrunken shadow of the powerful man he'd been.

Then he carried Duncan's frail body into the house, glad his anguished tears were lost in the rain.

Chapter 7

Signy had drifted off to sleep to the sounds of the rain and the rushing waves on the beach below her cottage. In Thorsay, people lived close to nature.

She was woken by pounding on her kitchen door. She came sharply alert, knowing that no visitor at this hour of the night would be bringing good news. As she swung from her bed, she pulled on a heavy robe and shoved her feet into fleece-lined slippers against the late-night drafts. Fiona came to her side, looking alert.

Her kitchen was dimly lit by the coals of the peat fire as the door swung open, revealing Ramsay. He was drenched, water running down his haggard face from his saturated hair and pouring from the cape of his oilcloth coat.

"He... he's gone," Ramsay said heavily. "The old laird is gone."

Signy's vision dimmed and she swayed, on the verge of collapse before Ramsay's arms came around her. His body was chilled but his embrace was strong. She clung to him until she had come to terms with his news. She had known the end was near, but not *now*, surely at some more distant time.

Sensing her distress, Fiona licked her hand in an offer of canine comfort. Signy scratched the dog's head gratefully, then stepped out of Ramsay's embrace, saying unsteadily, "We need to stop meeting like this. Most improper."

He smiled crookedly. "You mean mourning together over the death of someone we both loved?"

She nodded as she bent to add more peat to the coals and move the kettle from the hob to the fire. "If ever tea was needed, the time is now."

Ramsay took off his dripping coat and hung it on a peg by the door before he slumped heavily into one of the kitchen chairs. As Fiona lay down on his feet, he rested his elbows on the table so he could bury his face in his hands. "I can't believe that I've been back in Thorsay for less than a day. It seems so much longer."

"You've certainly had a very full day." They both had. "At least you made it home in time to say good-bye."

Voice muffled behind his hands, Ramsay said, "I think he was holding on until I returned. Then he simply... let go."

Signy had no trouble believing that. The laird had been fading for months, and she'd sensed that he was hanging on by sheer force of will. "How did it happen, and why wasn't I called over?"

"Mrs. Donovan organized a dinner to welcome me back. The weather sent people home early, and I went to sit with the laird. He ordered me to pour him some of Callan's best whisky and tell him stories of my travels, so I did.

"Then he asked me to take him outside to sit and watch the storm." Ramsay drew a ragged breath. "He said he wanted to die like a Viking, facing into the storm, but I thought that was just talk. He didn't seem that much weaker. He spoke of the past, and then... then he died in my arms."

As Gisela had died in Signy's arms. Such memories were as indelible as they were painful. "It sounds as if there was no time to call for me."

"No, his passing was swift and somewhat unexpected." After a long silence, Ramsay said softly, "One of the last things my grandfather said was that you were the daughter he'd never had."

She swallowed hard, her lungs constricting. "He was more my father than my real father."

"As he was my father also." Ramsay raised his head and gazed at her, his gray eyes steady. "But I'm glad that you and I are not blood kin."

"Why would it matter?" She poured boiling water into the teapot, inhaling the soothing fragrance as the leaves began to steep.

"The laird said again that you're a grand girl and I should marry you." As Signy's head shot up, Ramsay said dryly, "I think he wanted to ensure that there would be a strong hand at the tiller if I decided to return to exploring someday."

She sank onto the other chair as she studied Ramsay's cool gray eyes. Except that they weren't cool now. He burned with grief and intensity. "Will you go off again?"

He shook his head. "I gave my word that I'd return when I was needed. I won't go back on that promise."

She believed him. Many things about Kai had surely changed over the years, but he'd always been true to his word, and she sensed that he still was. "Since you don't plan on leaving, there's no rush to find a wife. I'm surprised that you'd consider a matchmaking suggestion from your grandfather."

"I'm surprised myself," he said with the hint of a smile. "But Duncan was as shrewd as they come, and he knew you very well. He knew your worth."

Her brows arched. "So you're looking to marry a permanent assistant? Why would either of us want that?"

"I don't know what you might see in me, but I know you will never be boring." His eyes gleamed. "Not to mention that my first thought when I saw you yesterday was that you'd gone from being a knobby little girl to a Nordic goddess. Surely you've noticed that you're beautiful enough to attract any man's attention, and that isn't even counting your intelligence, talent, and knowledge."

She felt herself flushing a color that would surely clash with her hair. "I see you've learned flattery on your travels."

He shook his head. "That's not flattery, but God's own truth. You're a strikingly attractive woman, Signy Matheson, and attraction is always an asset in marriage." He sighed. "But attraction and my grandfather's blessing aren't enough to make you want to marry me when you despise me."

She poured tea for them both, then brought out the tin of shortbread again. Serious discussions shouldn't be undertaken on an empty stomach. She sat and sipped her tea as she thought. "I don't despise you," she said at length. "But you're right that there is much history between us. Perhaps too much."

"There was pain and loss, but also friendship," he said quietly. "Though I was courting Gisela, it was also a pleasure to see you. You were a delightful girl who gave promise of great things, and you've grown up to fulfill that promise. I'm not proposing that we rush into marriage. But since we'll be working together, perhaps we can have an open mind about future possibilities?"

She raised her head and studied him. When he'd come ashore the day before, he'd been intimidatingly cool and polished, a sophisticated gentleman who looked out of place here at the end of the world.

Now he was gray with fatigue and very real. She'd been infatuated with him in an innocent way when he courted Gisela. Her interest was no longer innocent. She tried to look at him not as a man she'd known much of her life but as if he were a stranger. Handsome. Compelling. Vulnerable. And yes, unnervingly attractive.

At this moment, he seemed interested in her. Would it last? Or was he so unbalanced by all that was facing him that he merely saw her as a familiar face in a storm? Impossible to tell, but with sudden fierceness, she wanted to see if they might have a future together.

Keeping her voice calm, she said, "I intimidate most men, but I'm willing to be open to possibilities if you wish. We shall see."

"I'm glad," he said with a slight, sweet smile. Then his eyes closed and he rubbed his temple. "What a day this has been." His eyes opened and he rose unsteadily. "I should be leaving."

He swayed and looked ready to collapse, as if he'd reached the end of his strength. A new burst of wind rattled the windows.

"You shouldn't go out in this," Signy said briskly. "You'd fall over the bluff and drown. You need to stay here and rest."

"You're probably right," he muttered as he caught the back of the chair for support. "Where?"

She thought swiftly. The floor was cold, hard, and drafty. She didn't want the new laird to come down with lung fever before he'd even accepted his heritage. The only real place to lie down was her bed. It was wide and long enough for his height.

"Come along, Kai." She moved beside him and draped his arm over her shoulders so she could guide him. It wasn't far, just out into the wide front room and a right turn into the bedroom. The covers were tangled from when she'd awoken at the sound of his knock, so she flipped them over the end of the bed with her free hand. Then she sat him down on the edge of the mattress, pulled off his boots, and gently tipped him back onto the pillows.

He was half unconscious and didn't resist. His tension faded as he fell fully asleep. A light brown stubble was visible on his chin. Ramsay was a long way from the polished gentleman who had set foot at Skellig House the previous morning. She liked him better this way.

She pulled the covers over his long body and circled to the other side of the bed. She was almost as drained as Ramsay, and she'd be damned if she would sleep on the floor. Luckily the bed was wide enough to hold two people if they didn't thrash around. There was even room for a warm dog to lie at the foot of the mattress and settle down into soft snores.

She stretched out on her side of the bed and rolled so her back was turned to Ramsay. As she pulled the covers up, she reflected that at least she wouldn't go to her grave without ever having slept with a man.

Chapter 8

The brightening sky woke Ramsay at dawn. He lay still as he tried to figure out where he was. The bed wasn't moving, so he wasn't on a ship as he'd been for weeks.

And he definitely wondered why he was lying on his side with a warmly curved body tucked against him, her back to his front. His arm was around her waist. His eyes opened and he studied the red-gold hair that tickled his face. Signy, soft and yielding in sleep as she wasn't during the day.

With a deep ache, he remembered his grandfather's death and his journey through the storm to inform Signy. Had he braved the wind and rain because she had the right to know as soon as possible, or because he'd been drawn to her for comfort? Both, he supposed.

The storm had blown out in the night, and the light that entered the cottage through the open bedroom door was warm with soft early sunshine. Soon he'd have to get up and face all the complications of the laird's death, but for now he just wanted to lie still in the peace and warmth of Signy's bed. Being this close to her stirred gentle desire, all he had strength for at the moment.

She shifted, then suddenly stiffened as she came awake. "Don't worry," he murmured. "It's only me. Thank you for lending me your warm bed." When she rolled onto her back and studied him with narrowed eyes, he added,

"I won't misbehave. You have a dirk and you know how to use it, which I know because I taught you."

At that her lips curved into a smile. "You were a good teacher. It was startling for a moment to find you here, but it's hardly your fault when I put you to bed myself. I'm nowhere near unselfish enough to sleep on the floor, and I wasn't about to let you walk back to Skellig House in a storm."

He removed his arm from her waist and retreated as far as the bed would allow, which wasn't very. "You were right. I was so tired I might not have made it all the way back."

"When you arrived here you looked…" She searched for a word. "Shattered."

He sighed. "I hadn't realized how much I cared about the old laird until I lost him. We were always at odds when I was growing up, but now I recognize that he was my anchor. The man I measured myself against."

She nodded, her expression deeply sad. "It was the same for me. He saw me as myself, not a mere woman, and he gave me opportunities to learn and do as much as I was capable of. He used to say that Scots women have always been the equals of their men." Her brows arched. "Would you agree with him?"

"I hadn't thought of it in those terms," he said cautiously. "I do know that Scottish women are gloriously independent and capable, and that's doubly true for Thorsayian women."

"Very tactful." She reached across the bed and brushed her fingers over his stubbled jaw. "You're losing your London polish very quickly. Give your beard a week and you'll look like a proper Thorsayian fisherman."

Her gentle touch changed the atmosphere with shocking suddenness. There was great intimacy in sharing a bed, and the latent attraction between them flared into heated life. In her eyes he saw a surprise to equal his own.

His desire to lean forward into a kiss was almost overwhelming, but he knew with absolute certainty that doing so would be a disastrous mistake. There would be too much happening in the next weeks to attempt courtship.

He rolled onto his back, close to falling off the bed, his hands clenched under the covers. Courtship? Did he mean that? Yes, he did. But not now. *Later.*

"I plan on shaving when I have the opportunity," he said as he swung his legs over the side of the bed. "I still haven't been here for a full day."

"You'd best return to Skellig House now if you want to have time to shave," Signy said rather breathlessly as she rose, her braid of shining hair spilling over one shoulder. She'd worn her heavy blue robe to bed, and the fabric flowed sensuously around her as she slid her feet into her fleece slippers. A Nordic goddess, and unnervingly alluring.

He turned away from her and tugged on his boots, which were beside the bed. The leather was wet and heavy, but his rumpled clothing was reasonably dry, thanks to the long coat he'd worn. "You're right. I need to get back to the house before they start wondering what's happened to me."

He stood and stretched his cramped limbs, thinking that her bed wasn't quite large enough for two tall people. That was why it had been so cozy...

Needing a new subject, he said, "Odin came outside with us, and when the laird died, he howled and disappeared into the storm. I don't know if he'll ever come back. Was he like a witch's familiar? Duncan's familiar?"

Signy chuckled. "Just a cat, though one with more personality than most. But there's something primitive and warrior like in his saying good-bye that way. Vikings had ship's cats, you know. I can picture Duncan in Viking armor standing in the bow of a dragon-headed ship and Odin right beside him, paws on the gunwale, looking into the storm."

"I like that image." Ramsay plowed his fingers through his disordered hair and tried to concentrate on what would happen next. "Can you give me a general idea of the funeral proceedings? The laird was amused when I told him you and I had discussed sending him off in a flaming Viking boat, but he wanted a traditional funeral in St. Magnus Cathedral."

"It will probably be held four or five days from now. I'm sure word of his death is already going out all over Thorsay." She yanked the sash of her robe tight. "Many, many people will come to the funeral. It's lucky that you'll be there for them to meet and accept. It's a good foundation for traveling around the islands later."

The day of the funeral would be long and exhausting. "At the funeral, I hope someone will be standing nearby to remind me whom I'm meeting."

"Most likely that will be me. As the laird's assistant, I know a goodly number of Thorsayians." Her brow furrowed. "At some point you'll have to give a short memorial speech about your grandfather. Likely your cousin Roald will offer his house in Clanwick for the gathering after the funeral. He'll do that to prove how close he was to the old laird and the new, and it will give him a chance to show off his grand house. The house and grounds are spacious, and holding the gathering there will spare people having to travel out to Skellig House. We'll provide most of the food."

"So if he offers, I should accept no matter how annoying he is about it?" Ramsay moved into the kitchen and pulled on his coat.

"That would be my advice. He's a powerful man in Thorsay, so it's best to be on good terms with him."

Ramsay dug his knit hat from the coat pocket where he'd stuffed it the night before after reaching the cottage. "Luckily some of my time in Constantinople involved diplomatic duties."

"You'll need all your diplomacy," she said seriously. "Your grandfather was the laird for so long that many will be devastated by his death. They need to believe in you."

Spying in the Ottoman Empire had been easier than being the laird of Thorsay, with fewer people depending on him. "I'll do my best, and I'm thanking God for your help."

"I think the laird gets the credit for putting us together." She smiled wryly. "He was a grand chess player who always thought several moves ahead."

"If we're using chess metaphors, you're the queen, the most powerful piece on the board," he said thoughtfully. "That would make me the king, who has the grandest title but doesn't do much of anything."

"I'd make you a knight, who moves around the board in unpredictable ways," she said, amused. "After I dress and have breakfast, I'll join you at Skellig House to help deal with all the disruptions and arrangements."

"Until then," he said with a nod.

-

Fiona had gone out through her dog door early and would eventually return with muddy feet and an appetite. Signy put food in the dog's dish in anticipation of Fiona's return, then heated water for tea. When it was ready and steeped, she took her mug to her hooded chair and turned it to face the waves rolling in on the beach below. She never used the double chair Ramsay had made for Gisela. If any of her furniture was haunted, it was that chair.

The waves were larger than usual because of the storm. Seabirds swooped into the churning waters in search of fish. She could watch the hypnotic sea for hours.

The previous day had scrambled her as badly as Ramsay, she suspected. She'd met him with rage, which had erupted into her painful revelations about Gisela's death. Ramsay had deserved some of the blame, but Gisela had been a willing lover. She'd also forbidden her little sister to reveal the pregnancy to anyone.

Signy had wondered sometimes whether Gisela's life might have been saved if Signy had gone against her sister's wishes and summoned a midwife. It was true that Gisela was delicate, but an experienced midwife might have been able to stop the bleeding in time. Impossible to know, but Signy also carried some of the guilt.

As a girl, she'd adored her sister's sweetheart, Ramsay, who had seemed so strong and mature and confident. And he'd *seen* Signy, talked to her as if she mattered, and he looked forward to their being members of the same family. Now she realized how young he'd been, only twenty when Gisela died.

She'd hated him for abandoning Thorsay and thought him cold and selfish. But in the past day, he'd shown kindness, sympathy, and understanding. He'd grown in strength and maturity with the years, and now she saw him as a fully rounded human being. A man to respect.

And he was interested in her. He'd made that clear, but she doubted his interest ran very deep. Perhaps he was looking for another anchor now that Duncan was gone. She hoped he recovered quickly; she didn't want to be either an anchor or a wife.

She lifted her sketchbook and a piece of charcoal and did another swift sketch of Ramsay. This one was a little better than the first. The chiseled planes of his face and the bone-deep confidence were easy to capture, and this time she'd caught a hint of the vulnerability under his polished surface. But it wasn't a brilliant sketch.

With a shrug, she crumpled the page and tossed it into the fire. She didn't know him well enough yet to draw him properly. Maybe someday she'd do better.

She finished her tea, then determinedly rose and moved to get dressed so she could walk over to Skellig House. For now, she must continue one step at a time to do what must be done.

–

Ramsay left the cottage and made his way up the path to level ground. The air was bright and cool and bracing. He tugged on the knit hat and set off along the cliff path, thinking of everything that had happened in the hours since he'd arrived. Too much, and Signy was in the middle of it all. At least she didn't despise him anymore, and if he was any judge, she was feeling some of the same attraction he was.

They both needed time to move beyond the shadow of Gisela. Not to forget her—that couldn't and shouldn't happen. But they needed to build a relationship that was grounded in the present. That would take time. No matter, he wasn't going anywhere.

As Signy had said, he'd surely have to give a short speech about his grandfather. He must memorialize the things Duncan had done for Thorsay, and also convey who the laird had been as a grandfather.

He smiled a little, thinking of past whippings, all of which Ramsay had deserved. As he continued along the cliff path, phrases started to form in his head. His grandfather would have a fine send-off even if no burning boats were involved.

He felt composed by the time he reached Skellig House. When he entered the front hall, Mrs. Donovan bustled in. "There you are! I wondered where you got to after we laid the laird out."

"I'm sorry." He took off his coat and hung it in the hall closet. "I should have let you know that I was going to tell Signy the news. I thought she should know right away. One of the last things my grandfather said was that she was like the daughter he never had."

"Aye, she was," the housekeeper said, her expression softening. "The lass will miss him something fierce."

"As will you, since you spent so much time with him."

"Aye." Mrs. Donovan's eyes closed in a futile attempt to block tears. "Thirty years I've worked in Skellig House. Your grandfather was a stubborn old man, but a grand laird."

On impulse, Ramsay stepped forward and drew her into a comforting embrace. The top of her head barely reached his chin. He seemed to be doing a lot of hugging since he'd returned. He'd half forgotten how Thorsayians showed their feelings more readily than the English, but it was coming back to him.

The housekeeper rested her head on his shoulder as she shed more tears, then determinedly moved away. "Thanks, lad. What did he say at the very end?"

Ramsay hesitated a moment before saying, "His last words were 'Caitlin,' then 'Alastair.' He said the names with an air of... pleased surprise."

Mrs. Donovan nodded with satisfaction. "That's all right, then. He told me his wife and son would be waiting for him on the other side, and it sounds like they were."

"Do you have the second sight?" Ramsay asked a little warily. The ability to see more than the real world was not uncommon among Scots, but he found it disquieting.

"A bit of it. Enough to recognize that he saw the people he loved best on the other side."

Ramsay hoped that was true. "I need to make myself presentable. By the time I reached Signy's cottage with the news, I looked like a drowned ferret. She wouldn't let me come back here for fear I wouldn't make it safely."

Mrs. Donovan gave him a sharp look at that, but said only, "Wise of her, considering the storm and the shape you were in last night."

He grimaced. "Correct me if I'm wrong, but that was only an average Thorsay storm, wasn't it?"

"Aye, they can be much worse, but last night's storm was enough to see the laird out. Now get ready for the callers who will be coming to offer their condolences."

He nodded and turned to the stairs. "Signy said she'd be over to help out after she had breakfast."

"She's a good lass," the housekeeper said. "Did the old laird tell you that he thought you should wed her?"

Ramsay paused, his left hand on the railing of the stairs. "Several times. But the lady and I have doubts."

"Early days yet," Mrs. Donovan said. "Now along with you, my young laird."

As he made his way up to the room, Ramsay reflected that during his years of traveling, he'd been able to keep his private life private. Now he was recalling the drawbacks of living in a place where everyone knew your business, and usually had decided opinions about it. He needed to become used to that again.

After a swift wash and shave, he dressed in a black coat and trousers, an outfit suitable for greeting mourners. It was still early, so he headed down to the kitchen for a quick breakfast.

The cook, Mrs. Amundson, was grim-faced and the two kitchen maids were red eyed and sniffling. He introduced himself to all of them and accepted their condolences on his grandfather's death. The younger maid broke out into full-blown tears. It was going to be a long week as everyone around him mourned the loss of the man he would miss so much.

Mrs. Amundson produced a robust breakfast of eggs, ham, and fried potatoes, saying, "You'll need your strength, lad."

He wondered if the older servants would ever stop calling him "lad." Probably not. More significantly, he wondered how long it would take him to adjust to a place that no longer fit him.

Chapter 9

A servant was sent to attend the front door, and it wasn't long before the first knock. Ramsay moved into the entry hall and saw that his cousin Roald Ramsay had arrived, accompanied by two tall young people, one male and one female. Roald's children, presumably. They would be Ramsay's second cousins.

Determined to be hospitable, Ramsay approached the visitors and held out his hand. "Roald! Thank you for coming. It's been too many years."

"And whose fault is that?" his cousin said jovially as he shook Ramsay's hand. There was a touch of gray in his hair, but he looked sleek and prosperous. "I've been right here. Sorry we meet again under such unfortunate circumstances. I heard you only got home yesterday?"

"Yes, in time to say good-bye to my grandfather, though barely." Changing the subject, Ramsay continued, "I've heard you've done very well with your kelp business."

"So I have," Roald said complacently. "Come visit the works when you have time."

"I will. Once things settle down, I plan to travel around the islands to reacquaint myself with the people and places."

Roald nodded, then gestured at the young people. "You remember my son, Axel, and my daughter, Annabel?"

Ramsay offered his hand to Axel. "It's good to meet you again. I recall that you were a promising scholar. Have you been to university?"

There was a flash of annoyance in Axel's eyes, but his voice was steady as he replied. "No, it seemed better to stay in Thorsay and learn about running the family businesses."

Ramsay suspected that Axel would have preferred to go to Edinburgh rather than stay under his father's roof, which was understandable in a young man. Ramsay had been delighted to move into the wider world, and Duncan had encouraged his pursuit of knowledge.

Turning to Annabel, who had become a striking young beauty, Ramsay said, "I will refrain from saying, 'My, how you've grown.' But you certainly have!"

She smiled, her gaze on him frankly assessing. "I was in the schoolroom when you left. It's good to see you again, Kai." She cocked her head to one side. "They say you're going to marry Signy Matheson?"

"Where do these rumors come from?" a tart female voice interjected. Signy had entered the hall and was crossing to join them. She looked tall and commanding in a severely cut black gown, her red-gold hair restrained in a coronet of braids that made her look even taller. A Nordic goddess in the flesh. "Ramsay and I scarcely know each other."

"That will surely change," Annabel said, her gaze calculating as she studied Signy. "They say you were the old laird's right hand. I imagine you'll be assisting Kai as he learns his new duties?"

"Yes, but that won't take long, because Kai is a clever fellow," Signy said. "Then I'll be free to leave and follow my own interests."

Ramsay came sharply alert. She'd said nothing of the sort to him. "You may be overestimating my cleverness and underestimating your knowledge."

"We'll see." She gave him an amused glance, and he realized that she'd recognized Annabel's interest in him and was enjoying the sight of him as prey. He rolled his eyes at her. Annabel was very pretty but too young and, he suspected, rather shallow for his taste. Luckily he was good at avoiding pursuit.

Roald said, "I'd like to offer the use of my Sea Gift House for the gathering after the funeral. There's a great deal of space, and it's close to the cathedral."

"Thank you. That will be very convenient," Ramsay said, grateful for the offer even if it stemmed from Roald's political judgment rather than simple helpfulness. "I'm told an ox has been earmarked for roasting for the funeral feast."

"That will be a good start," Roald said, "and very welcome to those who haven't had much beef lately."

Ramsay wondered a little at the comment. The people of Thorsay lived largely on the sea's bounty, but cattle also did well on the islands, so beef wasn't uncommon. Before he could inquire further, the front door opened again and several more people entered.

Excusing himself from his cousin, he approached the newcomers with Signy at his side. She said in a low voice, "This is George and Bess Fielding, farmers from the south end of Mainland. Good folk, and their youngest daughter, Betsy, is the teacher in their village school."

The elder Fieldings looked as tough and weathered as seasoned oak. George offered his hand, saying gruffly, "I'm sorry for your loss, lad. We'll not see the like of your grandfather again."

"I doubt I am his equal, but I will do my best," Ramsay said quietly.

"Signy, we'll all miss the old laird, and none more than you will," Bess said as she clasped Signy's hand. "I don't know how we would have managed these last years without him. He was the heart and soul of Thorsay."

Ramsay turned to their shy young daughter. "Betsy, I'm told you teach in your village school. Do you enjoy it?"

"Oh yes, sir! I love teaching the little ones and watching them grow and learn new things," she said enthusiastically. "I never dreamed I could be a teacher, but Miss Matheson said I could do it and showed me how." She gazed at Signy with worshipful eyes. "She's done so much for Thorsay!"

Looking embarrassed, Signy said, "You were born to teach. You just needed a push in the right direction, like a nervous donkey facing a bridge."

They all laughed. The door opened again and more people arrived. Some were strangers to Ramsay, others dimly remembered. Using his best diplomatic skills, he spoke with everyone and listened carefully. Signy stayed by his side, offering introductions and occasional suggestions for how some visitors should be treated. She would have done well in the diplomatic service.

When the flow of callers subsided, Ramsay said, "Thank you for saving me from making a fearful muddle of this."

"You've done well," she said. "Your listening has made a good impression."

"Many of them mentioned how grateful they were for the old laird's help," he said thoughtfully. "It sounded very specific, not just general appreciation."

Signy hesitated before replying. "As I said yesterday, the last two years have been difficult. Many households were on the verge of starvation. Your grandfather arranged for food supplies and other kinds of aid as needed. It was always done quietly so as not to damage people's pride."

"Men can have too much pride. Women are often more practical." Making an educated guess, Ramsay continued. "Were you his agent for assessing needs and seeing that people received what they needed?"

She made a dismissive gesture. "Yes, but your grandfather was the one who made it all possible."

"I'm going to continue learning about him for a long time, I see."

"He was a man of many facets." She smiled at Ramsay and for a fierce, visceral moment he remembered how it had felt to hold her in his arms. So natural, so right. Was she really planning to leave once she'd trained him in his new duties? Not something he could ask her anytime soon.

Callers thinned out in the late afternoon. Then the door opened to an auburn-haired man with military bearing and a very familiar face. "Broc Mackenzie!" Ramsay exclaimed as he came forward with an outstretched hand. "Damn, but it's good to see you! Have you said good-bye to the army?"

"Good-bye and good riddance!" his old friend said as he seized Ramsay's hand and clapped him on the shoulder for good measure. He had a thin white scar arcing down his left cheek and there was ancient weariness in his eye, but his broad smile lit up the room. "I can hardly believe I survived the Peninsula and Waterloo intact."

"Broc, I didn't know you were back in Thorsay!" Signy said warmly. "When did you return?"

"Only a week ago, and you've been busy. You're a sight for sore eyes, Signy." Not content to shake hands, Broc gave her a thorough hug.

The Mackenzie farm was just north of Skellig House, and Ramsay and Broc and the Matheson sisters had played together as children. Broc and Ramsay went on to attend the grammar school in Clanwick, studying and getting into mischief regularly. Then Ramsay had gone off to the University of Edinburgh and Broc to the army. Ramsay said, "My grandfather's letters included occasional mentions of your progress up through the ranks of the cavalry and your continued survival."

"And I heard similar reports of you, visiting faraway places with strange sounding names, most of them hot and sunny," Broc said with a grin. "I envied you when I was camped in muddy fields in Portugal!"

"I don't envy you that," Ramsay retorted. "What brings you back now?"

His friend's face sobered. "My father died last year. My family needed me, so it was time to sell out and come home."

"I'm so sorry about your father," Signy said softly. "Your mother has been doing her best, but the farm is more than she and the younger children can manage."

"When I walked in the door, she gave me one hug, then said the milking needed to be done." Broc chuckled. "That's how I knew I was home."

Though Broc was making light of it, Ramsay was sure that his friend's adjustment to his childhood home would be as jarring as Ramsay's. Another group of people were entering, so he said, "After the funeral, we need to sit down with a bottle of Callan's whisky and catch up."

"I'd like that." Broc turned to examine the long table of refreshments that Mrs. Donovan had set out earlier in the day. It was somewhat depleted, but there was enough to feed a hungry young man. Ramsay saw Broc greet Mrs. Donovan, who promptly served him a sizable piece of fish pie while they exchanged news.

Then it was time to turn to the new arrivals, a family of fisherfolk who'd come all the way from Holsay, the most distant inhabited island of Thorsay. Duncan would have been pleased by this outpouring of respect and affection.

Ramsay just hoped his smile and his ability to listen thoughtfully would survive the next three days.

–

Tired but too restless to sleep after the long day, Ramsay made his way to the small family sitting room. Someone, probably Mrs. Donovan, had set up several bottles of drink and glasses on the table between the two wing chairs that faced the fire. He added a couple more blocks of peat to the embers, then inspected the bottles. The whisky would probably flatten him in his present state, so he poured claret from the decanter and settled down to watch the flames as he tried to sort out all the people he'd met that day.

It was near midnight when the door opened and Signy entered, dark circles under her eyes. "Do you mind if I join you?" she asked.

Ramsay rose politely. "Of course not, as long as you don't expect dazzling conversation from me. Would you like a glass of Duncan's excellent claret?"

"Yes, please." She sank into the other wing chair and stretched her feet toward the fire. "I am thoroughly talked out. You must be too."

"Indeed." He poured her a glass of the wine and handed it over. The starkness of her black gown had been modified by a richly colored shawl woven of burgundy and gold and green yarns. She accepted the wine with murmured thanks and drank a third of it with one swallow. He topped her glass up before resuming his seat. "I thought you'd gone home several hours ago."

"I did but only to collect a few of my things." She released her braids from the coronet she'd worn all day, then began combing her fingers through her thick hair to loosen it. "Mrs. Donovan suggested that I stay at Skellig House until after the funeral. I agreed since she needs the extra help and it's more convenient if I'm here."

"You are always helping others, Signy," he said softly as he admired the highlights glinting in the cascade of her red-gold hair. "Everyone seems to depend on you. Do you ever get tired of it?"

"Frequently." She sighed. "But when things need doing and there's no one else, I must do what I can. As the old laird aged, he could no longer manage everything. Since I'm good at organization and getting things done, I gradually took over a great deal of his work. It was often interesting, but there was no end to it."

"It feels wrong that I'm being treated as the old laird's chief mourner because I'm his grandson," Ramsay mused. "But he hasn't been part of my daily life for many years. You were with him all the time. Surely you miss him more deeply than I can."

"Yes, he was the closest thing I had to a father." She gave a soft chuckle. "And like a real father, he could be an annoying old devil! But we understood each other well."

There was intimacy in enjoying a fire together after a long day of shared work, which made it easy to say, "Earlier today you said that after you've trained me, you'll be free to pursue your own interests. What did you mean by that?"

After a long silence, she said, "I'd like more training so I can become a real artist. I want to learn to use oils and spend hours lost in painting. Most of my work now is quick sketching and watercolors. There's never time for more."

"You're very talented and you have a gift for capturing the essence of what you see," he said thoughtfully. "I can imagine the appeal of burying yourself in your work and not always taking care of others. You've earned the right to be your own woman."

"I don't want to bury myself altogether," she said. "The world and people interest me. But I'd like to be selfish sometimes."

"As I said, you've earned the right. Remind me of that if I become too demanding during our training sessions."

"I imagine it will be easier to ignore you than it was to ignore the old laird," she said with amusement. "You are warned."

"Is Sea Cottage a good place for you to work when you have more time?"

"Yes, it's why the laird said I could live there. I have room for a studio and I'm surrounded by the sea and sand and sky that I love to draw and paint." She made a face. "The only thing I haven't had is time. It's the one thing the laird couldn't give me."

Another question had been tickling his mind all day. "You said that with all the bad luck Thorsay suffered, the laird was providing people extra help as needed and that you were his agent. How did that work?"

"I traveled around the islands regularly," she explained. "In theory I was visiting the teachers I trained to see how they were doing, but since they're an important part of their communities, they usually had a good idea which households needed help."

"Clever," he said approvingly. "What form did aid take?"

She shrugged. "Whatever was needed. Sometimes money but most often food. Potatoes, flour, dried fish. Sometimes labor for planting or sheep shearing or the harvest. In many cases, neighbors were willing to help with the work, but they were having difficulties of their own, so paying them for their labor helped both households."

"No wonder everyone in Thorsay seems to know you," he observed. "The aid you brought sounds necessary. Also expensive."

"I'm sure it was, but I don't know the costs. I'd tell the laird what was needed and he'd give me money or tell me to take food out of the storehouse. I know that he imported basic foods from the South and Norway when the troubles became serious." She slanted a wry glance at him over her glass of wine. "You didn't think you'd come back to great riches, did you?"

He laughed a little. "Never that. I never knew much about the family finances. The laird's lands are extensive but not his bank accounts, I think. It will be interesting to hear what the laird's lawyer has to say. Is that still Fergus Maclean?"

She nodded. "He's bald as an egg now, but his mind is as sharp as ever. I expect he'll want to talk to you after the funeral."

"Something else to look forward to," Ramsay said dryly.

"How long do you think it will take us to stop talking about your grandfather as 'the laird'?" she asked with amusement. "After all, you're the laird now."

He hesitated. "That's going to take time. Right now, the title is like an old coat that doesn't fit because it's been shaped to the form of a different man." After a long silence, he added, "I'm not sure it will ever fit."

"In time you'll tailor it to a style that suits you. Keep listening to people and act confident," she said seriously. "Confidence is vitally important. The last years have been difficult, and now Thorsay has lost the man who led us for over four decades. Many people remember no other laird. You need to look as if you have a sure hand on the tiller." She smiled slightly. "And try not to flinch when someone says 'the laird' and they mean you."

"I'll do my best." Raising his wineglass in a salute, he said, "Thank you for all you've done for Thorsay, Signy. And here's to the day when you'll have the time to be the artist you want to be!"

"I'll drink to that." She raised her glass, then swallowed the rest of her wine. "And may both our dreams come true!"

Chapter 10

As Signy had predicted, the day of Duncan's funeral was the longest of a series of very long days. As the funeral feast wound down, most of the Thorsayians who had gathered to mourn the old laird left before dark, but pipers could be still be heard playing in the distance when Ramsay and Signy walked to the residence of the family lawyer, Fergus Maclean, who had asked them to stop by before returning home.

Despite the dark circles under his eyes, Fergus welcomed them warmly and ushered them to his study. "Thank you for meeting with me tonight," he said. "You must both be exhausted, but I thought you should have a general idea how matters stand. Care for a drink?" He opened a cabinet well stocked with bottles and decanters. As a maid came in with a tea tray, he added, "Or you could have a nice hot cup of tea."

The steaming teapot was wearing a knitted cozy designed to look like a puffin. Signy smiled when she saw it. "Tea, please. After being surrounded by so much food and drink for hours, simplicity is appealing."

"The same for me," Ramsay said. He looked tired, but he'd done an admirable job in his role as the new laird. Signy noticed that he'd drunk very little during the funeral feast, which had been a wise choice for a man trying to impress several islands' worth of Thorsayians.

"Will you pour, Signy? I'm for tea also," Fergus said. "And there's a bottle of brandy there to add a bit of extra warmth for anyone who desires that."

Signy did as he asked, adding dashes of brandy since everyone thought that sounded like a good idea. After serving the two men, she added cream and sugar to her cup and settled into a chair, curious what Fergus would have to say.

"That was a fine eulogy you gave for your grandfather," the lawyer began.

"Signy warned me that a short speech would be expected, so I had time to think about it." Ramsay tilted his cup at her in a salute. "I also asked her questions since she knew Duncan so well."

Fergus nodded. "Indeed you did, Signy. The old laird was lucky to have you by his side. He realized that, which is why he left you Sea Cottage. The property is now yours."

She felt a rush of pleasure at the news. "I'm glad," she said simply. Not that she would have expected Ramsay to evict her, but it was good to know that she now owned her own home.

Ramsay took a deep swallow of tea and visibly relaxed. "I'm sure you had good reasons to ask us here tonight. Time for the bad news."

He meant the comment jokingly, but Fergus's expression was grave when he answered. "The financial situation is not good. You've surely heard how badly the islands were struck by bad weather and disease?"

Ramsay nodded. "Signy told me something about it, and how the old laird supplied aid where needed. I gather she did most of the assessing and distribution."

"Yes, it was needful but the estate is near bankruptcy," Fergus said bluntly. "Not only was he spending a great deal of money to help people, but many tenants couldn't pay their rents, so the estate's income is well below what it should be in normal times."

Signy frowned. "I was sometimes surprised but mostly just grateful at how much money the laird was spending on people in need. I didn't realize how great a strain he was putting on the estate."

Fergus sighed, his face tired. "When matters were at their worst, he asked me if it might be possible to get a loan from an Edinburgh bank. I warned him about the risks of borrowing, but he said there was no point in being the laird if half of Thorsay died of disease and starvation."

"It's impossible to argue with that," Ramsay observed. "Just how badly do matters stand? Are there massive debts?"

"I don't really know," Fergus said, sounding annoyed. "Your grandfather was secretive about money and handled all his finances himself. The records should be in his office."

"They're in a locked box," Signy said. "I know where the key is kept. I did have the sense that money has been in very short supply for the past couple of years."

"It will be interesting to look at his record books," Ramsay said thoughtfully. "Luckily I have some money of my own thanks to the work I did for the government. Not vast wealth, but it should be enough to keep the estate running while we figure out how to make the islands more prosperous. Is there anything more I should know?"

Fergus shook his head. "There is much more detail to go over, but that's for another day. Tonight I just wanted to give an overview of what you'll be facing." He slid open the top drawer of his desk and pulled out two letters. "Duncan left these for you two."

The lawyer handed Signy and Ramsay letters sealed with red wax embossed with the fierce sea creature that was the emblem of Thorsay. Signy had always wondered if it was a sea dragon or the mythical selkie, a man upon the land and a seal upon the ocean. Gisela said it was just an imaginary sea beast so Signy could call it whatever she wanted.

Signy drew a deep breath and broke the seal. The brief lines inside were shaky, but in the old laird's distinctive hand.

> *My dearest girl,*
> *I'm not a very pious man, but I have often given thanks to God for bringing you into my life, though I regret that it was because of the tragic loss of your sister. You have been my right hand as well as my best loved child. I don't know how I would have managed without you these last years. I have been selfish in using your strength; don't let Kai do the same.*
> *I wish I could give you more, but I know you have the strength and talent and courage to achieve what your heart craves. Be happy, my dear girl.*
> *Duncan Ramsay, your Old Laird*

By the time she finished reading, there were tears in her eyes. Duncan had never been so openly affectionate, and his farewell tore at her heart.

She closed her eyes while she composed herself. When she opened them again, she saw that Ramsay was carefully folding up his letter, his expression tight. Letters from the dead were bound to have an impact.

The old order had ended. The new was just beginning.

—

Ramsay rose and tucked his letter inside his coat. "I'll be heading for home. I could use the fresh air and exercise of walking there. Signy, will you join me, or would you prefer to ride in a cart? You must be exhausted."

She also stood. "No more than you. I can also use the fresh air. Good night, Mr. Maclean." She smiled. "I want to spend the night in my newly acquired home."

After their farewells, Ramsay escorted Signy outside and away from the town. Clanwick wasn't very large, so it didn't take long to reach the cliff path that led to Skellig House, and beyond that to Sea Cottage. The moon was almost full, and the cool light illuminated the path clearly. The sea was to their right, and the moon touched the foaming waves below with silver.

As the lights of town faded behind them, Ramsay drew in a deep lungful of air and felt himself begin to relax. "I'm so glad that's over. Given a choice, I prefer to lurk quietly in the background rather than be the center of attention. I presume that now I'll be dealing with people a few at a time rather than in crowds."

"Most of the time that will be true," Signy agreed. "But there will always be gatherings and celebrations where you'll be a central figure. Though you might not like being onstage, you managed everything well. That really was a first-rate commemoration of your grandfather. You honored his virtues while not ignoring his gruff, stubborn side. It's particularly impressive considering you hadn't seen him in so many years."

Even when Ramsay was thousands of miles away, Duncan had been a dominant figure in his life. "I suppose

I've been mentally writing that eulogy for most of my life. Now it's time to settle into a more normal routine, whatever that will turn out to be."

"What did your letter say?" she asked quietly.

He didn't want to quote those brief lines, so he said only, "He apologized for leaving what would be a difficult job but said he knew I was up for it. I found that a welcome vote of confidence. What about your letter?"

"He said he was glad I was in his life," she said tersely, as reluctant to say more as Ramsay had been. He understood; words from another's heart were meant to be cherished privately.

"You'll have your hands full, my young laird," Signy said. "But you didn't seem to be too upset about the estate's financial problems."

"Things may be tight for a while, but it sounds like the worst of Thorsay's problems are over. As I mentioned to Maclean, I have enough money to ease the transition while we find ways to make the islands more prosperous."

"Your grandfather said several times that you'd done well for yourself. Have you come back from your travels rich as a nabob?"

He laughed. "Hardly that. I've earned a fair amount of money working for the government, but it's not cheap to outfit expeditions to search for lost ruins. I have a modest fortune that would enable me to live as a comfortable country gentleman under other circumstances. That's not enough to fix everything that needs fixing in Thorsay, but it will give me a good start. Where did Duncan keep his locked box of financial records? You said you know where it is, and where the key is."

"The box is in his office, the small room at the back of the house," she replied. "One wall is taken up with bookcases. The record box is on the bottom shelf all the way to the left end. The key is in an antique pot you sent him that sits on the desk. The pot is Egyptian, I think."

He nodded in recognition. "I bought it in Cairo but it came from farther south, the kingdom of Nubia. Lovely workmanship and very, very old."

"A suitable repository for mysterious keys," she murmured.

Ramsay chuckled. "I'm sure the maker of the pot never imagined his work ending up here in the far north so many years later. Thank you, I'll look at the records tomorrow. While we're talking about money, where do you think it would best be invested to improve the islands' economy?"

"I've been considering that. Better breeding stock for the cattle and sheep would be good," she said thoughtfully. "The storms and livestock diseases reduced the herds badly, and some of the best bulls and rams were lost."

"That makes sense," he agreed. "Rebuilding the herds will take time, so it's best that we get started. I've also been thinking that the roads could use improvement. Most of them now are very poor. Better transportation would have a number of benefits."

"Yes, and road work is a good project for the quiet months after the harvest," Signy said. "That can be a hungry time for some families if there is no other work."

The path crested one of the higher hills between the town and Skellig House. Ramsay halted on the top of the hill, the wind tugging at his hair and garments and the sounds of the sea filling his senses. "I was never really conscious of what it meant to be an islander when I was a boy," he said softly. "The sea was always there in all its moods, offering both bounty and hazard. Now that I've lived in other places, I'm much more aware of how the sea defines the islands and all of us islanders."

Signy moved beside him, tightening her woven shawl against the wind as she gazed at the waves swirling in below them. "I've never lived inland, and I'm sure I'd not be happy out of sight and sound of the sea. We're islanders in our bones, Kai."

He turned and resumed walking along the path. "In the next couple of days, I should start my travels around the islands. Are you game to be my guide? And if so, where should we begin?"

"Is there a particular place you'd like to start?"

"It makes sense to travel Mainland first since I'm here and it's the largest island," he said slowly. "I should also visit Cousin Roald's kelp works since it's probably the most profitable business in Thorsay. After Mainland, Cronsay. I spoke with Jean Olson very briefly after the funeral, and I see why you suggested her as a possible magistrate. I'd like to talk with her at greater length."

"She has the most successful linen works in Thorsay," Signy said. "She runs it as a model of efficiency and good business practices, and she pays her girls better than the other linen manufacturers." A cloud drifted across the moon, darkening their path, and Signy stumbled on a rock. Ramsay caught her hand to steady her.

"Thank you," she murmured.

He found that he liked holding her strong, capable hand. Hand holding was the simplest of intimacies, so why did he feel such a rush of emotion when she didn't pull her hand away?

Because he was increasingly attracted to her. As they continued along the path, they discussed other issues and ideas for Thorsay, but he was always profoundly aware of their clasped hands.

When they neared Skellig House, Signy said, "I'll continue along to Sea Cottage. I want to sleep in my own bed."

"I'll walk you there," he said, reluctant to let go of her.

"That's hardly necessary," she protested.

"True, but it's the gentlemanly thing to do," he said with mock hauteur.

She chuckled and didn't release his hand while they continued along the path. As they neared her home, he asked, "Are you pleased to inherit Sea Cottage?"

"Yes, surprisingly so," she said thoughtfully. "I didn't imagine you'd evict me, but it means a great deal to me that it's *mine*. I own my own home. Before now, there was very little that was mine." She glanced at him. "Do you wish your grandfather hadn't made that bequest? It comes from the overall estate, after all."

"Not at all. You deserve it." As they descended the path that led to the cottage, he said seriously, "I'm going to be relying on you a great deal for some time to come, but don't let me take too much of your time. You should have a couple of days a week that are yours alone, when you can paint or walk along the beach and conjure new pictures. Start by not coming to Skellig House tomorrow. Sleep late, fish from the rocks, anything that makes you happy."

She turned to look up at him, her lovely face appearing surprised in the cool moonlight. "Thank you, I'll do that. I seldom worked on Sundays, but other than that, the old laird never suggested I take a day off even though he said I worked too hard."

"He didn't see the connection between you being overworked and the fact that you worked for him?" Ramsay said, amused. "He was being deliberately obtuse, I think."

"True, but in the last couple of years, he needed a great deal of help."

"No wonder he said several times what a grand girl you are," Ramsay said softly. "Because you are."

Unable to resist, he bent his head into a light, careful kiss. He didn't want to drive her away, but he really, really wanted to kiss her.

Signy caught her breath but didn't retreat. Instead she leaned into him so that their bodies were pressed together. She was intoxicatingly warm and desirable. "You are so lovely," he murmured. "When I caught my first sight of you on my return, I thought you looked like a Nordic goddess."

"Hardly that. Perhaps a scowling shield maiden." She pulled her head away from his. "I'm having trouble remembering why this is a bad idea."

"It's too soon, we're both too tired and emotionally drained by the last days," he explained. "Of course, those reasons could be considered good cause to kiss you again."

So he did.

-

Being kissed by Ramsay and enjoying it was the perfect strange end to a very strange week. After the second kiss, Signy whispered, "Good night," and retreated into Sea Cottage. Once inside, she leaned against the door and closed her eyes. A Nordic goddess? The man had more imagination than she'd realized. And he kissed very well, with light invitation rather than grabby demand. It made her wonder what the next stage of kissing would be like.

Her reverie was interrupted when Fiona emerged yawning from the front room, then nuzzled Signy's ankle in a clear suggestion that her supper was overdue. Signy smiled as she scratched her dog's head. Then she moved into the kitchen and put on water for tea before putting out food and fresh water for Fiona.

After months of watching Duncan decline, it was as much relief as sorrow that he was finally gone. She hoped that wherever he was, he'd enjoyed watching the grand send-off Thorsay had given him.

She pulled out her sketchbook and did a swift drawing of Gisela. Her sister had been shorter and softer and sweeter than Signy. Generous of heart and quick to laugh, she'd been Signy's best friend. Gisela had been so young when she died, just a girl.

What would she have thought of the uncertain relationship growing between Signy and Ramsay? She might have been surprised, but not condemning. She would have thought that enough years had passed that her sister and her beloved should have moved on with their lives.

Or perhaps Signy was just fooling herself. The water was boiling, so she poured it on the leaves in her teapot. As the tea steeped, she wondered where she would go the next day. It had been so long since she'd had free time that she'd lost the habit.

She looked into the lidded jar that held shortbread and found one battered piece left. She collected it and took a bite. Tomorrow she'd bake and not feel rushed, as if she should be somewhere else.

Bake, take a walk, and then paint the sea...

Chapter 11

When Ramsay reached his bedroom, he barely managed to strip his clothes off before falling into the bed and sleeping like a hibernating bear.

He awoke with the dawn after dreaming of Signy in his bed. Alas, she wasn't, but he spent several pleasant moments remembering their kiss and the intoxicating feel of her in his arms.

With a sigh, he swung his feet from the bed and turned his thoughts to the day ahead. Now that he knew where the record box and key were, he should study the estate finances after breakfast. It was not an enthralling prospect.

He stood and moved to the window. The sky was clear and tinted with delicate shades of pink and orange. This was not a morning to be wasted studying accounts.

Decision made, he swiftly dressed in riding clothes and descended to the kitchen. Ordinarily it would be bustling at this hour, but after the days of backbreaking work that had been put in by the cook and her assistants to prepare for the funeral feast, he'd told everyone to take the day off.

He looked in the pantry and smiled to find a bere-meal bannock. Bere was an ancient, fast-growing strain of barley that did well in the short summers of these far northern islands. He hadn't had bere since he'd left Scotland on his travels. He cut a sizable wedge and spread sweet butter on it, then grabbed a slightly withered apple and strode off to the stables. The nutty flavor of the beremeal took him back to his childhood.

Now it was time to make the acquaintance of Duncan's horse, Thor the Fifth. The laird's personal mount was always kept in a large loosebox at the far end of the stables. A sign above simply said THOR without specifying what number he was.

Ramsay caught his breath when he saw the dapple gray stallion. He was a splendid example of the Thorsayian horse, which was descended from a variety of breeds and included a large amount of Icelandic blood. Thorsayian horses were larger than their Icelandic ancestors, but with similar stamina, bold personalities, and equally full, flowing manes and tails. Ramsay had ridden many horse breeds over the years, but he thought none surpassed the Thorsayian. The fabled Arabians came closest, though they were very different.

Thor raised his head and whickered enthusiastically when he saw Ramsay. As he got a closer look at his visitor, he snorted with disgust and lowered his head. Ramsay wasn't surprised that the horse had briefly thought he was Duncan, because in height and build he looked very like his grandfather. "Sorry, Thor," he said softly. "The old laird is gone. You're mine now. I know it won't be the same, but I hope we can be friends."

He held the apple out on his palm. Thor approached and sniffed the apple, then chomped it down in one quick bite.

"How about we go for a ride, my lad?" Ramsay asked as he patted the stallion's neck and scratched behind his ears. "I imagine you haven't been getting as much exercise as you'd like, so today you can have a good run."

He continued talking as he saddled and bridled the horse. Thor showed restless excitement at the prospect of a run. Ramsay led him out to the yard and swiftly mounted. "You're going to want to try to throw me off just to show who's in charge, but don't be too sure you'll succeed."

Thor exploded into a series of kicks and bucks, but Ramsay suspected that the horse wasn't trying as hard as he might have. Surely Duncan hadn't been strong enough to ride Thor for some time, so someone else must have been exercising him regularly.

When Thor had finished performing and settled down, Ramsay patted him on the neck approvingly. "One of the stable lads has been riding you, hasn't he? I'll have to find which one and thank him for keeping you in such good shape.

"Now we'll head out and I'll see how many gaits you have." True Icelandic horses had two more gaits than most horses—the tölt and the flying pace. Ramsay walked Thor out of the yard and turned inland, wanting to see more of the island. It was good to be on a horse again after the weeks at sea on the voyage from Constantinople.

Ramsay signaled Thor to go from the walk to a tölt, which was a gait similar to a walk but which could be performed at a wide range of speeds. He gave the stallion his head, and soon they were skimming up a long slope at the speed of a fast canter. Swift, smooth, lovely. Ramsay laughed aloud, saying, "My grandfather was right—you really are the best of your breed!"

He slowed the horse at the top of the hill so he could admire the stunning views of the sea and distant surrounding islands. But the evidence of poverty was disturbing as he continued across the island. The herds of livestock were smaller than they should be, especially the cattle, and several farms seemed to have been abandoned. The sights were grim confirmation of the troubles Thorsay had endured in recent years.

He must ask Signy how much worse matters would be if not for Duncan's aid to those most in need. As he headed north, parallel to the coast, he passed one of the larger peat cuttings. No one was working this early, but there were sizable stacks of drying peat. Without peat as a fuel source, these northern islands would be uninhabitable.

He halted briefly at one of his favorite historic sites, the crumbled circular remains of a stone broch built on a headland above the sea. A hundred yards out in the water was a stack—a tall, irregularly shaped pillar that had once been part of the cliff until the relentless pounding of the waves had eroded away the rest of the stone, leaving this imposing monument to the power of the North Sea.

He didn't dismount to study the broch more closely, but as always he wondered how old it was. Who were the people who had built it, and whom had they been defending themselves against? The answers were lost in time, but he looked forward to doing the inventory of ancient sites he and Signy had discussed on his first day back. That seemed a long time ago, though it was less than a week.

He turned Thor back toward Skellig House. "Let's see if you can do the flying pace, my lad." This extra gait was possessed by the best Icelandic horses, and not all Thorsayians had it. It was a sprinting gait, very fast and smooth, though not designed for long distance.

As Thor moved easily from a tölt into the flying pace, the crack of a rifle echoed across the hills, and the shot sounded damned close. Swearing, Ramsay leaned forward and urged Thor into his top speed. Another shot rang out, as if it came from one of the hills above. It wasn't as close as the first shot, because Ramsay and Thor were racing away from the shooter.

No more shots sounded, but Ramsay kept Thor at his top pace until they were well away down the path that edged the sea. Then he slowed the horse down, frowning as he considered the shots. There weren't a lot of rifles in Thorsay. The larger landowners would have them, and it was likely that some of the returned soldiers might have managed to come away with their weapons. Could that have been a poacher? They usually preferred stealth.

It was certainly damned careless shooting. One of the first lessons of firearms use was never fire without a clear view of the target.

Maybe the shooter did have a clear view, and his target was Ramsay. It was a chilling thought, and he swore again. Surely he hadn't been in Thorsay long enough to acquire murderous new enemies! More likely the shooting was accidental, or perhaps someone with an ugly sense of humor who liked scaring people.

Ramsay pulled Thor to a halt and turned to study the hills behind him. There weren't a lot of trees in Thorsay, but the landscape had shrubs and boulders and irregularities where a shooter could conceal himself. Impossible to guess where those bullets had come from.

His earlier exhilaration gone, Ramsay continued south along the cliff path at a walk to cool Thor down. There was an itchiness between his shoulder blades, but no more shots disturbed the island's peace.

The sun had risen high enough for islanders to be stirring. He was nearing Thorfield, the Mackenzie family farm, when it occurred to him that since he wanted to talk to a wide range of people, he might as well start with his old friends. He'd seen Broc and his mother and sister at Duncan's funeral, but there had been no opportunity to talk.

The Thorfield house and farm building were set in a protected cup of land on the edge of the sea. As Ramsay rode down the slope toward the house, he was pleased to see a familiar-looking man leaving the house and heading to the barn. He gave the low, sharp whistle that he and Broc had used as boys.

Hearing the whistle, Broc looked up and waved a hand. He greeted Ramsay with a broad smile as Thor trotted into the yard. "You're a sight for sore eyes! Have you come to help me with the morning chores?"

Ramsay laughed. "Dream on! This is the first day that I can do anything except try to stay afloat in the middle of an uproar. I'm more interested in talking and maybe begging one of your mother's excellent breakfasts."

"That could be arranged." Broc ran an admiring cavalryman's gaze over Ramsay's mount. "This is one superb piece of horseflesh. One of the Thors?"

"Yes, Thor the Fifth. The laird said he's the best Thor yet, and I'm inclined to agree." Ramsay swung from the saddle and offered Broc his hand. "How are you adjusting to your return home?"

"A mixture of pleasure and shock." Broc's handshake was firm. "Is Thor the Fifth and Best available for stud service?"

Ramsay considered as he led Thor into the barn. "I hadn't thought that far ahead, but it makes sense to breed more horses like him. Do you have any mares worthy of his divine self?"

Broc sighed as he settled Thor in a stall with water and hay. "A couple are. The farm lost several of our best mares in the late troubles. We need to rebuild, but it will be a long struggle. What kind of stud fees will you charge?"

"One of your mother's breakfasts will do for the first mare. We can negotiate future fees later."

Smiling, Broc said, "Thank you!" Then his gaze went to Thor's hindquarters and he frowned. "Did you have an accident?"

Ramsay followed Broc's gaze, then swore under his breath. Just behind the saddle was a thin line of blood. "A couple of shots were fired in my direction when I was testing Thor's paces up island. I thought they'd missed, but it looks like a bullet grazed him."

Broc frowned, looking very military. "That is not a good thing."

"Do you know of anyone who might hate me?"

"Of course not. Many people mourned the old laird, but most seem pleased that you've made your way home to take up your responsibilities." After a pause, Broc said, "It could be a poacher, or maybe a careless shooter who didn't think anyone was around. The land is pretty open up there."

"I hope you're right." Ramsay's gaze moved from Thor to Broc. "But if you hear anything suspicious or threatening, please let me know."

"Of course," Broc said, his gaze steady. "But now that wound needs tending. I'll be right back."

Ramsay removed Thor's saddle and saddle cloth. The bullet had come from the right side. If he hadn't just kicked Thor into the fast pace gait at that moment, the bullet would have struck him. He and Thor had both been very lucky. So had it been an accident, or was he going to have to watch his back from now on? Because he certainly wasn't going to stay inside Skellig House.

Broc returned and efficiently cleaned the graze, then spread salve over it. Thor was remarkably unconcerned about the whole process. "This one would have made a great cavalry horse," Broc said admiringly.

"Yes, but I'm sure he'll prefer being a great stud. What male wouldn't?"

Broc laughed, and they didn't mention the shooting again. With Thor contentedly munching his hay, Ramsay accompanied Broc across the yard to the farmhouse. It was a sprawling building, but the main entrance and the heart of the house was the kitchen. Broc swung the door open, saying, "A stray who wandered in wants feeding. Do we have enough to satisfy him?"

The room was spacious, with a vast fireplace and abundant cooking implements hanging from hooks. The end wall sported a splendid cast iron stove that Dougal Mackenzie had bought when the farm had had a particularly good year. It was probably the only one in Thorsay and was greatly admired when it was first installed.

Flora Mackenzie, Broc's mother, glanced up from cracking eggs into a bowl, her smile lighting up her face. "There might not be enough food when I think of your appetites as boys! But it's good to see you, my lad. Do you plan to eat me out of house and home this morning?"

"I'll do my best," Ramsay promised. As children he and Broc had been continually in and out of the house, and Flora was like a favorite aunt. She'd aged more than her share of years in the time he'd been gone, and her hair had gone silver, but her smile was genuine.

She stepped back, her face serious. "I'm sorry your grandfather is gone, Kai. I don't know how we'd have survived without his help after Dougal died."

Broc's father had been a broad, cheerful man who always welcomed friends and family to the homestead. "I'm so sorry Dougal is gone," Ramsay said gravely. "There have been too many losses here in recent years."

Drawn by voices, a young woman with dark hair emerged from the pantry carrying a plate of oatcakes. Seeing Ramsay, she squealed and set the plate on the table before hurling herself at him. "Kai, you really are here! I didn't quite believe it."

Laughing, he hugged her back. "And I can't quite believe that Broc's little sister has grown into a beautiful young lady, Maeve!"

"You're lying, but I like it," she said mischievously. She must be about eighteen now. She'd been just a little bit of a thing when Ramsay knew her before.

Ramsay was wondering if he dared ask about Broc's younger brother when Flora said, "Jamie is now a second officer on a Hudson's Bay ship, so we don't see much of him, but he gets back to Thorsay every few months."

"Next time he's here, I hope to see him," Ramsay said. "He was always getting onto boats whenever he could, so I'm not surprised that he chose the sea."

While they chatted of memories and stories of days gone by, Flora and Maeve were brewing tea and producing plates of scrambled eggs with cheese and herbs, fried potatoes, and toasted oatcakes. Broc told some hair-raising stories of life in the cavalry. Ramsay suspected that Broc had barely escaped death in battle multiple times, though he spoke easily about what had happened.

Ramsay kept his own stories light and entertaining, with descriptions of what it was like to ride camels and how it was possible to get tired of endless sunshine. The

Thorsayians scoffed at that since they'd never seen too much sunshine.

But he noted that although the breakfast was substantial and satisfying, no meat was served. In the past, such a breakfast would have included bacon, sausage, or ham, and quite possibly all three. The tea was also unexpected, the China blend extended with mint. Money was obviously in short supply.

When the breakfast had been demolished, he said, "Mrs. Mackenzie, seeing you is a great pleasure, but I'd also like to ask you some questions in my capacity as a newly hatched laird. Are you willing, or will you give me my marching orders?"

She sighed and turned her gaze to her daughter, who had just finished clearing the breakfast dishes. "Maeve, isn't it time you gathered the eggs, and after that did some weeding in the vegetable garden?"

Maeve scowled at her mother. "You want to get rid of me."

"Exactly," her mother said. "So off with you!"

Maeve finished stacking the dishes, then flounced from the room. She flounced very prettily.

After his sister left, Broc asked dryly, "Are you going to throw me out also?"

His mother shook her head. "No, some of this you know, and there is more you need to know. Ask your questions, my young laird."

"I've heard of the climate and disease problems, but only in general terms. Now I need to learn more so I better understand what must be done to help. I want to talk to people all over the islands to hear what they have to say, and I'm starting with you."

"Aren't I the lucky one?" Flora said with a flash of her old humor. She pulled a knitting basket from under the table and began working on a scarf in the soft natural colors of sheep's wool, ranging from white to dark brown.

"At least you'll get rid of me quickly this way." Ramsay's brow furrowed. Where to start? "Your farm was one of the largest and most prosperous on Mainland. It was always bustling with people. Today it seems deserted. What happened to everyone? I hope to God that they aren't all dead!"

"A few died of the fever. A few who were able left Thorsay to work elsewhere, in Shetland or Orkney or somewhere South. But a good many are at your cousin's kelp works since it's high season for kelp cutting and extra help is needed."

Ramsay's brows rose. "Surely that work doesn't pay well."

"It doesn't, but something is better than nothing." Her needles clicked in the silence until she continued, "Some islanders who've lost their homes are staying here at the farm. The quarters aren't fancy, but at least they have a roof over their heads."

He frowned. "Are many people homeless?"

"I can't say how many, but there have been families doubling up and moving into barns." Her hands stilled. "We'd had some good years, so Dougal borrowed money from the Bank of Clanwick to buy a fine flock of Irish sheep and a first-class bull. It seemed like a good idea at the time, but it cost Dougal his life and almost cost us the farm."

Startled, Ramsay said, "I'm sorry, I don't understand. Could you tell me more about what went wrong?"

"The cattle disease took out the bull and most of our herd. And the sheep…" She stopped speaking, her face rigid. "You've heard of the devil storm that did so much damage? Those damn fool sheep were huddling on a headland in the full force of the storm. Dougal went to gather the herd and take them back to the barns. The end of the headland collapsed into the sea, taking Dougal and most of the flock and two sheepdogs."

Ramsay swore under his breath at the vicious unfairness of it. "So you lost your husband and your investment in livestock in one blow. Was the bank unwilling to work with you until the farm recovered from the damage and could pay off the loan?"

"The bank demanded repayment immediately." Her mouth twisted. "The manager was apologetic but said the troubles had strained the bank's resources so badly that he couldn't afford to give us more time. I was told that there was someone ready to buy Thorfield. That's when your grandfather stepped in." Her gaze turned fierce as she glanced at her son. "We *will* repay you! I swear it."

"Indeed we will," Broc said quietly.

"I know you will," Ramsay said as he rose. "Thank you for your directness. And the breakfast."

"I don't envy you the task ahead, laddie," Flora said. "But I know you'll be up for it."

He wished he shared her faith in him. As he mounted Thor and turned south along the cliff path that ran toward Skellig House, he started making lists and calculating how far his savings could go toward fixing what needed to be fixed. Not far enough, but he could make a good start.

The path took him past Sea Cottage, and he saw a figure walking along the beach below. Signy enjoying her day off with her dog at her heels.

He wasn't the only one who recognized her. Thor gave a happy whinny and darted down the angled path that led to Sea Cottage. Bemused, Ramsay gave his mount his head. Thor circled the cottage and picked his way down to the beach, sure-footed as a mountain goat.

Signy turned at the sound of hooves. She was glorious, her tall figure swathed in a wrap that matched her hazel eyes, tendrils of red-gold hair dancing in the breeze, and her face bright with healthy color.

Unexpected joy surged through him. Seeing Signy smile with welcome made everything he faced seem manageable.

Chapter 12

Signy laughed aloud as Thor dashed up to her and skidded to a stop in a flurry of sand and pebbles, Fiona giving a yip of welcome. "Thor!" She reached up to caress the elegant neck and ears. "How are you, my beautiful boy? I'm sorry I don't have an apple or carrot for you."

Ramsay grinned. "I wondered who exercised Thor after my grandfather became too weak to ride. Obviously it wasn't one of the grooms."

Signy glanced up as the stallion nudged her with his muzzle, then touched noses with the dog. "I had to do a lot of riding on the laird's behalf, and Thor needed the exercise. He and I had always had a special relationship, so it worked out very well. But now he's your horse, of course."

"I'm not so sure about that," Ramsay said with amusement. "Thor was quite determined to say hello."

"I haven't been able to go out riding with him for a week, so he probably missed me." She patted the glossy neck again.

"Hard to believe that a week ago I was still sailing north from Aberdeen." He collected Thor's reins in preparation for leaving. "How are you spending your day off?"

She chuckled. "I slept late, baked a new batch of short-bread, and decided to take a walk. I could become used to this."

His brows rose. "How long would it be before you became restless and needed more tasks to keep you busy?"

"Two days? Perhaps three." Enjoying his company, she said on impulse, "But for now, would you like some shortbread and tea?"

He hesitated a moment. "I probably shouldn't intrude on your leisure time, but tea and shortbread would be lovely."

Ramsay dismounted and led Thor back along the beach, walking on the opposite side of the horse from Signy. She enjoyed watching him, not just because he was tall and fit and handsome but because of the easy confidence with which he moved. He had a quality of being at home in his body that was appealing. She smiled to herself, thinking that was rather like the way Thor moved.

Reminding herself that she shouldn't stare, she asked, "Were you riding somewhere in particular, or just riding for pleasure?"

"I woke very early and decided to check out Thor's gaits."

"Which are flawless," she said. "I've never seen a finer Thorsayian horse, though your grandfather has several others that are almost as good."

"On the way home, I stopped by Thorfield and almost the first thing Broc did was ask me about stud fees."

"Your grandfather would approve," Signy said. "He talked about setting Thor up as a stud but hadn't got around to it. What will you charge for Thor's services?"

"I told Broc that one of his mother's breakfasts would do for the first mare Thor covers, but I'll have to think more about fees for the future." He frowned. "I'm glad

I didn't give Broc a cash price. Over breakfast I learned what a hard time the Mackenzies have had."

That was an understatement. Even Flora, who had a spine of pure steel, had come close to breaking down when threatened with the loss of Thorfield. Thank heaven the old laird had been able to prevent that. "A ghastly time, but they've survived the worst of it, I think."

She guided them around the cottage to the flattened area at the bottom of the path down the bluff. With the cottage on one side and the bluff on the other, it was protected from the wind, and Signy had installed a small watering trough and an iron ring in the wall of the house. "Will you tether Thor while I get water and his blanket?"

As Ramsay obeyed, he said, "This seems to be Thor's second home."

"He's spent several nights here when it made more sense than returning him to Skellig House and collecting him again in the morning," she admitted as she headed inside, Fiona on her heels. She filled a bucket with water and collected Thor's horse blanket, which was fine enough for a Derby winner.

As she emptied the bucket into the trough, Ramsay spread the blanket over Thor's back. When they entered the cottage, he said, "I hadn't thought about it, but where does your water come from?"

"There's a spring on the bluff above. Some years ago, your grandfather installed pipes to bring fresh water to the cottage. Since it comes from higher ground, a simple stopcock controls the water." Signy turned the stopcock to fill the kettle, then set it over the fire. "Did you know your grandmother used this cottage as a retreat from the busyness of Skellig House?"

He looked surprised. "I recall that she regularly disappeared for several hours at a time, but I never thought much about it. I assumed she'd withdrawn to her sewing room."

Signy waved him to a chair. "Sometimes she did that, but when she really wanted privacy, she came here because she was harder to find. No one was allowed in the cottage without her invitation." Signy opened a pottery jar and pulled out a mixed handful of shortbread and gingerbread bars. She tossed a little piece of shortbread to Fiona, then set the rest on a small plate.

"It's remarkable how oblivious a child can be to those around him," he observed. "Skellig House was usually busy with people coming and going, so I didn't notice when my grandmother wasn't visible."

"She enjoyed peace and quiet and the sound of the sea. She'd come here to read or do the household accounts. Or weave." Signy gestured at the small loom in the corner of the long front room. "That loom was hers. She was a much better weaver than I, but I like to use it in winter and imagine that she's sitting next to me."

"No wonder I'm so comfortable here," Ramsay said quietly. "She must have filled this space with her own warmth."

"I've often thought the same. It's one of the reasons I asked the old laird if I could live here." Signy rose and poured boiling water into her favorite teapot. "And now Sea Cottage is mine."

"As it should be." He gazed out the windows at the endless rolling waves. "This seems so much your place."

"It is," she said quietly as she set out mugs and poured tea into them. "Now come and have your tea."

He settled in one of the chairs and skimmed his fingertips over the curving side of the teapot. "I love this redware and look forward to visiting the Jansen pottery."

Signy had a swift, hot image of him caressing her bare skin the same way he was touching the teapot. Ramsay glanced up, and their gazes met for an unnervingly intense moment. She forgot to breathe as she wondered if he was thinking something similar...

He swallowed hard, then helped himself to a square of shortbread. "I need to start my traveling over the islands. I'm thinking of leaving day after tomorrow for a first journey of a week or so. Will you be able to come with me?"

She nodded casually, not wanting to show how much she liked the idea of being his traveling companion and guide over the next weeks. "Yes, I think it's wise to be away for only a few days at a time. You'll have work coming at you from all directions."

"I'm sure you're right. Our first call will be on Cousin Roald's kelp works. I'd like to get to know him better in a less formal setting than a funeral." He consumed a piece of gingerbread. "This is as good as your shortbread. Hard to choose, so I'll have one more of each." After he'd consumed a second piece of shortbread, he asked, "What do you think of Roald?"

"He's a good businessman and a hard worker." Signy stirred honey into her tea as she considered her answer. "Thorsay is not an easy land, and most islanders look out for their neighbors because we need one another. But Roald is interested only in himself and how to increase his wealth and power. He's not evil, but if he has to choose between his own interests and those of his neighbors, he'll choose himself every time."

"I thought that about him when I was young, and it sounds like he hasn't changed much," Ramsay commented. "What about his children?"

"From what I've seen, they're both restless here and would prefer to go to Edinburgh. Annabel wants to cut a dash in society and catch a rich husband and live in Edinburgh or even London. I think Axel feels much the same. He'd like the money and freedom to be a young man about town, but Roald keeps them here on Thorsay. They're at the top of local society, but Thorsay isn't grand enough for them. Expect Annabel to flirt with you madly and Axel to try to prove his superiority," Signy said dryly.

"Blunt and true, I suspect," Ramsay said thoughtfully. "So I need to keep my distance when possible and handle with care when I can't avoid them."

"That's much how your grandfather handled Roald and his family. If you leave him alone, he'll leave you alone."

"But what if his interests conflict with my plans for Thorsay?" he asked, thinking out loud. "What happens then?"

"Then you and Roald fight," Signy said calmly.

"Who would win?"

She studied his face. "Roald would cheat, but even so, I think you'd win. Either way, conflict between the two of you would probably be bad for Thorsay."

"So better to keep the peace if possible," Ramsay said. "I will if I can." He drained the mug of tea and stood. "I'd best be getting back to Skellig House. As you said, work will be coming from all directions."

She also rose.

"After visiting the kelp works, we can spend the night at an inn in Skillness, which is the largest Mainland town after Clanwick. The fishing fleet has grown, and a fair number of trading ships call there as well. On the way back here, there are several farmers you might want to call on. I'll make a list of suggestions."

"I should have thought of this before," Ramsay said hesitantly as he donned his hat. "Will it be considered scandalous that I'm traveling with an attractive young woman? I don't want to ruin your reputation."

She laughed. "After all my journeys on behalf of the old laird, I think I'm considered an honorary man. I'm not the kind of marriageable young female who needs protecting."

"Anyone who thinks of you as an honorary man isn't paying attention," he said as he opened the door. "Thank you for the tea, cakes, and insights. They'll help sustain me this afternoon as I dig into my grandfather's financial records."

"Imagine me taking a long and lazy walk on the beach," she said cheerfully. "I'll leave the accounts to you. I'll come to Skellig House tomorrow and we can work out the details of your first journey."

She and Fiona followed him outside and said their good-byes to Thor. As Ramsay removed the horse blanket and swung into the saddle, he remarked, "It hasn't escaped my attention that it's Thor who holds your heart."

"Well, he's very fine looking," she pointed out.

"And he has five gaits. I admit his superiority." With a smile, he rode up the path to the bluff and disappeared to the south.

She folded the horse blanket and went into the cottage. It was going to be interesting traveling with Ramsay. The key question was whether she *wanted* their time together to become scandalous.

The sky clouded up on the ride back to Skellig House, and it was mizzling by the time he returned Thor to the stables. He remembered the searing heat and thirst of traveling the desert and decided that he much preferred the rain.

As he took Thor to the stallion's loosebox, he was greeted by Jamie Donovan, the robust head groom whose wife was the housekeeper. "What do you think of Thor the Fifth, lad?"

Still another old retainer who called him lad. "He's magnificent," Ramsay said good-humoredly as he removed the tack and began to groom the horse. "He has all the Thorsayian gaits and performs them perfectly. He's also very well behaved for a stallion."

"That's Miss Signy's influence," Donovan said. "He purrs like a kitten when she's mounted on him."

"I noticed," Ramsay said as he brushed out the horse's neck and back in easy circles. "In fact, he insisted on visiting her at Sea Cottage when I was on the way home."

Donovan chuckled. "Aye, he's in love with her."

"Technically Thor belongs to me, but it seems wrong to break up such a beautiful romance," he said dryly as he started combing Thor's mane.

"No matter, all the horses love her. The laird gave her Loki, Thor's half brother. He's a gelding, the chestnut in that stall there." He gestured with his chin. "He's a fine horse, but smaller. Thor is better for your weight."

Ramsay glanced over. The gelding was a handsome red chestnut whose coloring complemented Signy's. He smiled at the thought. "Among the Norse gods, Loki is Thor's half brother. Is the horse Loki a mischief maker like Loki the god?"

"Nay, he's a fine riding horse who dotes on Miss Signy," Donovan said. "I'd hire her to work in the stables if the laird hadn't claimed her time first."

As Ramsay circled to Thor's other side and resumed grooming, he was startled by a flash of gray to his left. He turned and saw that Odin had leaped onto the wall of the box and now stared unblinkingly at Ramsay with his one golden eye.

"Odin!" he exclaimed, surprised at how glad he was to see the cat. "I thought you were gone for good."

He reached out to scratch the cat's head and was swatted by Odin's long paw. But it was a friendly swat, followed by Odin presenting his head in an obvious bid for ear scratching. Ramsay complied, saying, "Has Odin been living in the stables? I haven't seen him since the night the old laird died."

"He's not been here." Donovan surveyed the cat, who had begun purring under Ramsay's ministrations. "He used to spend most of his time in the stables and a fine catcher of mice and rats he is. But he moved into the house when the laird became so ill. Kept him good company."

"He howled and ran into the night when my grandfather died," Ramsay said. "I was afraid he might have been swept off the bluff in that storm."

"I expect he had to mourn in his own way," Donovan said thoughtfully. "Now he's back and has accepted you as the new laird. You should feel honored."

"What I feel is manipulated," Ramsay said with amusement as he continued scratching the cat's gray head and throat. "He has an impressive purr."

"And he knows how to use it," the old groom said with a chuckle. "He seems to be winning you over pretty easily."

"Let's see how long he stays with me when I go in the house and start looking at accounts."

"If there's food involved, he'll be there," Donovan predicted.

"Want to join me?" Ramsay asked Odin. "There might be some cheese in it for you."

The cat jumped to the floor and sauntered away in the direction of the house. Smiling, Ramsay followed Odin inside and cut a thin slice of cheese when he passed by the kitchen. The cat wolfed it down, then joined Ramsay in the old laird's study, where he flopped into a patch of sunshine and began to snore.

Ramsay skimmed the most recent account books to get a sense of how the finances looked. The accounts were straightforward, with listings for income and expenditures. Not much of the former in the last three years, though he could see the steady deterioration of his grandfather's health reflected in the old man's handwriting.

Then he fished the key to the private file box from the vase that Signy had told him about. These documents were much less clear. Scribbled notes listed names and amounts of money but provided no clue as to what they were for.

He also found a statement showing almost five thousand pounds in the Bank of Scotland, which was headquartered in Edinburgh. If the statement was up-to-date, the money would prove useful, but where had it come from? It didn't show up in the regular accounts.

His gaze went to Odin, who had shifted to follow the sunshine across the carpet. "What was the old laird up to, Odin?"

The cat rolled over so his back was to Ramsay. No help from him. Ramsay locked the papers up again and hoped that Signy could provide some insights.

Chapter 13

Ramsay blinked in surprise at Signy's manner of dress when she showed up the next morning for the start of their expedition. She wore a split skirt that fell just past her knees over what looked like heavy black knit stockings and well-worn riding boots. The sight of her shapely legs briefly interfered with his breathing.

Forcing himself to drag his gaze away, he said, "That looks like a very sensible riding costume."

"It is," she said imperturbably. "Thorsayian roads are mostly not good enough for carriages, so any woman who wants to travel very far needs to ride, and astride is better." She gestured at her split skirt and leggings. "This has become quite the costume for fashionable Thorsayian female riders since I came up with the idea."

He suspected that the outfit had become fashionable not only because it made riding easier but because Signy had the courage to wear it. Where she led, other women followed. He commented, "Englishwomen should adopt something similar."

He lifted his saddlebags, which had been sitting lopsidedly in the front hall. "I have my notes and some clothing, and the kitchen has provided us with a generous luncheon. I've also remembered the first rule of travel on Thorsay."

Signy chuckled. "Have several layers of clothing, including a waterproofed outer garment, because on any given day it will certainly rain at least a little."

"Exactly." He slung the saddlebags over one shoulder. "Shall we set off? I'm anxious to meet Loki, the god of mischief."

"My Loki is actually quite a sweetheart." Signy lifted her own saddlebags before giving Ramsay a glance. "The old laird gave him to me outright several years ago since I was doing so much riding on official business. I didn't start riding Thor until your grandfather wasn't able to."

"You've more than earned a horse of your own," he said mildly.

They walked together the short distance to the stables and found that Donovan had both mounts saddled and ready to go. As Signy approached, the two horses crowded toward her enthusiastically. She laughed and petted one with each hand. "Thor is the epitome of the Thorsayian breed, while Loki is a throwback to his Arabian ancestors. He can't do the extra gaits of a true Thorsayian, but they're both lovely horses."

"Can't beat a Thorsayian horse for good temperament," Donovan agreed as he took Signy's saddlebags and set them onto Loki.

Ramsay swung his saddlebags onto Thor. "As I recall, the main road across the island goes from Clanwick to Skillness and Roald's kelp works, but I'd like to take the old road over the hills. There were some ruins along that route."

"As you wish. I haven't traveled that way for years, so it will make a pleasant ride." Signy used a mounting block to get onto Loki, denying Ramsay the opportunity to help her himself. Reminding himself there would be more opportunities, he mounted Thor.

He looked forward to rediscovering Thorsay, to meeting people and surveying some old ruins. But most of all, he looked forward to spending time alone with Signy.

—

Signy found that riding with Ramsay was interesting. He was in a constant state of quiet alertness, a habit he'd likely developed when traveling in dangerous terrain, possibly on camelback. They saw few people, but when they did, he introduced himself and chatted for a few minutes.

Everyone had heard of the old laird's death, and people were curious about his long-absent grandson. Most were wary at first, but Ramsay soon won them over with his easy charm and interested questions about their lives and what changes they'd like to see on Thorsay.

When they rode on after one such encounter, Signy observed, "You're a born politician, Kai."

He looked pained. "I see you're back to hurling insults at me."

She laughed. "That was actually a compliment. You're good at talking to people and winning their approval. That's a fine skill for the leader of Thorsay since Thorsayians are independent and opinionated. I know this isn't the life you wanted, yet here you are, talking and listening seriously, and making friends."

He was silent while they circled a tumble of rocks. "No, it isn't the life I would have chosen," he said finally. "But it's always been my destiny, assuming I didn't get myself killed somewhere along the way. I regret ending my travels, but this..." He glanced across the short distance that separated them, his gaze intent. "This feels right."

She looked away, wondering if there was any special meaning in his words. "I'm glad for everyone's sake. A sullen laird would be dreadfully annoying."

He chuckled. "I'm sure he would be. I'll try not to inflict sullenness upon you."

She pointed at the hill ahead. "The ruins are on top of Sky Hill. I think it's the highest point on Mainland. A good place to stop for lunch."

"I'm ready to eat and so are the horses, I imagine. I poked around among the old stones up there once or twice when I was young, but the place seemed to be the remains of an old farmstead and didn't interest me much. I've visited a lot of ruins since then, so maybe I'll be more perceptive about this site now."

A brief rain squall swept over them as they ascended the winding road to the top of the hill, which was crowned by a scattering of low, irregular stone walls, plus the remains of a tower. Ramsay pulled Thor to a stop. "Look at the view from here! We can see all of Mainland and the seas around. I wonder if this might have been used as a watchtower."

She halted Loki beside him. "I hadn't thought of that before, but you might be right. This would be a prime location for spotting dragon ships or other invaders. I'm trying to remember if there are any old tales that refer to a watchtower and watch fires."

"I'll have to find some of the old storytellers." He swung from his horse. "But now, lunch!"

—

Ramsay set the horses to grazing while Signy laid out their lunch next to a crumbled wall that provided some protection from the wind. It faced south, so it caught warmth from the fitfully visible sun. The ground was wet from the earlier rain, but several stones were suitable for sitting and kept them off the damp grass.

The meal of bread, cheese, and pickled onions was simple and tasty, especially when washed down with ale. Ramsay had always had an appetite, and Signy was amused to see that hadn't changed. After she finished the last of her cheese, she asked, "Did you find anything interesting in the laird's accounts?"

He frowned. "The regular account books were straightforward, but there was a private file that I didn't understand. A number of local names were listed, followed by a notation of something like 'Fifty pound loan, to be repaid when possible.' No terms, no interest rate, just the name and the amount."

He pulled a folded paper from his inside coat pocket and handed it to Signy. "Here's one page. Does it mean anything to you?"

She scanned the names and numbers. "It looks like money he gave to people in dire straits, and the outlays are described as loans because many Thorsayians hate the idea of taking charity."

"I wondered if it might be something like that. Tactful of him."

Signy nodded. "When someone has nothing left but his pride, it is cruel to take that away as well."

He accepted the paper and returned it to his inside pocket. "More surprising was a statement from the Bank of Scotland showing a balance of just over five thousand pounds."

Signy stared. "That's a small fortune."

"Yes, and I wonder where it came from given how low revenues have been in the last several years." Ramsay frowned. "The Bank of Clanwick was my grandfather's bank. I wonder if he went to the Bank of Scotland for a loan that he couldn't get in Clanwick. But there are no loan documents describing the terms or repayment."

"I know nothing of this," Signy said. "I wish he hadn't been so secretive!"

"So do I. I'll have to write Edinburgh to see what the bank says."

"Would you try to collect on those loans?" she asked uneasily.

His brows arched. "What kind of man do you think I am? Of course not."

"I didn't think you would, but Roald would if he'd made those loans." She swallowed the last of her ale. "He'd say it was a simple matter of business."

"True, but Thorsay isn't a business. It's a sacred trust."

She blinked at his words. She agreed but hadn't realized that Ramsay felt the same way. She supposed he wouldn't be here if he didn't.

As she packed away the cups and the remnants of the meal, she said, "I brought my sketchbook since you're interested in having drawings of the various ruins. I can do some quick drawings before we move on."

"Do we have time? I'm not sure how long it will take to reach the kelp works."

"This is the narrowest part of the island, so we can explore more here and still reach the works before the afternoon is over."

"Excellent! I'd love to get a closer look at the ruins." Ramsay crossed to his saddlebags and took out a notebook and an odd implement.

"What's that device you have?" Signy asked as she retrieved her sketching kit from her own saddlebags.

He unfolded the handle to reveal a small shovel. "Bare hands aren't much good for poking around ruins. I came up with the idea, and a smith in Constantinople made this for me. Small enough to carry easily and very useful for investigating."

"Just what every antiquarian needs," she said with a smile.

"As long as they don't mind getting their hands dirty. I want to see how much of the original structures remain." He headed around the wall that had blocked the wind, his expression enthusiastic.

The gleam in his eyes was proof of the antiquarian interests that had driven him so far from his home. Signy hoped that Thorsay had enough ruins to hold his attention.

She followed him around the wall, sketching kit in hand. The kit was a flat waterproofed pouch that contained her tablet, a thin board to support the tablet, and several types of sketching pencils. Ramsay beckoned her closer. "You can see the outlines of this main building. It's sizable and it looks as though there are several outbuildings as well. A pity so many of the stones were scavenged for other uses, but there are enough left to get a sense of the place. It looks as if there was a defensive ditch around the area, though it's mostly filled in now."

As she followed his gestures, what had seemed like random bits of stone took on a clear, obviously manmade outline.

"What would you like me to draw?" she asked. "The ruins of the tower are the most appealing from a scenic point of view, but I assume you're more interested in an accurate record of the site."

"Exactly." He paced several yards to the right. "I think this would be a good view. Would you like to walk the site with me first?"

She nodded. "That will give me a better idea of what to draw." Glad she was wearing boots, she accompanied him around the remnants of the farm. It was surprisingly interesting as he pointed out faint lines or depressions that made it possible to imagine the structure in its prime. Probably an entrance here, perhaps a storeroom here. His suggestions made the site come alive.

She asked, "Do you have any idea how old these ruins are?"

"*Old!* Many centuries." He gazed across the grassy turf whose scattered stones sketched outlines of the past. "There might well have been multiple buildings on this site over a very long period of time."

Her brow furrowed. "How can you learn whether that's true?"

"By digging down to see if there are more layers of ruins below, then spending a long time studying what is found." He brandished his little shovel. "Antiquarian studies are not for the impatient."

"Why do you do it?" she asked, intrigued.

"The simple answer is that I find old ruins fascinating." He paused thoughtfully. "The fascination comes from curiosity about the past. Who lived here, and what were their lives like? Were they people we would recognize as kin, or were they so different in language and thought and appearance that they would seem utterly alien? For that matter, have there been several different peoples who lived here in different ages? Very likely, but we'll never know unless we study what they've left behind."

"You would make an excellent university lecturer," she said admiringly. "You're arousing my interest in learning more. Thorsay has any number of ruins and standing stones and towers scattered over all the islands, yet I've never thought much about them. But these stones have countless tales to tell, don't they?"

He grinned. "I'll make an antiquarian out of you yet."

"Perhaps," she said, returning his smile. Then she made her way across the wet, springy turf to a stone perch that would give her a good view of the overall site.

She began sketching in pencil. Later she could finalize the drawing in ink, but pencil was quicker and easier to correct. As she sketched the visible stones, she found herself thinking about the people who had lived here. What had their world been like? Surely there had been families, loving couples and mischievous children. What did they wear? Warm clothing this far north. Surely they had sheep and could make woolen fabrics? She was beginning to understand Ramsay's fascination with the past.

After she finished the overview sketch, she moved to a good view of the ruined tower, which was the most interesting single structure and would make a good close-up. No windows were visible in the lower section of the tower—all that remained—perhaps to keep attackers from gaining easy access.

She was almost finished with the sketch when Ramsay called, "Signy? I have something interesting to show you."

She packed her materials into the pouch and followed his voice. His head was barely visible just beyond the farthest edge of the structure.

When she reached the low irregular wall, she saw that he was standing in a kind of pit and digging enthusiastically at the opposite wall. "What have you found?" she asked. "Buried treasure?"

He laughed. "Antiquarian treasure. This is a midden."

"A trash heap?" she said doubtfully. "What makes it interesting?"

"It shows how people lived. What they ate, what they used, what they threw away. Treasure indeed. Come down for a look." He extended his hand up to her.

She stepped over the low wall and reached for his hand, but the grass at the edge of the pit was wet and slippery from the earlier rain. Before she could catch his hand, she slid on the wet grass and went tumbling down on top of him.

He fell backward and she fell with him, landing on top in a tangle of limbs, with her face only a few inches from his. "I'm so sorry!" she exclaimed, all too aware of the warmth and strength of his lean body under hers. "Have I hurt you?"

She tried to scramble off him, but his right arm went around her waist, and he held her there as close as a lover's embrace.

His gaze caught hers, the gray depths intense, locking them both into this intimate moment. "As I said, middens can contain unexpected treasure," he said huskily. Then he pulled her down into a kiss.

Chapter 14

After her first moment of surprise, Signy found Ramsay's kiss a swift, spontaneous pleasure. When he'd kissed her before, it had been a sweet embrace of discovery. Lying along his warm, strong frame stirred her blood in shocking new ways.

She wriggled against him to a more comfortable position. He sucked in his breath, and his hands skimmed down her body, smoothing her back and shaping the curve of her waist before coming to rest on her hips, drawing them tight against him. Her lower body began pulsing against him, wanting more. Wanting... what?

Shocked at her own reactions, she pushed herself away from him and scrambled back so that she was sitting pressed against the end of the pit. For the first time she really understood how Gisela had thrown good sense to the winds and lain with Ramsay, with catastrophic consequences. Gisela had loved him, and Ramsay had loved her back.

Voice unsteady, she said, "Didn't we decide this was a bad idea?"

He closed his eyes and drew a shuddering breath before opening them and moving away from her until his back was pressed against the other end of the pit, which put him about six feet away. "Yes, but I'm having trouble remembering why," he said, his face taut.

"Because it's too soon. Too many complicating factors." She drew an unsteady breath. "Too much doubt on my side."

"Those are all good reasons," he said quietly. "Time will help us sort them out."

"Is there an *us*? I thought we were you and me, separately." Though she had an uneasy feeling that maybe they were becoming an *us*. She brushed back her loosened hair and tried to lighten the atmosphere. "And really, Kai, a midden? Is this the seduction place of choice for sophisticated men of the world?"

He gave a choke of laughter, and his expression eased. "It does lack *savoir faire*," he agreed. "But what's a man to do when assaulted by a goddess?"

She snorted. "Flattery does not a goddess make. A better topic would be whatever interesting thing you called me over to see."

"Yes! I temporarily forgot." His expression became focused, and he leaned over to retrieve a fragment of pottery near his right knee. After brushing off some loose earth, he handed it to her. "Look."

She turned the fragment over in her hands as she studied it. About six inches across, it appeared to be one third of a shallow bowl. The color was the soft tan of natural clay, and the surface was hard and smooth, though she didn't think it was glazed. The rim of the bowl was patterned with sets of grooved lines that crisscrossed first to the left, then to the right. "Why is this special?"

"It's very old," he replied.

She frowned at the fragment. "How old, and how can you tell?"

He hesitated. "Very, very old, I think, though it's hard to explain why I feel that way. It's a kind of sixth sense

I've developed from handling so many potshards and other artifacts in my explorations. A couple of years ago I tested myself by visiting a private antiquarian museum where the age of most items was known. I held various objects and found that if they felt old to me, they really were old. My guesses about how old were in the right range. Though it was a range of centuries."

"That is interesting," she admitted. "Maybe you started developing that sixth sense early by living in Thorsay, because there are old artifacts all over the islands."

"If so, you might have acquired a similar sense. Close your eyes and concentrate on that piece of bowl and see if you can get a sense of its age."

Obediently she closed her eyes and focused on the potshard. She thought of hands making the bowl, women laughing over food preparation, the bowl a treasured possession in a very modest home. Surprised, she opened her eyes. "I see what you mean. This broken bowl has been in this midden for a long time. Do you have any idea how old it might be?"

He shook his head. "Centuries, probably many of them. I've never seen a potshard quite like this."

"I have a bowl that looks similar, only it's intact and a little smaller," she told him as she handed the piece back. "I've never thought about its age."

He became instantly alert. "Really? Where did it come from?"

"I found it in the ruins of an old fort on Sandsay. I was calling on a farm family there and found the bowl when one of the children asked me to play with her among the old stones. Pure luck that I found the bowl. The farmer and his wife said I could keep it. I use it when I need a bowl that size."

He laughed. "I'd like to see it. Does it feel old?"

She considered. "I've never thought about that, but considering where I found it, I'm sure it is. I'll take a closer look when I get home." She scrambled to her feet. "And it's about time we got out of this midden!"

Ramsay rose to his feet and brushed dirt from his boots, but his gaze was on the side wall of the pit. "I wonder what I might find if I do a little more digging?"

"Not today," she said firmly. "We need to get going if we want to reach the kelp works at a reasonable hour."

"No time for just a little more digging?" he asked, a mischievous glint in his eyes. He tossed his little shovel onto level ground, then scrambled up to the surface and turned to offer her his hand.

The pit was deep enough that his aid was useful. He easily helped her up to level ground, then continued to hold her hand. Smiling with dangerous charm, he said softly, "I think there really is an *us*."

"That's in the same category as your nonsense about goddesses," she said pleasantly. "And if you don't release my hand, I'll push you back into the midden."

He laughed and let her go. "If you do, I'll ask you to toss my shovel down so I can start digging again."

She rolled her eyes, but she was smiling. "On your horse, Ramsay. The midden has been here for a very long time, and it will be here next time you come by."

"Yes, madam schoolteacher," he said with mock obedience.

She could have pointed out that he was being foolish, but she didn't. It was good to see him smile.

—

They smelled the kelp works before they saw it. Ramsay wrinkled his nose as they crested the final hill above the sea and drew the horses to a halt so they could survey the site. "I haven't smelled kelp being burned since I left Thorsay, but that acrid odor instantly brings me back here."

"The wind is blowing in from the sea, so we're getting the full effect," Signy observed. "Did you ever visit the works before you left Thorsay?"

"A time or two." He studied the long, sweeping curve of shingled beach. Kelp was harvested from the shallows when the tide was out. A low islet lay several hundred yards out from the shore, and the area between islet and shore was an abundant source of rippling seaweed. A couple of dozen laborers of both sexes were harvesting the kelp with short sickles, and two burly men were pushing wheelbarrows piled with kelp to the shore.

"That building at the far left end of the beach contains offices and storage," Signy explained.

Ramsay noted a short pier by the storage area, though no boats were currently docked there. Scattered along the shingle were a number of kilns for burning kelp down to the valuable slag. Unlike enclosed pottery kilns, these kilns were shallow, stone-edged fire pits about four feet across and a foot or so deep. Sooty figures tended the fires, pushing kelp from the edges into the flames. Observing the dark plumes of smoke rising from the kilns, Ramsay remarked, "The beach looks like the volcanic plains around Mount Etna in Sicily."

"At least there's no spewing of lava." Signy's nose wrinkled. "Only bad smells."

"Is the water always this rough?" he asked. "Here on the Atlantic side of the island, I know the currents are strong and often treacherous."

"Usually the water is calmer," Signy said. "These high waves must be the result of a storm out over the ocean."

"With the tide rising, the cutters will have to come in soon." Ramsay studied the workers in the water. "The place is busier than I remember. More laborers cutting kelp. More kelp spread out to dry on the hillside. More kilns and more smoke yellowing all the plants around. That building on the far right is new, isn't it?"

"Yes, there's been quite a bit of expansion since you left. The building to the right is a rest area for the laborers to use when the tide is up and they can't work. People who don't live close enough to go home until the tide falls again can stay in the shelter and warm themselves by the fire, make tea, and nap or play cards."

Surprised, Ramsay said, "How enlightened of Roald."

"The old laird suggested it to Roald rather strongly," Signy said. "I believe he offered to suspend certain taxes for a year as an encouragement to build the rest shed."

Ramsay wasn't surprised to hear that. His grandfather had always tried to improve the lives of Thorsayians. "Good for the laird. Gathering kelp is demanding work."

"Harvesting is mostly done in the high summer when the daylight lasts seventeen or eighteen hours, but the work is very intense. Some people get up in the middle of the night to cut the kelp during early low tides." Signy shaded her eyes with one hand while she studied the people harvesting the seaweed. "The tide is coming in fast, so they'll have to quit soon and wait for it to go out again."

"Time to go down and say hello." Ramsay set Thor in motion along the track that led down to the works.

"Does Roald spend much time here?" he asked as they headed down.

"A couple of days a week, I think," she replied. "Axel spends time here as well."

"I would have thought the kelp works were not his style," Ramsay said dryly.

"My guess is that he hates the place but knows where the family money comes from," she said with equal dryness. "There's a general manager, Mr. Drummond, under Roald and Axel. He supervises all the day-to-day work and is very capable." She pointed to the right. "You can just see the roofs of his house over there. It's set back from the sea as protection from the winds."

As they approached the works, Ramsay saw that the people who tended the kilns stood upwind to avoid the smoke and stench. At least they were warm, unlike the workers in the water.

Ramsay and Signy dismounted by the office building. Looking a little wary, Axel emerged with a broadly built older man behind him. "Hello, Cousin," Axel said. "We weren't expecting you."

"I'm reacquainting myself with the islands," Ramsay said pleasantly as he offered his hand. "Since your kelp works are one of the most important businesses in Thorsay, this seemed a reasonable place to start."

Signy greeted the older man. "Mr. Drummond, it's good to see you. Have you met Kai Ramsay, the new laird?"

"Nay, I saw him from a distance at his granddad's funeral, but we haven't met properly." Drummond shook Ramsay's hand, his gaze direct as they exchanged greetings. "I'm sorry for your loss. He was a grand laird, and he'll be missed."

"Indeed he will. I've much to learn as his successor."

"Will you come into the office and have a cup of tea with us?" the manager asked.

"We'd like that," Signy said warmly.

"Just a moment." Drummond glanced out at the water. "Time to call people in." Raising his voice, he bellowed, "Come ashore before the tide takes you away!"

Hearing the call, most of the workers began moving toward shore, dripping with water and laden with cut kelp. They were coming none too soon because a powerful current was building between the islet and the shore, pushing the workers to the right.

A few workers lingered to cut a little more. Drummond muttered a curse under his breath. "There's always a couple who stay out longer to get a larger load and earn that bit of extra money."

Signy said sharply, "Someone's in trouble!"

Ramsay's eyes narrowed as he saw the person farthest from the shore. A small female, he thought, and she was clearly having trouble keeping her footing.

A sudden surge swept her off her feet, and the current caught her. She gave a strangled cry, and others turned to look. One man started splashing toward her. "Tilda! Tilda!"

Another man grabbed his arm to keep him from risking his own life. The current was increasing with vicious force, and few islanders were strong swimmers.

Ramsay was an exception. Swearing, he bolted along the shore, dragging off his coat and boots as he estimated where he might be able to intercept the struggling girl. He launched himself into the cold water with a flat dive and drove forward with powerful strokes. Thank God he'd grown up swimming in these northern waters.

The girl's head disappeared briefly, then reappeared again. She tried to scream, swallowed water, and began to cough convulsively. "Hang on, Tilda!" Ramsay called out to her. "I'm coming!"

She heard his voice and looked up desperately, but she was losing her battle to stay afloat. Ramsay swam harder, afraid that she was being pulled away so quickly that he might miss her.

With one last spurt of strength, he reached the girl and caught one of her flailing arms. She grabbed at him and they both went under, but she was clear-headed enough to realize that she risked both of their lives. She loosened her grip, and he managed to get both their heads above water.

"Good girl, Tilda! Now lie on your back and let me tow you ashore." As she obeyed, he looped his left arm across her thin chest and began heading toward the beach, stroking with his right arm and kicking.

But one arm had much less power than two, and the current was dragging them farther from shore. Raised beside the sea, he'd respected the water but never feared it. He became grimly aware that he was slowly losing his battle against the cold, rushing current. They might both drown within sight of land.

It was a damn fool way to die.

Chapter 15

Signy hardly had time to register that a kelp cutter was
in danger before Ramsay was off, throwing aside his coat
and boots so they wouldn't drag him down in the water.
He'd always loved the water and was a strong swimmer,
but her breathing almost stopped when she recognized the
power of the currents he was battling. Though the tides
were always strong here, today the waves were fiercer than
usual.

Drummond and Axel and the kelp cutters looked
worried and a woman was weeping, but no one was *doing*
anything. What was needed was a life boat, and there were
none available.

Ramsay had caught up with the girl and was trying to
return to the shore but was making scant headway against
the increasing currents. Panic threatened to paralyze Signy
when she thought how quickly a swimmer would tire in
the cold water.

Her mouth tightened. She didn't have a boat but she
had Thor, and Thorsayian horses loved the water. They
were also larger and stronger than humans. As soon as the
thought formed, she gave an ear-splitting whistle.

Thor had been only lightly tethered, and when he
heard her summons, he jerked the reins free and raced
down the beach toward her. The simple shed used for

resting between tides was nearby, and she saw that a fishing net had been hung to dry on the outside wall.

By the time Thor reached her, she'd yanked the net from the wall. The stallion skidded to a stop beside her, kicking up pebbles from the shingle beach and looking pleased with himself.

"Good boy!" she exclaimed as she swung up into the saddle. Luckily the stirrups were only a little long for her. They'd do.

She'd seen this shore at low tide and knew that at the far right end of the beach a sand bar ran out to sea. It wasn't visible in this high water, but she thought that if she and Thor followed it out, the water would be shallow enough that the horse would be able to keep his footing for a good part of the distance to the swimmers.

Praying to God that she was right about the location of the bar, she urged Thor into the water as she shouted, "Kai! *Kai!*"

Thor plunged into the waves happily, enjoying this new game. She yelled Kai's name again, and this time he heard her. He shifted his direction so that he was moving toward her, though with painful slowness.

The water was getting deeper, up to Thor's back, and Kai and the girl were about to be swept past Signy. If that happened, they'd be lost. Praying that she could throw the net far enough, Signy hurled one end toward Kai while hanging on to the other end.

Kai lunged toward the net, his long body and right arm outstretched. For a horrifying instant Signy thought he'd missed, but then the net jerked with a ferocity that almost yanked her from her saddle.

Heart hammering, she pulled Thor to a stop. The water was up to her hips and the net was swinging to her right from the weight of the two people on the other end.

So far, so good. Carefully she turned Thor and headed back to shore at a walk as they hauled the net and its precious cargo behind them. She didn't realize how exhausted she was until Thor scrambled onto the shingle beach.

Drummond and several cutters had caught up with her, and they took over the job of pulling the net ashore. Drummond himself caught Tilda in his arms and carried her out of the water. "Someone get a fire going in the rest shed!" he barked.

Ramsay staggered to his feet and lurched over to Signy, collapsing onto Thor's neck. "Best. Horse. Ever," he gasped.

His shoulder was by her knee, so she put a hand on it, chilled to the heart by the knowledge of what a near-run thing it had been. "How are you?"

"No damage done, but I may never go swimming again." He raised his head and gazed at her with exhausted gray eyes. "Rán is the Norse goddess of the sea, isn't she? If I recall correctly, she had a net she used to catch people. Apparently she's your goddess."

Signy laughed and brushed her fingers over his saturated hair, intensely grateful that he was alive. "You remember well. I'd have preferred a nice dinghy, but a net was all that was available."

Axel Ramsay's cool voice said, "A fine job of swimming, Cousin. And a very fine horse. Is he for sale?"

Ramsay shook his head. "I think he's probably part of the estate's entail. He belongs to Skellig House and the lairdship." He patted Thor's neck. "Amazing, as is his rider. We would have drowned without Signy and Thor."

She slid off Thor on the opposite side from Ramsay. "It's pure luck we were here. The next time, we won't be here and someone will likely drown. Axel, I think you should keep a couple of dinghies here as a safety precaution. One at the pier by the warehouse and another down at this end of the beach."

"We have no dinghies to spare," he protested. "This sort of thing doesn't happen regularly."

"No, but it has happened before and it's God's mercy no one has drowned yet," Drummond said as he joined them. "Having a pair of dinghies is an excellent idea, Miss Signy. With a life buoy attached to a rope in each of them."

"Sounds like a waste of money," Axel grumbled. "And unnecessary."

"People drowning unnecessarily is wasteful too," Drummond said in a steely voice.

Signy sensed the underlying tension between the men, with Drummond concerned about his people and Axel about his profits. Which man would Roald support? He was more pragmatic than his son, and a better businessman. A couple of life boats wouldn't cost much and would be good for his reputation.

Ramsay said pleasantly, "If you don't install two dinghies and lifesaving equipment, I'll give an order requiring it. Being a good employer is good business."

Mouth tight, Axel said, "I suppose you're right."

"I'll take care of it," Drummond said. Turning to Signy and Ramsay, he continued, "You must be chilled to the bone. Come into the rest shed and warm up."

Signy realized that she was shivering in the chill wind. "Here's hoping the tea kettle is already boiling."

"And that there's a bottle of good whisky to splash into the tea," Ramsay agreed as they began walking the short distance to the shed with Thor between them.

"There usually aren't spirits in the shed," Drummond said, pulling a silver flask from an inside coat pocket. "But this time, yes."

A young man Signy recognized as Drummond's oldest son came toward them. He said, "I'm Harald Drummond, sir. I'll take your horse to our barn and rub him down and make sure he's fed."

Ramsay offered his hand. "Thank you. It's a pleasure to meet you."

"Could you also collect my horse, Loki?" Signy asked. "He hasn't rescued anyone, but he and Thor both had long rides today."

"With pleasure. They're both grand horses." Harald took the reins and led Thor away, heading down the beach to the office building where Loki was tethered.

They reached the rest shed, and the door swung open to admit them. It was crowded inside, and the air was damp from all the wet people drying off.

Two women came forward and handed Signy and Ramsay dry blankets. "God bless you both!" the older of the women said intensely. "Tilda is my cousin's child and a lovely girl. I said she wasn't strong enough for kelp cutting, but she insisted on working to help the household out."

"Tilda is a brave girl," Ramsay said. "And intelligent. She cooperated instead of drowning both of us in panic."

As Signy wrapped the blanket tightly around her, Drummond ushered them through the crowd. "Come sit by the fire. Tea is coming up. With whisky."

"Thank you," Ramsay said. "But where is Tilda? Is she all right?"

"Yes, sir," a girlish voice said with a hint of chattering teeth. It came from a bundled-up figure in another chair by the fire.

This time Signy recognized the girl's elfin face and white-blond hair. "Tilda!" she exclaimed. "I didn't realize that you'd joined the kelp cutters."

"My grandda died," the girl said tersely. "My cousin took me in, but I needed to help out."

Signy took the chair next to Tilda and caught the girl's cold hand. "I'm sorry you dropped out of teacher training. You were doing so well."

Tilda shrugged her shoulders, her face pinched. "'Twasn't meant to be, miss."

Signy frowned. Tilda was young but had the instincts of a real teacher. Being a kelp cutter was heavy work for such a small, slight girl. A thought occurred to her. "A friend of mine who lives in Skillness told me that she'd like to find someone who would help with her children in the nursery and teach them the basics of reading and writing. Would you be interested?"

"I'd love that!" Tilda glanced in the direction of the sea and gave a shiver. "I wasn't a very good kelp cutter, but I do love working with the little ones."

Drummond appeared with their drinks, strong hot tea liberally dosed with whisky. Signy sipped cautiously, not wanting to burn her mouth, then gave a sigh of pleasure as warmth spread through her.

Drummond said, "Would the two of you wish to stay at my house tonight? We've plenty of room, and you can borrow dry clothes while yours are dried."

Signy glanced at Ramsay, who nodded agreement. "We'd like that, Mr. Drummond. It's been a long day."

"I'll send a message to my wife," Drummond said, looking pleased.

As the manager moved off, Ramsay said in a low voice, "Do you actually have someone who is looking for a combination nursery maid and teacher?"

"One of the teachers I trained is married and lives in Skillness. She has three children now and helps her husband in his business. She said in her last letter that she could use help with the children. I'm sure she'll be happy to have Tilda."

"Your network of teachers really covers the whole of Thorsay," he observed. "Very useful."

"The network keeps growing because my teachers have a lamentable tendency to get married, so more are always needed," she said with a smile.

"If Thorsay were a republic like the United States and women could vote, you'd be elected the laird," he said seriously.

She laughed. "You have a fantastical imagination."

"I don't know how I'd manage without you," he said seriously.

"You would have figured out how to be laird soon enough. Three months from now, you'll have no need of me."

And when that day came, Signy would be free to leave the islands. It was a discussion she really needed to have with Ramsay, and soon.

—

The Drummonds' house was sizable and modern, and their dinner with the family was informal, friendly, and educational. Ramsay learned more about the kelp trade, including where the product was shipped in the South for use in the manufacture of soap and glass. He also discussed safety issues with Mr. Drummond, who listened with real interest and had several good ideas of his own.

Ramsay and Signy and the older Drummonds ended up talking around the drawing room fire until the mantel clock struck ten times and their hosts rose to say good night. Signy covered a yawn, saying, "I'll soon call it a night also, but I want to talk to the laird about our itinerary over the next few days."

Mrs. Drummond shook her head with a smile. "What would the Lairds of Thorsay do without you, Signy?"

"They'd manage," Signy said, returning the smile, "but not as well."

After their hosts retired, Ramsay said, "I hope the discussion will be short. I have barely enough energy to climb the stairs."

"I feel much the same, so I'll keep this brief." Signy took a small sip of her watered-down local whisky. "What do you think of your first day reacquainting yourself with Thorsay?"

Ramsay laughed. "I am hoping that none of the future visits are so exhausting! But it was worthwhile. I have a better understanding of the kelp trade, and I've met good people who I hope will become friends."

"You've also gone a long way toward winning over all Thorsayians," she observed. "The story of you risking your life to save a young girl will have spread to all the islands by the end of the week. You're a hero, and our islanders like their laird to be heroic. Larger than life, like your grandfather."

"I'd have been a dead hero if not for your quick thinking and horsemanship." He sipped at his less-watered-down whisky. "Horsewomanship."

Signy shuddered visibly. "It was a very near-run thing. Harald Drummond told me that Thor is getting oats tonight."

"So we all dined well. Mrs. Drummond has a fine cook." He gave a tired sigh. "What can I expect in future days?"

"In Skillness, you'll meet some of Thorsay's most important ship owners to learn of their concerns and what they would like the laird to do. After that, we'll follow the coast south and you can visit some fishing villages, the largest linen works on Mainland, and a couple of smaller kelp works."

He nodded. "Will I be meeting some farmers before we return to Skellig House?"

"Yes, we'll pay a call on Mr. Smithson. He has the most acreage under cultivation of any farmer in Thorsay. He's keen to discuss a change in the traditional five-year crop rotation. Something about planting white clover in what is usually the year for raising grass for grazing."

Ramsay's brow furrowed. "I believe I read something about how clover improves the soil substantially, so it sounds like a good idea. Why would Mr. Smithson need to discuss that with me? Presumably he can do what he likes with his own fields."

"I think he would like moral and financial support from the new laird."

Ramsay looked pained. "Moral support is easy, but I don't know about the financial part. I'll be happy to talk to him, of course. What else?"

"If we time it right," she said mischievously, "you can be in Clanwick on the summer solstice for the annual playing of the ba'."

Ramsay groaned. The ba' was a riotous affair in which teams from opposing geographical areas such as North and South struggled furiously to move a ball to the harbor. "Last time I played I cracked my collarbone. Having survived near drowning in the Atlantic, I have no desire to risk breaking my neck in an insane scramble through the streets of Clanwick in pursuit of a feather-stuffed ball."

Signy laughed. "No one has been killed in years, though there are generally some broken bones."

She was lovely in the firelight, her hair shining like dark copper and her long body elegantly alluring. Since her own clothing was drying, she wore a loose gray robe that belonged to the eldest Drummond daughter. The robe was short on her, and her graceful ankles were visible between the hem and her warm socks.

He felt a stirring of energy and realized that he was less tired than he'd thought. "I'll leave this year's ba' to the young fools. What I really want is to investigate some new ruins. My grandfather mentioned the discovery of an ancient church somewhere south of Skillness?"

"Yes, at Burnbray. The ancient church probably goes back to the earliest days of Christianity in Thorsay. A more recent church dedicated to St. James was built on top of it, and the older ruins have only recently been discovered below."

Ramsay's eyes gleamed. "That sounds really intriguing. Can I have, say, one ruin for every incident of sober lairdly duty?"

Signy contemplated. "One ruin for every three official visits."

"How about one ruin for every two official duties?" he argued.

"We'll see," Signy said. "It depends on the distribution of ruins. There's no shortage. You have your choice of old churches, old farms, and old fortresses. I imagine you'll find some more worthy of study than others. I look forward to sketching the church at Burnbray, which is very interesting. Luckily my drawings of the farm on Sky Hill survived since Loki didn't go swimming."

Ramsay stood and stretched his tired muscles. "I suppose after our grand tour of Mainland we'll spend a few days at home, then visit some of the outer islands?"

She nodded. "Yes, people who live on the other islands want to see you, and you can meet the potential magistrates I suggested."

"But now for bed." He extended a hand to help her from her chair. She rose easily, and it was somehow natural that she came into his arms.

At first he just held her, enjoying the softness and strength of her wonderfully female form. "In case I didn't mention it earlier," he murmured, "thank you for saving my life."

"Thor gets most of the credit," she replied with a soft laugh.

"He supplied the brawn, but you supplied the brains. I'm told you summoned him from the far end of the beach with an ear-piercing whistle. You taught him to do that?"

"Yes, he loves learning new tricks, so I taught him some that I thought might be useful."

"If you whistle like that for me, I'll always come," he breathed before he kissed her. His goddess. Strong, womanly, irresistible.

She responded with the intensity of a woman who had faced death this day, and her open-mouthed kiss triggered equal intensity in him. She filled him with desire and yearning such as he'd never known in his younger years.

His hands slid down her back, pulling her hard into his body, but it wasn't enough. He wanted more. "We could share that bed upstairs," he said huskily. "And share a bed forever if we marry. The better I come to know you, the more I realize that my grandfather was right. You would be the best of all possible wives. Will you marry me?"

Chapter 16

Signy froze at his words, jarred out of her sensual haze. Marriage. Forever. Indignantly she pushed herself away from him. "*No!* You may think I'm the perfect wife for you, but that doesn't mean that *you're* the perfect husband for me. I've spent my whole life taking care of other people and their needs. I'm *tired* of putting everyone else first!"

She hadn't realized how much anger she'd buried until the words came blazing out of her. "I want to be selfish and let everyone solve their own problems rather than letting me do the work so they can then tell me how wonderful I am! I want to be *free!*"

Ramsay flinched and his arms dropped. "You're right," he said, his voice tight. "My grandfather and I have been far too willing to take advantage of your talents and loyalty."

His words calmed some of her anger. "My service was offered willingly, but I've reached the end of my willingness."

He nodded acceptance. "How can the balance be righted? What do you want? What, if anything, would you like from me?"

No one had ever asked her that, so she had to stop and think. "I've spent my whole life living at the end of the world, and I don't want to die here without ever seeing any other places. I want to travel. I doubt I'll make it to Constantinople, but at least Paris? First I want to go to London and study with an artist who will teach me how to really paint, and I want to have the time to learn how to do it properly."

His face like carved marble, he said, "You're right. It's unfair that I had all the opportunities because I'm male."

"I have often thought the same," Signy said dryly.

"When do you want to leave Thorsay?"

She hadn't thought much about leaving because the future was so unclear, but Ramsay's acceptance was making it seem possible. "I'm willing to stay another three months to help you become settled into your position as the laird. Then I'll be off."

His voice low, he asked, "Will you ever return, or will you be gone for good?"

The thought of leaving Thorsay forever was like an icicle in her heart. She drew a deep breath, a little unnerved that her vague dreams were somehow becoming concrete. "I'll return someday. Thorsay is my home. I have a house and a horse and friends. Maybe you can take Fiona? I don't think she'd enjoy traveling."

"Of course. I'll enjoy her company, though I'm not sure how Odin will feel. He might storm off to the stables and ignore me ever after." He hesitated. "Forgive me for asking, but do you have enough money to travel as you wish?"

"I've saved most of the salary the old laird paid me, and in London I can stay in Thorsay House indefinitely. I've handled the laird's correspondence with the couple who run the house. I look forward to meeting them in person."

"You'll like the Browns and the house is pleasant and well located." He drew himself up. "So for now, we continue on our journey, with you introducing me to people and places while I attempt to keep my hands off you. Is that correct?"

Remembering the warmth of his embrace gave her a sharp pang of regret. "That would be best."

He put his hand on the doorknob, then paused. "Is there a particular artist you'd like to study with?"

"Sophie Macleod. She was a student of Turner and is wonderful with landscape and wild weather. Since she's a woman, she's not well known, but she does take students. I have a book that includes prints of her work. She's brilliant."

"I saw some of her work at my friend Richard's gallery in London," Ramsay said with interest. "She's very talented and she's interested in similar subjects as you. Since Thorsay has plenty of landscape and wild weather, she sounds like an ideal choice for a teacher. I hope she takes you on. She should, given your talent." He opened the door and departed.

Signy was left with an odd mixture of emotions. Elation that leaving Thorsay and studying painting in London suddenly seemed possible, combined with anxiety about the unknown and a disturbing sense of loss. For years she'd dreamed of traveling away to different worlds, but she hadn't realized the price she would pay to attain her dreams.

Chapter 17

Ramsay and Signy delivered a nervous Tilda to Hilda Barnes, Signy's friend in Skillness, who welcomed the girl into the household warmly. She then invited Signy and the new laird to stay at her home while they were in Skillness.

Signy introduced him to merchants and ship owners and sailors, most of whom were willing to accept him, though the owner of a fishing smack who carried live lobsters to London challenged the new laird to a wrestling match. Ramsay won, barely.

Afterward, the lobster man stood Ramsay and the sailors who'd witnessed the challenge to drinks at the local tavern. They were all grand friends by the time Ramsay proceeded rather unsteadily back to the Barnes house. It was impossible to imagine a political situation more different from the insanely complex protocol of the Sublime Porte in Constantinople. Ramsay much preferred the informality and directness of Thorsay.

He visited one of the most successful linen works in Thorsay, which was run by a ferocious old lady with high standards and a sharp tongue who reminded him of his grandmother, Caitlin. She informed him that flax had been grown in Thorsay since Viking times, and her spinners and weavers produced the best linen in Britain. He wouldn't have dared to argue with her.

They visited the Burnbray site of the old church with the truly ancient church below. Ramsay would have spent the next week studying the ruins and taking more notes if Signy hadn't dragged him away. Fortunately her drawings of the site were as precise as they were elegant, so he'd study them more later.

Most nights they stayed in the homes of prominent local people, though they spent one night in a barn that turned out to be occupied by a rooster who was quite willing to get up and crow his heart out at the dreadfully early dawn of the long summer solstice day. Signy laughed and poked Ramsay in the ribs when he tried to roll over and bury his head in the hay so he could get more sleep.

His favorite part of this journey was discovering that he and Signy could regain much of their relaxed companionship, though they always kept physical distance between them. He hated knowing that she'd soon leave. Yet how could he ask her to stay when he'd been lucky enough to travel across the world?

He could only hope that she wouldn't stay away for a long time. The more time he spent with her, the more he wanted her to be with him always, both in his bed and at his breakfast table every morning. She made every day brighter, a valuable trait in this stormy northern land.

They took the ferry to the smaller island of Cronsay for an overnight trip so he could meet Jean Olson, one of Signy's suggestions to become a magistrate. He'd met her briefly at his grandfather's funeral. Further conversation impressed him so much with her intelligence and balanced thinking that he appointed her as Thorsay's first female magistrate.

Before they left Cronsay, they paid a visit to a famous cliff that was home to thousands of seabirds. The colonies were raucous, smelly, and beautiful. He'd loved visiting such colonies as a boy and hadn't realized how much he'd missed them. Best of all were the puffins. Their comic coloring and fearless acceptance of human visitors were a delight. Signy enjoyed them as much as he did.

It was all interesting and rewarding, but after a week his heart leaped when he saw the towering stones of the Ring of Skellig in the distance. Almost home.

The horses were equally keen, and they quickened their pace when Skellig House became visible. Loki whickered happily as Ramsay and Signy pulled up in front of the stables. The wide doors were open, and Jamie Donovan, the head groom, came out to greet them, a bridle he was cleaning in one hand. "Good to see you home! I hear you went swimming in the Atlantic, lad."

Signy hadn't been joking about how far and fast the story of his rescuing Tilda would travel. "So did Thor and Signy, or you'd be looking forward to training a different new laird, Mr. Donovan."

"One new laird every thirty or forty years is easier." Donovan grinned. "They're difficult to train."

Signy dismounted as Fiona emerged from the stables barking excitedly. "Oh, my darling dog!" She bent and ruffled Fiona's head and neck with both hands. "You missed me?"

"She obviously did," Ramsay said. "I wonder if Odin noticed I was gone?"

Signy straightened. "Even if he missed you, he won't admit it. Cats prefer to keep their humans guessing. Come along, Fiona. We're going back to Sea Cottage."

Ramsay asked, "Do you want me to ride with you to your cottage so I can lead Loki back here?"

"No, I've spent enough time on horseback for now. I want to walk the last distance and feel the sea breezes. Mr. Donovan, will you take care of Loki? There's a storm coming and I'm anxious to get home. I'll collect my saddlebags tomorrow."

Donovan took the reins. "Of course, Miss Signy." His eyes narrowed as he looked at Ramsay. "You, laddie, have to groom your own horse!"

"Yes, sir," Ramsay said obediently, but he frowned when he looked at the sky to the west. Dark clouds were piling up, and he thought he saw a flash of lightning. "The storm looks like it will be a big one."

"Good. I love listening to the waves crashing when I'm tucked up in my snug little cottage." Signy gave him a quick smile. "I'll see you tomorrow. Come along, Fiona. We're going home."

"Sleep well tonight." Ramsay led Thor into the stables behind Loki. Considering how much Signy loved her home, surely she wouldn't stay away for too long?

–

Signy stopped in the Skellig House kitchen to get milk for her tea and left with a basket of provisions, including a piece of warm mutton pie, ginger cake and bread, and a nice meaty bone for Fiona.

She set off along the cliff path at a brisk pace, with Fiona bouncing happily ahead of her. The storm was moving in fast, and the first drops of rain were falling as she entered her cottage.

She set the basket on the kitchen table and tossed the bone to Fiona, who fell on it gleefully. After filling the dog's dish with water, she crossed the front room to gaze out the wide window. The light was fading fast, but she could still see the rising waves crashing along the narrow beach.

She loved storms. If she could study with Sophie Macleod, perhaps she might learn how to capture the power and majesty of nature's fury as well as Sophie did.

Signy bit her lip, thinking how much she'd miss Thorsay when she moved to London. The city had a river, but it wasn't on the sea. It also had masses of people greater than she could really imagine. Yet much as she loved her home, she also yearned to see a wider world. To meet people who were complete strangers and who had no expectations of her. She doubted that she would make a career out of selfishness, but she loved the idea of being free to put her own desires first.

Which would be easier if she didn't desire Ramsay. During her days of traveling with him, she'd found herself increasingly tempted to drag him to the nearest bed, or even a midden if it was clean and grassy. There she could explore that lean, strong body while he explored hers with equal thoroughness. He aroused heated thoughts she'd never had before. It was exciting to imagine him as her husband...

But if she succumbed to that desire, she'd be trapped on Thorsay forever. Best to go now while she still could. The future—she'd worry about that later.

She turned determinedly from the window and prepared her supper. After a week of riding around Mainland and talking to hordes of people, she was *tired*. She enjoyed a leisurely meal, then decided to go to bed early. Chores could wait till the morning. "Come sleep with me, Fiona?"

The dog didn't need a second invitation. She jumped onto the bed and curled up by her mistress's ankles. Signy smiled as she wondered if Skellig House had a bed large enough for her, Ramsay, Fiona, and Odin. Probably not, a further reason for her to leave. He'd find some other strong, opinionated Thorsayian woman to share his life and his bed.

Which was a thought that didn't please Signy at all. She sighed and relaxed her body muscle by muscle, then fell asleep to sounds of the wind and the waves. Thorsay in all its stormy glory.

—

After Ramsay finished dinner, he retired to his room, but the power of the rising storm was too electrifying to allow rest. His room had a window on the sea, and since Skellig House was on a bluff well above it, he was high enough to see the waves in all their magnificence.

He didn't think he'd ever seen waves as high and powerful. Was this like the devil storm that had done so much damage to Thorsay? He hoped not; he had enough other problems to worry about.

He should try to get some sleep because the morning would arrive with a full share of problems, but he was still too restless to relax. Succumbing to the allure of the storm, he went downstairs to the closet that held foul weather gear and donned his waterproof boots and oilcloth coat. Then he went outside to enjoy nature's fury.

—

Signy was jarred awake by the sounds of shattering glass and rushing water. After an instant of disorientation, she realized that her beautiful front window must have been destroyed. She lurched from the bed. Broken glass. Her feet needed protection, so she shoved them into the light slippers she wore around the house before racing into the front room. Fiona was already there, whining as water washed around her paws.

Faint light from outside was enough to show the catastrophic damage. Something long and dark lay across the lower windowsill. A tree trunk thrown through the window by the waves?

There was water everywhere, and as she watched, another huge wave hurled itself against her house. Signy gave a low moan as she saw her easel wash away. The paints and materials on the table had vanished. The water was ankle deep and rising with every monster wave.

"Fiona! Outside!" she said sharply. A scrabbling of claws indicated that Fiona was using the small dog door at the back of the house.

Another wave crashed through the remains of the window, and the water rushed around Signy knee-high. She realized with anguish that there was nothing she could do here. She must escape while she could.

As she swung around to the back door, she heard a deep, ominous sound overhead. A groan, a crack.

And then... blackness.

—

Ramsay collected a bottle of his grandfather's favorite whisky, then went outside to the bench in the sheltered alcove on the side of the house where his grandfather had died. Most of the wind was blocked, so it was a comfortable place to watch the churning waves. He uncorked the bottle and raised it in a toast. "To you, Duncan Ramsay, a legend here in the land you loved so well. I hope you're enjoying Valhalla!"

He could almost hear the old man laughing in his ear. With a smile, Ramsay took a deep swallow, then corked the bottle and gazed over the sea. He still had much to learn about his islands, but he already had a deep connection to this land of his fathers. That connection had been latent inside him for all his traveling years, so deeply buried he didn't realize it was there until he returned home.

Home. He pictured himself living in Skellig House with Signy, sleeping and making love and arguing as they raised tall stubborn children with Viking blood in their veins. He couldn't imagine another woman as his wife, yet if she never returned, he'd have to try.

He took another swallow of whisky, his gaze on the hypnotic swirl and crash of the waves. Signy, his goddess of the sea. In Thorsay everything came down to the sea...

His reverie was broken by a frantic bark as a furry body emerged from the rain and cannoned into him. "Fiona, are you afraid of storms?" he asked as he tried to pat her comfortingly.

She rose onto her hind legs and barked frantically in his face.

Signy! Sea Cottage was lower than Skellig House— could she be in danger?

"Take me to Signy!" he ordered as he leaped to his feet and rounded the house to the cliff path that led to Sea Cottage, while Fiona bounded ahead of him.

He wanted to run, but the wind and lashing rain made the footing treacherous, and, unlike Fiona, he didn't have four feet for stability.

If Signy had escaped the cottage, surely she would have headed to Skellig House and he'd have met her by now. His heart was hammering by the time he reached the path that angled down to Sea Cottage. Dear God, half the roof had caved in!

Fiona dashed down the path to the rear door, barking all the way. Ramsay followed, grateful for the railing Signy had installed. If he hadn't had that to hold, he'd have pitched down the bluff into the roiling waters.

Grimly afraid of what he'd find, he opened the door to Signy's home and found the broken chaos of Sea Cottage. Though there was barely enough light to see, he could make out water pouring through the shattered window. The cottage was flooded to nearly waist height, and the front right corner and side had collapsed, crushing the bedroom. If she hadn't managed to get out before that... "Signy! *Signy, are you here?*"

Fiona was almost covered by the water, but she forged into what remained of the kitchen, still barking. Ramsay followed, terrified that he'd find Signy's body in the wreckage.

Fiona rose and braced her front paws against... something, whimpering piteously. Ramsay closed the distance between him and the dog and reached out, trying to identify by touch. Cold, wet softness—a wash of hair over his hand as the water surged.

It was Signy, wedged between the table and the work counter. Her body was held partially upright, just enough that her head was barely above the rising water.

Not knowing if she was dead or alive, he wrenched the table away. It moved only a few inches, blocked by a fallen beam, but it was enough to release Signy's body from where it was trapped.

He grabbed her as she slipped into the water. As soon as his grip was secure, he pivoted and waded to the back door. Fiona ran ahead, splashing in the water and yipping anxiously.

He held Signy's limp body with his left arm while using his right hand to grasp the railing. He used it to haul them both up the path, praying it wouldn't pull loose from the side of the bluff. An enormous wave crashed over them and almost dragged them both down into the waters, but he held on with every ounce of his strength until the wave retreated. Sliding his hand up the railing and moving only inches at a time, he continued their slow progress upward.

He was dizzy from the strain by the time he scrambled over the lip of the bluff onto the saturated turf. He laid Signy down and bent over her, his back blocking the worst of the wind and the rain. She was as cold and white as death. Fiona licked her face with a long frantic tongue, but there was no response.

"Signy," he gasped hoarsely. "Signy, can you hear me?" He tried to find a pulse in her throat, but his fingers were too numb with cold to feel anything.

Remembering an incident when he'd witnessed a Greek fisherman revived after nearly drowning, he rolled her onto her side and pounded on her back with his open hand.

He was giving in to despair when she convulsed and began coughing up water. Dear God, she was alive, *alive*!

"Signy," he said, pitching his voice above the wind. "Can you hear me?"

"Kai?" she said in a dazed voice.

"In person. Fiona came and found me." He put an arm behind her and gently raised her to a sitting position.

She bent her head and had another fit of coughing before whispering, "My house?"

"Damaged," he said tersely. "I don't know how badly. We'll find out tomorrow, but now I have to get you to Skellig House."

She cried out as he tried to raise her to her feet. "My right leg!" she gasped. "I think it's broken."

He winced at the pain in her voice. He wished he could carry her all the way back to safety, but she was a tall, strong woman, not a featherweight. He wouldn't be able to get her that far in the fierce winds and lashing rain.

"If I support you so your right foot doesn't have to touch the ground, do you think you can make it back to Skellig House?"

"I don't have much choice, do I? Help me up," she said tartly.

He dragged off his oilskin coat and draped it over her shoulders. Then he slid an arm around her waist and lifted her from the right side.

Despite his best care, she cried out again but quickly swallowed the sound. He steadied her as she got her balance on her left foot. When she was steady, he said, "This is like a three-legged race. We'll be home in no time."

She muttered, "Bloody optimist!"

He almost laughed at the evidence that she was still Signy. "Feel free to swear as much as you want. You're entitled."

Slowly and with weaving steps, they made their way back, Fiona trotting ahead and looking worriedly over her shoulder. The trek seemed interminable.

By the time they reached the house, Fiona had reached the front steps and was barking to raise the dead. A dog worth her weight in gold.

The door swung open to reveal Mrs. Donovan, the housekeeper, with her husband beside her. The head groom moved forward just in time to get another arm around Signy's waist and keep both the refugees of the storm from collapsing.

"Thanks," Ramsay choked out. He'd never been so glad to arrive home in his life.

Chapter 18

Signy was barely conscious when she was helped into the house, but she heard Donovan, the head groom, say comfortingly, "Steady on, lass, you're almost home."

From her other side, Kai said, "Mrs. Donovan, what room can we put her in?"

"The laird's room upstairs is the only one made up," the housekeeper said. "I'll light the fire and warm the sheets." She immediately left to take care of the preparations.

Signy did not like the idea of being hauled upstairs like a sack of potatoes, so she tried to speak up to assure everyone that she was all right. But she couldn't manage to find the words. Everything seemed to be happening at a great distance...

"Let's settle her down in this chair." Kai again. His voice was close, and she could hear the strain in it, but his grip was gentle as he and Donovan lowered her into a wooden Windsor chair. "Will you examine her?"

"I'm better with horses," Donovan murmured, "but the principles are the same. From the blood here, she was struck a blow on her head."

A gentle touch above her right temple. She flinched away, but he continued with his careful examination. She was grateful when he stopped.

"She banged her head hard. Her skull isn't broken, but she'll have an almighty headache tomorrow." She felt like telling the head groom she had an almighty headache already, but it was too much effort.

"She may have broken her right ankle," Kai said. "She couldn't walk, and it seemed very painful."

"I'll have to examine your ankle, lass," Donovan said with the same gentle voice he would use on a nervous filly. "I'll try not to hurt you more than necessary."

She was glad he warned her but even so, when he began examining her ankle, she couldn't prevent herself from crying out. Kai caught her hands, and she held his fingers so tightly that she must have cut off his circulation.

"This won't take long," Kai said soothingly. "Soon you can go to sleep in a warm, comfortable bed. Tomorrow this will be just a bad dream."

He was probably lying, but it sounded good…

—

Signy awoke to pale sunshine coming in the window at an angle suggesting it was well into the next day. She recognized the warm weight on her left side as Fiona, and she reached down automatically to ruffle the dog's ears. She got her hand licked in response. She realized that she was in the laird's bedroom, the most spacious and light-filled room in the house. It felt somehow sacrilegious to be in his bed, but the mattress was undeniably comfortable.

Her right ankle ached ferociously, and she realized that her lower leg was heavily bandaged. Trying to move it made her suck her breath in.

A low masculine voice asked, "How are you feeling?"

Ramsay. She turned her head to see him sprawled on the chair by the bed, looking tired and bruised, but composed. She said in a thin voice, "I feel as if a herd of kelpies galloped out of the sea and stampeded over me."

"They're a rough lot, those kelpies," he said with a glint of amusement. "Though I thought they lived in lakes, not the sea."

"These were definitely sea kelpies." She frowned at his rumpled and unshaven appearance. "Did you get any sleep last night? I hope you weren't sitting up with me."

He shook his head. "After you were settled here, I went straight to my room and slept like the dead till this morning. I was wakened by a rough-tongued feline face wash."

She smiled and stroked her dog again. "Has Odin met Fiona yet?"

"I heard a brief altercation in the corridor this morning, but I didn't see any blood or fur, so they may have worked things out." He stood. "I've ordered breakfast for us both, but this pot of tea is still hot. Would you like some?"

She realized her mouth and throat were parched. "Please."

He prepared her tea and handed it over. She swallowed the hot liquid with pleasure, feeling warmed and steadier. "How damaged am I?"

"A bump on your head and an injured ankle. Good horse doctor that he is, Donovan said you have a bad sprain of the right foreleg, but he bandaged it and applied a horse salve that he said should dull the pain some."

"My foreleg?" she asked, bemused.

"Donovan doesn't know the names of body parts for humans," Ramsay said solemnly, "but he's a first-class horse doctor. He said your ankle should heal with no problems if you take it easy."

"I am *not* a horse," she muttered as she straightened up and put pillows between her back and the headboard.

"Donovan seems a little unclear on that. He warned me that you're a restless filly and gave stern orders that you aren't to get out of this bed today." Ramsay smiled. "I told him that I wasn't a strong enough man to enforce that prescription."

"Wise words," she said, unable to resist a smile. It faded quickly. "How much damage was there across Thorsay?"

"I received a few reports this morning. It looks like there will be a fair amount of cleanup, and in some places chunks of the bluffs fell into the sea, but so far I haven't heard of anything catastrophic."

"Since the devil storm, most Thorsayians have taken extra precautions to reduce storm damage. I'm glad they seem to be working." She braced herself before asking the next question, afraid to hear the answer. "What about my house? How badly is it damaged?"

"I haven't been out this morning, so I'm not sure," he said, his gaze level. "It was a dark and chaotic night. The front window was smashed and part of the roof caved in, but I couldn't see much more."

She frowned, trying to remember what had happened. "The breaking glass woke me up. It looked as if the waves slammed a tree trunk through the window. When I saw how much water was pouring in, I turned to escape through the back door. That's when the roof fell in." She touched her sore head and felt a small bandage above her temple.

He nodded. "When the beam came down, you were trapped in the kitchen between your table and the work counter. Fortunately, you were held in place with your head fairly high." He paused, his expression darkening. "If you'd fallen on the floor, you would have drowned in the rising water. Thank God Fiona found me!"

Signy's hand tightened around the dog's neck. So Fiona was her savior. Her fur was dry, so someone must have toweled her off the night before. "Did she bark under your window?"

"No, I was outside enjoying the storm when she galloped up and told me in no uncertain terms that help was needed *right now*!" He drew a deep breath. "It was very close. Five minutes more and you would have drowned."

She winced at the pain in his voice. "Sorry. I've always felt safe in Sea Cottage. There was no major damage from the devil storm, and I thought last night would be the same. I didn't expect the waves to be so fierce or for the water to rise so quickly."

"No need to apologize," he said wryly. "I owed you a sea rescue."

She shrugged. "You didn't owe me anything. Thorsayians help each other. But I do think this demonstrates that it's a good thing to have animals around us." She petted Fiona again. "Especially rescue dogs!"

A soft knock announced the arrival of a kitchen maid with a tray holding covered dishes, toast, preserves, and more tea. "Here's your breakfast, sir, and enough for both of you. Would you like some nice eggs and toast, Miss Signy?"

"That would be lovely, Janet." Signy pushed herself as upright as she could manage against the pillows. "Ramsay, what would you have done with all this food if I hadn't woken up?"

"Eaten most of it myself. Shared some with Fiona. Luckily there's enough for all three of us."

"That's good, because I'm hungry." Signy accepted a refill on her tea. "And after breakfast, I'm going to see if there's anything left of my house."

"Stubborn filly," Ramsay said without surprise. "There is the question of how you'll get there. You shouldn't walk that far. I suppose that one of the grooms and I could carry you over in a litter."

Like a blasted invalid. *No.* "I'll ride. There's a sweet old pony in the stables, Puff. She's patiently carried every child who grew up near here. She has a very broad back. I can ride her sideways."

He considered. "That sounds slow but possible."

"Slow is the only speed Puff has. I'll take a cane to help on the ground. Mrs. Donovan has canes and crutches of various sizes."

She glanced down at the unfamiliar nightgown she was wearing and wondered who had removed what she'd had on and dressed her in this. Not Ramsay, she hoped. The idea of him undressing her was… unnerving. She bit into her toast and ordered herself to change the direction of her thoughts.

She'd think of Fiona, who was gazing at the toast with deep hope. Signy tossed the dog a piece, which was snapped out of the air.

Dogs were more reliable than men.

—

Signy was right about the suitability of Puff, who was more of a pony-shaped sofa than a serious riding horse. Donovan produced a wide old saddle with a horn that could be used for extra security and saddlebags to bring back some of her clothing if possible. It was easy for Signy to perch sideways on the old saddle, though she winced whenever her ankle was jostled.

For simplicity's sake, Ramsay led the pony and carried the knotted wood cane while Fiona trotted along next to him. As they set off along the cliff path, he said, "I feel like Joseph leading Mary to Bethlehem."

Signy chuckled. "I'm feeling a great deal of sympathy for Mary at having to ride a long way like this. And in her condition!"

Puff's main and possibly only gait was a gentle ambling walk, which gave Ramsay time to survey the shoreline below. The storm had thrown up masses of seaweed and branches, shells and dead fish. About halfway to Sea Cottage, a stretch of the path had disappeared, and they pioneered a new path around the cliff edge.

Even so, it didn't take long to reach their destination. Ramsay halted the pony on the bluff above, and they both stared down at the damaged cottage that had been such a bright and welcoming little home. Signy's face was like granite.

"The walls are still standing," said Ramsay, who had wondered if the whole structure might have disappeared. "And more than half of the roof is still in place."

"It looks like one of the ancient ruins that are scattered all over Thorsay," Signy said tightly. "Help me down."

He obeyed, feeling her warrior spirit despite her pain and grief and the damage to her much-loved home. When he'd eased her to the ground, he held her close for a long moment, wishing he could shield her from all physical and emotional pain. "Are you sure you're up to this?" he asked quietly.

"I have to know." She took the cane and limped away from him. "In the moments I watched, I saw the waves sweep away my easel and all my paints."

"A good thing so many of your paintings are in Skellig House," he said pragmatically. "The easel and paints can be replaced."

She didn't reply, just moved in small steps toward the railing where it curved down the bluff to the path. Before she started down, he said, "Let me check how well the railing is holding. It seemed all right last night, but more damage might have happened later."

She nodded and he moved down the slanting path, testing the railing at every step. At the bottom he called up. "It seems solid as ever. Ready to give it a try?"

She grasped the railing with her left hand and held the cane in her right to help with balance and to spare her injured ankle. Fiona followed, looking concerned. Ramsay stayed alert in case Signy slipped and needed help, but she didn't. She hung on to the railing with white-knuckled determination.

She was panting and there was pain in her face by the time she reached the level area behind the cottage. He suggested, "This wooden bench survived, so why not sit down and catch your breath while I walk around outside and see if the structure seems solid?"

Seeing that she was about to protest, he said, "At least give Fiona a chance to rest. She had a hard night."

"She's a sheepdog and has more endurance than both of us put together." Signy smiled wryly and settled gingerly on the bench, stretching her right leg out in front of her. Fiona jumped up and settled with her furry chin on Signy's thigh.

The cottage door was open because Ramsay hadn't bothered to close it the night before, but the interior was too dark to see anything. Careful of his footing, he worked his way around the cottage. The stones of the walls and the mortar that held them together were solid and undamaged. As Signy had said, there was a medium-sized tree trunk tilted inward on the sill of the large window. Most of the trunk was inside the cottage with the roots sticking up outside. It was an odd sight.

When he'd finished his circuit and reached Signy again, he said, "No catastrophic damage. A couple of stones were loosened when the roof beam went down and where the tree trunk is lying across the windowsill. It's a fairly sizable tree. Given how few trees are on Thorsay, it might have sailed over from Norway. I'll go inside now."

"So the roof can drop on your head instead of mine?" she asked dryly. "Thorsay needs you more than it does me, unless you like the idea of Roald becoming the laird."

"If the ceiling starts collapsing, I can move faster than you," he pointed out.

"There is that." She used the cane to help herself to her feet. "It's time to see what, if anything, is left."

Chapter 19

Signy moved past Ramsay and stepped warily into the remains of what had been her warm and welcoming kitchen. There was crunching underfoot. She looked down and saw small shells that had been washed into the cottage. The floor was still wet.

Behind her Ramsay pushed the door wide open to allow more light, and she saw the narrow space between the table and counter, where she'd apparently been trapped the night before. Ramsay was right: If she'd fallen to the floor rather than being caught there, she would have drowned. She had major bruising on both sides, but it was a small price to pay for her life.

Ramsay said, "Your kitchen cupboard seems intact. Maybe some of your dishes survived."

"Perhaps. I'll look later." She turned sideways and inched her way through the narrow passage between table and counter and the cupboard next to the counter. Behind her, the fallen roof beam slanted down toward the front of the cottage.

She stepped into the front room and shuddered at the sight of the tree trunk that had smashed its way into her home. It was large enough to be used as a bench on the beach. Then again, maybe she should turn the blasted thing over to a carpenter so it could be cut into pieces.

The floor was littered with rubble. The only furniture left was the table that she used for her painting materials. It hurt to see the empty space that had held her easel. Also gone was the hooded two-person Orkney chair Ramsay had made for Gisela so they could cuddle by the fire. Her solidly built loom appeared intact, though it had been swept across the front room. Through the broken window she could see the rolling waves she'd always loved, larger than usual in the aftermath of the storm.

A warm arm came around her shoulders. "You're shivering," Ramsay said quietly. "There's a painful amount of damage and loss, but flooding is better than fire because fires consume everything. Sea Cottage can be rebuilt. These stone walls have been standing for centuries and will stand for centuries more if the cottage is cared for."

She looked at the wet sand and soggy broken objects that littered the floor. The broken, empty frame of the miniature portrait of Signy, Gisela, and their mother when the girls were young and they'd all been happy… "Where does one even start?"

"The first thing to repair will be the roof," he replied calmly. "The main roof beams are intact, so when the fallen one is lifted back in place and secured, it's just a matter of some shingles. You'll need a new window, of course, and I'd suggest sturdy shutters that can be closed and latched on the outside when big storms blow up."

She thought of the cleaning that would be needed, the replacement of furniture and kitchenware and linens. "It will be expensive," she said wearily. "Maybe this is a sign that I should take my savings and move to London permanently."

"Nonsense!" he said firmly. "The official property transfer hasn't taken place yet, so the cottage still belongs to the estate, which will pay for the repairs."

She looked up at him, frowning. "The estate is you and you can't afford it either. There are better uses for your money than one badly located cottage."

"The location turned out to be more vulnerable than you thought, but the setting is also what makes the cottage so special," he said. "Worth repairing. Use your savings for the trip to London and come back when Sea Cottage is ready for you."

Her brows arched. "Very gallant of you to offer, but I can't let you pay for a major rebuilding project. The property transfer might not be finalized, but we both know that the cottage is my responsibility."

"I can use my personal funds to cover repair costs so I won't have to take anything from the estate," he offered.

"That's very generous of you, but not necessary." Signy thought of the people of Thorsay, whom she'd loved and served for so many years. Knowing how much help they needed, she said, "This is not a good use of your limited funds when there are so many greater priorities. Seeds for farmers, better breeding stock, repairs to cottages that shelter whole families. Sea Cottage is more like one of the garden follies beloved of English aristocrats."

He shook his head. "Sea Cottage is a special place. My grandmother loved it and so do you. It's important to cherish what we love."

"I've lost many things I loved," she said flatly. "This cottage is not a good investment in rational terms."

She looked again at the rubble around her and wondered if the cottage could ever be so special again. "It makes more sense for me to walk away and go to London. You can fix the cottage up at a better time."

"You need to travel. You'll probably love and hate London in equal measure, but you said yourself that Thorsay is your home. I'm learning how powerful such bonds can be," he said, his voice dangerously persuasive. "I want to give you a good reason to return here after you've fed your appetite for escape."

"It took you a dozen years to return," she pointed out.

"I hope you won't be gone as long as that," he said with a rueful smile.

"Why does where I live matter to you, Kai?" she asked softly.

"When I found you last night, I thought you were dead." His voice cracked. He drew a deep breath before continuing. "The thought was... unbearable. You need a chance to test your wings in wider skies, my goddess of the sea. But in the end, I want you to fly home to me." He cupped her face in his hands, his intense gaze holding hers before he bent into a yearning kiss.

His words melted a cold, lonely place deep inside her. She opened to the kiss and slid her arms around him, dropping the cane in the process.

Each time they embraced, the sensations were more intense. More emotion, more desire, more yearning for completion. His kiss deepened, and she stepped into him so their bodies would be pressed together...

...and pain blazed through her ankle. "Owwww!"

Ramsay pulled back, startled. "Sorry! I forgot about your injury."

"So did I." She clung to his arms until the pain had diminished. "Could you pick up my cane? I'd probably fall over if I tried."

"Of course." He bent over and picked it up for her. "I seem to choose the worst possible places to try to court you. A midden, a recently flooded cottage. Next time will probably be in the middle of a flock of sheep."

She had to smile. "I find your bad judgment about such things to be rather endearing. It makes me feel that you mean it." She leaned on the cane. "So you're courting me?"

"Rather badly since I'm trying to be reasonable and sensitive to your needs when what I really want to do is sweep you onto my white horse and carry you off to my castle," he said ruefully. "Instead it was you on the white horse and you were saving me from drowning in a sea of kelp."

"But you're making a future for us seem more possible," she said hesitantly. "And I think it's not just because the old laird said you should marry me."

"Definitely not, but this is not the time and place for a serious discussion," he said. "Now that we've seen what the cottage needs, there's no reason to linger. How about I try to get into the remains of your bedroom to collect some clothing while you look in your kitchen cupboard to see what might have survived?"

"That's a good idea. My clothes are in a small wardrobe in the corner." She turned and started painfully making her way back to the kitchen. "I'll check my cupboard. The waves probably knocked it about so much that everything inside is broken."

"It's heavy so it might not have moved much." He touched her cheek, then turned to pick a path through the rubble and over the fallen beam toward her bedroom.

Signy made her careful way back to the kitchen. Nothing large blocked the cupboard, though she saw that the waves had twisted it partially away from the wall.

The cupboard was about six feet high and had two doors. Water had swollen the wood, so it was difficult to open the upper door. She tugged at the handle carefully, not wanting to cause more damage. Even so, when the upper door opened abruptly, the contents within rattled. She peered inside, expecting to find broken fragments, and was delighted to see that her redware was intact. She took out the teapot, which was coated with a thin layer of silty sand, but when she brushed the grime away the dark red ceramic had its usual warm glow. The mugs and small plates were also intact. The sight cheered her amazingly.

The top shelf held drinking glasses, and they hadn't fared as well. Two had broken and one was cracked, but the last had survived. Her small cooking aids—a mill and mortar and pestle—were sturdy and undamaged.

The door of the lower half was also stubborn, but it opened a little more easily than the top. The shelves contained kitchen items that she seldom used. The skillet and cooking pots that were in regular use had hung by the fireplace, and they might be part of the clutter that had landed on the floor. Being metal, they should have survived if they hadn't washed away. At the moment Signy didn't have the energy to search for them.

She bent to study the lower shelves better and spotted the buff-colored old bowl she'd found in the ruins of the old fort. She pulled it out and found it unbroken, though it was as covered with silt and sand as everything else in the cupboard.

She was brushing off the decorative grooves around the rim when Ramsay reappeared carrying several sodden garments. "Success! I'm not sure that your leather boots will survive, but most of your clothing will be fine when taken to Skellig House and properly washed and dried. I'll bring a cart out here later today so that everything worth saving can be taken back and cleaned properly. How did you do in the kitchen?"

"Better than I expected. All my redware china and cookware survived. Plus I found this." She handed him the old bowl.

His eyes widened as he accepted the bowl. "It's in perfect condition!" He closed his eyes for a long moment. "And old. So old. An ancient piece from the distant past."

"Unfortunate that it can't talk," Signy said. "It would have tales to tell."

Ramsay smiled. "It would probably complain of how boring it was to be buried by that fort for a few centuries."

"Perhaps the bowl found it restful," she said thoughtfully. "I'm not going to have the energy to make a return trip today, but when you come back with the cart, make sure that there is material for packing the china."

"Of course." He surveyed her and was probably unimpressed. "You look tired. I need to get you home."

It was proof of Signy's fatigue that she didn't argue the point. "Do you want to carry my old bowl with you?"

"Indeed I do. Puff's saddlebags have room for it and some of your sodden garments. After you, my lady."

She wanted to point out that she wasn't his lady. But she didn't have the energy for that either. She closed the doors of the cupboard, then picked her way across the kitchen to the door, keeping as much weight as possible off her damaged ankle.

It was a relief to get out into the fresh air. Everything worth saving must be removed and cleaned before mold set in. For that matter, the whole cottage needed to be cleared out. Ramsay would probably lend her a couple of people to do the job.

Fiona hadn't liked being in the ruined cottage, so she'd withdrawn to the outside bench. Her head came up when she saw Signy. "Yes, we're leaving now, Fee."

The dog jumped from the bench and trotted over to the path, then looked to see if her mistress was following. Signy was, though much more slowly. She hauled herself upward with the railing while Ramsay positioned himself directly behind to catch her if she fell.

She was panting by the time she reached the top. Ramsay stepped around her and tucked the bowl and the garments he'd collected in the saddlebags, then swooped her up in his arms and planted her on Puff. She suppressed a squeak. Then glared at him.

He chuckled. "Even a goddess doesn't have to do everything herself. That's what minions are for."

She had to smile. "So you're a minion?"

"When one is required." He took the reins, since her position made it difficult to direct the pony herself. He turned toward Skellig House, then paused when Fiona began yipping and heading up the coastal path in the opposite direction. "I wonder if someone else needs rescuing."

Signy glanced over her shoulder and saw nothing but grassy turf and the coastal path. "We should probably follow and see what has caught her attention. It's likely just a hare."

As they ambled after the dog, Signy shaded her eyes and looked ahead. "I think there's been another cliff fall ahead, because the path used to rise a little here. Maybe someone fell over the edge and needs help?"

She was proved right when the path ended abruptly at a new, wave-carved cliff. The storm tide had ripped away a stretch of grass-covered dunes.

And cupped in the curve of the newly made cove were three ancient, connected stone buildings that looked older than time.

Chapter 20

"Dear God in heaven," Ramsay said in a stunned whisper as he stared down at the newly revealed site. Thorsay abounded with ancient ruins, but he'd never seen anything like these buildings.

"Buried homes that have been revealed by the storm," Signy said, her voice showing the same awe that he felt. "The way the houses are connected makes this place look like an ancient village or family compound. There could be more houses still hidden in the hill. Do you have any idea how old they must be?"

"Two thousand years? Four thousand? I have no idea." He studied the solid walls made of flat stones laid on top of each other. The roofs were gone, allowing the two of them a bird's-eye view of the rooms and passageways. "As old as anything I've seen in the Middle East, I think. Perhaps older."

"Older than the pyramids of Egypt?" she asked incredulously.

"Perhaps. I wish we had a good way of judging the age of ancient sites like this. Maybe someday we will, but now it's mostly guesswork."

"Let's go down there for a closer look," Signy said, almost vibrating with excitement.

Surprised, he said, "But you said you're tired. I need to get you back to Skellig House."

"And not explore this amazing piece of the past?" She grinned. "You know you're itching to see more."

"True." He studied the site to determine whether going down was feasible, then pointed. "That slope to the left looks like it wouldn't be too hard to climb down and then scramble back."

"I wonder if Puff could manage it both ways," she said thoughtfully.

"I think that would be asking too much of the old girl. What about you? Can you navigate the slope?"

She brandished her walking stick. "With my cane, I am able!"

He laughed. "Don't say I didn't warn you when your ankle is giving you fits later."

"Some pains are worth it."

He guided the pony around the rim of the cove until they were above the area where the slope was gentler. "Stay here with Puff while I check to see if the hillside is stable."

"Blasted sprained ankle!" she said. "If I hadn't injured it, I'd race you down."

"But injured it is. Be grateful it wasn't broken. That would slow you down for a lot longer." He glanced at the dog. "Do you want to go exploring, Fiona?"

She looked bright eyed and interested and scampered ahead when he started down the slope. The sandy soil was loose in a couple of places but not seriously treacherous. Luckily, the bluff wasn't very high here. When he got to the bottom he turned to call up to Signy—and found that she was already halfway down the hillside, cane in hand.

Near the bottom she slipped and ended up skidding the last few yards on her backside. Alarmed, he strode to her, but she was laughing as she levered herself up with the help of the cane.

"Idiot!" Ramsay assisted her to her feet and steadied her.

She grinned. "How could I miss out on this?"

He brushed the dirt off her back, forcing himself not to spend extra time stroking her delectable backside. "You don't look as tired as you did."

"It's the excitement of visiting Thorsay's ancient history." Limping with her cane, she made her way to the closest of the dwellings.

Though the storm waves had done a reasonably good job of washing away the sand and soil that had buried the buildings, it would take a good deal more work to completely clear them. She stopped in the open doorway and examined the inside. "It looks like there are furnishings made of stone. Or are they for some other purpose?"

"I think you're right." Ramsay pointed at the rectangular structure built out from the opposite wall. It was made of the same kind of piled rocks as the walls, though lower. The top was flat, and there were four large square openings on the front of the structure. "This was surely for storage."

"Since the hearth is in the middle of the room, there must have been a smoke hole in the roof above," Signy said. "I wonder what they used for roofing. I'm guessing turf. If the roof was made of stone, it would have collapsed onto the floor after the community abandoned the village. There would be a pile of rubble on the floor."

"You're thinking like an antiquarian," he said approvingly. "I agree that turf or possibly thatch seem to be the most likely materials."

She brushed her hand down the stacked stones on the left side of the doorway. "I'm beginning to understand your passion for antiquities. Perhaps these buildings speak to me because this is our history. What do you think these people were like?"

"It's hard to say. My guess is that the houses were here long before our Viking ancestors. But there might well be some blood of these ancients in our veins."

She stepped through the open door into the roughly square room and sank onto a low stone wall. "I'm tired. I hope any ghosts that remain won't mind me sitting down here."

He sat next to her and put his arm around her shoulders again, glad when she didn't object. "Resting here is appropriate, because I think these are beds, one on each side of the entrance. The stone pillars at the end corners might have held canopies over the beds to keep the warmth in."

"If the roof was turf, the canopies might also have kept small creatures from falling on sleeping people in the middle of the night," she pointed out.

He laughed. "That is one of the drawbacks of turf and thatched roofs. The stone bed enclosures must have had some sort of mattress and probably sleeping furs as well. They'd be wonderful to cuddle up in on cold northern nights."

She glanced up, and he had the sense that they were both intrigued by the idea of cuddling down amidst the furs. They both looked away quickly. She pointed at a door opening in a side wall. "Some kind of storeroom?"

"Perhaps." He rose and looked into the tiny room. "Hard to tell what's here without cleaning out the corners and bottom." He bent over and poked in the dirt, then froze at the sight of the pale curving object he'd spotted. Surely not…

He bent over and worked the object out of the dirt holding it in place, then simply gazed at it. Collecting himself, he crossed the main room and held out his find to Signy.

She gasped and took the shallow bowl from his hand. "This bowl is almost identical to mine, right down to the grooves around the rim!"

"And it feels very, very old."

She ran her fingers around the grooved rim, feeling the texture and sensing that it was of great age. "It's easy to imagine people living here. Talking, cooking, sleeping, raising children just as people do now."

"I'm sure you're right," Ramsay said thoughtfully. "I've seen people in many different lands. The cultures vary greatly, but the basic human desires and challenges are much the same." He gestured to encompass the ruins around them. "That's why studying the past is so interesting. It's only a step away from the present. Both different and the same."

"A good reason to visit foreign lands to see more myself. But here and now, I'd love to make drawings of this place." She made a face. "And I will after I get more drawing materials."

"Didn't you say that there's a shop in Clanwick that carries some basic supplies? That should be a priority," Ramsay said. "Anything they don't carry can be ordered from Edinburgh or London."

She looked ruefully at her injured ankle. "I'd love to go into Clanwick tomorrow, but I'd better stay home for another day or two." She rose with some difficulty from her perch on the edge of the stone bed. "Do you think there are more buildings here that remain to be dug out?"

"I'm sure of it, but this will be a long-term project." Enough fascinating discoveries to keep him interested for many years. He hoped that Signy would truly share his interest, because he loved the idea of working side by side with her.

"Time to head back to Skellig House," Signy said. "Getting out of here will be harder than getting in."

"But the visit has been worth it." Ramsay offered his arm. "We'll go up together. Think of me as a second cane."

"We'll have to figure out a better way to come and go," Signy said as she took his arm. "Railings to hang on to while one gasps for breath?"

"Or perhaps a long ladder. Maybe stairs later." Ramsay glanced back at the small group of houses. "For now, it's probably best we don't tell anyone of our discovery. I'd rather keep the souvenir hunters away until we have a better idea of what's here."

"That's wise. Lucky that not many people come along this section of the coast path since there's a shorter road inland."

With her cane in one hand and Ramsay's arm in the other, she grimly tackled the hillside. It looked steeper from the bottom than it had from the top. The ascent was an ordeal that left every fiber of her body limp and shaking. Twice they almost lost their footing and fell, but Ramsay had a good sense of balance as well as sheer physical strength.

Signy was grateful to find Puff grazing only a few feet away when they finally reached the top of the bluff. She crossed to the pony and draped herself over the warm, solid flank. After she caught her breath, she rasped, "I don't think this exploration would fit your horse doctor's recommendation to take it easy."

"Probably not," Ramsay said. "I hope you haven't made your ankle worse."

"I don't think so, but I hadn't realized how tiring pain is. I want to sleep the clock around."

"And so you shall." This time she was less surprised when Ramsay scooped her up and set her on the pony's broad saddle.

"What shall we name this site?" she asked as Ramsay took the pony's reins and started the trek back.

He considered. "Fiona found it, so how about Fiona Brae?"

"I like it. Fiona's Hill. We're making her immortal."

Signy was hazy for the ride back to Skellig House. Every step the pony took jarred her ankle agonizingly, which left little energy for conversation or thought. Well, she'd insisted on going to Sea Cottage, and then climbing down to the newly discovered ancient homes. She wasn't sorry for doing either thing, but she was paying the price.

—

On the journey back, Ramsay kept a hand on Signy's back to steady her since she seemed halfway unconscious. When they reached Skellig House, he asked, "Are you awake?"

"Reasonably so." She slid from Puff's back, and her ankle collapsed under her.

Ramsay caught her before she hit the ground. When he lifted her in his arms and carried her up the steps, she muttered, "Being helpless and having you carry me around is very annoying."

"I'm rather enjoying it." An understatement. It had been far too long since he'd been with a woman, and Signy wasn't just any woman. She was beautiful and warm and intelligent, strong and deeply feminine, and it was increasingly difficult to behave with any restraint. He wanted to take her to the bed and lie down with her and kiss her into a state of passionate need.

But not today. She closed her eyes and rested her head on his shoulder. "Odd tastes you have, Ramsay."

He managed to get them through the door and into the front hall without dropping her. Once inside, he called for Mrs. Donovan, who appeared quickly.

The housekeeper clucked her tongue at the sight of Signy. "The lass has done too much, I see."

"Would you expect anything else?" he asked wryly.

"No," she agreed. "I'll bring up some willow bark tea and fresh bandages."

"Don't forget your husband's numbing horse salve, since that seemed to help before." He headed to the stairs. "Could you also organize a cart and a work crew of three or four people to go to Sea Cottage? It was badly damaged by the storm. We need to salvage what we can of Signy's belongings and clean the place up so it can be repaired."

"Yes, sir, I'll arrange that now." She bustled off to make the plans. Ramsay realized it was the first time she'd called him "sir." He must be growing into the role.

By the time he'd carried Signy to the top of the stairs, he was panting. It was very fine to hold her in his arms, but he'd be glad when her ankle healed.

When he carried her into his grandfather's suite, she said, "It still feels wrong to be in the laird's rooms."

"There's no one he would rather have here than you," he assured her as he laid her on the bed and deftly removed her left shoe.

"But these rooms should be yours. Don't you want to live here?" she asked earnestly. "This suite has the best views and the most space of any in Skellig House."

"I'll live here someday perhaps, but not now." He brushed a kiss on her forehead. "I'd really like to share these rooms with you."

She blinked. "You're so persistent."

"I am. Most people find me very annoying." He kissed her lips more seriously.

She responded, sliding her hand around his neck. "When you're annoying me, I forget how much my ankle hurts," she breathed.

"Pleased to be of service." He kissed her again, sure he'd never tire of her lips when their kissing had so much intimacy and desire.

He had to wrench himself away. "Our discussion of who occupies this room will have to wait for another day since Mrs. Donovan will be here soon. For now, I think the sitting room will make a good studio for you until Sea Cottage is fit to live in again." He shook out the quilt that was folded over on the foot of the bed and laid it over her. "Tell me what you want me to buy in Clanwick tomorrow, and where I can find it."

"Olson's Bookshop on the High Street. You must remember it. Greta Olson is in charge of art supplies. Do you have a piece of paper so I can make a list of what I'd like? There should be notepaper in the laird's desk."

"A good idea to give me a list." Ramsay walked through the open archway that led to the adjoining room, which could be either sitting room or office. His grandfather's massive desk was a family heirloom. He should look through it when he had the time.

He opened the top right door and found his grandfather's notebook inside. That could be interesting, because Duncan was always jotting down ideas, notes to himself, and reminders of what needed to be done.

He paged through to the most recent entries. His grandfather's handwriting had become shaky by then, but the words were clear. *Ask Roald to extend the repayment time.*

Ramsay stared at the simple sentence, knowing that whatever it referred to couldn't be good. He'd need to talk to Roald as soon as possible to find out what was owed and when it was due.

"Did you find any paper?" Signy called. "He usually kept scrap paper in the top left drawer."

He shoved thoughts of debts aside and looked into the left drawer. The piece of paper on top would do. "Fire away."

"I'll start with what should be in stock, and then add several other supplies she might have available if I'm lucky." Signy began listing items by description and manufacturer because all drawing papers were not the same.

By the time Signy was finished, Mrs. Donovan had arrived with willow tea and honey cakes and what turned out to be her medical kit. As she opened it, she explained, "Generally I take care of the people in the household and Donovan does for the horses. But he's better with bone setting, which is why he was the one who looked at her ankle." She poured a cup of willow tea for Signy.

Ramsay nodded. "I'll get a bite to eat and then go out with the work crew. Thanks for all your efforts."

He went down to the kitchen, where a ham sandwich and hot tea revived him while he reviewed the storm reports that had come from different parts of the island. Mainland had been lucky. So far there didn't seem to be any casualties beyond a couple of sheep who had managed to get themselves drowned. Signy and her cottage might have been the worst hit.

By the time he finished eating, his work crew was ready. Donovan himself came with the cart and a young stable hand as well as rags, brooms, buckets, and a large tarpaulin. Two housemaids joined them, and they set off to Sea Cottage.

All of the helpers loved Signy, and they set to work energetically after their exclamations of dismay. The housemaids dove into the kitchen and found that the water pipe and stopcock above the counter still worked, so they were able to rinse off all the kitchen china and utensils before packing them carefully in baskets.

Ramsay and Donovan collected the rest of Signy's sodden clothing from the bedroom as well as her modest personal possessions. There were several books that might never recover, but Ramsay packed them up anyhow.

Then he and Donovan joined with the stable hand, who was clearing the front room and the other floors. Broken furniture was stacked outside. Some might be fixable. The loom was mercifully undamaged.

In a corner of the front room, one of the maids found a wet but otherwise intact piece of canvas that was painted with the images of Gisela, Signy, and their mother. She took it to Ramsay. "Miss Signy will want this back, I'm thinking."

"You're right." Ramsay took the picture and carefully flattened it into a coat pocket. "I'll tell her you found it." It was a good omen for Signy's future, he thought.

Ramsay and Donovan discussed the repairs needed. Then the large tarpaulin was fastened over the broken window and open areas of the front room, and none too soon. By the time they left, a misty rain was falling.

As the group headed back, Ramsay said, "Many thanks to you all. Signy will be very grateful."

The smaller housemaid piped up, "I'm that pleased to help, sir. Miss Signy has done so much for me and my family."

As Ramsay had told Signy, she should have been the new laird. He hoped he was making progress toward convincing her that she would make a splendid Lady of Thorsay. It was a grand good title for a Nordic goddess.

Chapter 21

Signy woke after a long night's sleep feeling much better. She moved her right leg cautiously under the covers. Her ankle certainly ached, but it was nothing like the agony of the day before. The new bandage and Donovan's horse salve had performed a minor miracle. Not that she was going to take a chance by going out again today. She was impatient but not stupid.

A wet nose poked her left ear. Signy's eyes shot open. "Fiona! Such a good girl you are."

Signy swung her legs carefully from the bed. She had a vague memory of Mrs. Donovan telling her the night before that they'd wash and dry her clothing and bring some garments up. The housekeeper had done her job. A nearby chair held folded items that Signy recognized. And sitting on top of her clothing was one-eyed Odin, who was eyeing her and Fiona balefully.

Signy laughed. "Odin, my old friend. Come join us on the bed."

After another glare at Fiona, Odin launched himself from chair to bed, kicking her clothes to the floor before he landed on her right side and presented his head for petting. Signy obliged, stroking the cat with her right hand and scratching her dog's neck with the left.

"You two must learn to get along," she said soothingly. "You're not Vikings fighting the English. You're both good Thorsayian beasties and should be friends. I won't ask you to shake paws, but you should become better acquainted. Accept each other's differences. Sniff each other's backsides."

She heard warm male laughter and looked up to see that Ramsay had entered the room carrying a basket of tantalizingly scented breakfast. "Blessed are the peacemakers?" he commented. "The antagonism between cats and dogs is eons old, though some individuals of the warring breeds learn to negotiate a truce."

"I hope these two will manage that." She had no desire to seduce Ramsay just now. Actually, it would be more accurate to say that she had no intention of doing so. But she wished that she wasn't wearing a long shapeless nightshirt that must have been borrowed from a man. She hoped Mrs. Donovan was the one who'd put it on her.

"You look like you're doing much better today," Ramsay commented. "I've brought breakfast for two. How about if I take Fiona for a brief walk while you wash up and get dressed? Unless you need help with that?" He gave her an exaggerated leer.

Signy's cane was leaning against the headboard, so she picked it up and carefully got to her feet. "Fiona, go with the lecherous gentleman and come back to protect me from him later."

Ramsay grinned and set the basket on the table that sat by the window with the best view. "Come with me, Fiona. I'm sure you'd like a breath of fresh air."

He snapped his fingers and Fiona happily followed him out. True to his feline nature, Odin abandoned the bed and jumped on the table for a closer investigation of the food. Luckily, the basket had a lid.

The laird's suite had a small washroom, which was a good reason for Signy to accept Ramsay's offer to stay in these rooms for now. She washed up with the lukewarm water in the pitcher brought to the washroom by a maid. Everyone was taking such good care of her. Signy wasn't used to being pampered, but she could get to like this.

She collected the garments that Odin had kicked onto the floor, and dressed. Since she wouldn't be doing any riding or walking today, she put on a simple dark blue morning gown. Then she sat in one of the two chairs by the window table and poured a steaming hot cup of tea from the pot that had come in the basket of food. Bliss.

There was a knock on the door, followed by Ramsay and Fiona. Impeccable timing.

"Good news. I checked the laird's office downstairs and found the sketchbooks you used on our journey around south Mainland. This one is mostly empty."

Signy almost stood to collect the sketchbook, then remembered her ankle and said, "Lovely! Put it on this desk, please. Later I'll see how well I can remember what we found at Fiona Brae."

"I'm guessing that you have a very good memory for how things look," he said as he set down the sketchbook, then joined her at the table.

She poured tea for him. "I do, though I'll need to sit there and study the stones to do good detail drawings."

"I've received more reports of storm damage around the islands. There's a fair amount of crop damage but no serious injuries." He took a deep swallow of tea. "I'll be off to Clanwick after breakfast. Is there anything else you'd like me to get for you?"

"No, just the art supplies. I hope Greta is well stocked now. What she carries varies a lot depending on who has been buying what." Signy slipped a piece of bacon to Odin, who had been watching her with his gimlet eye.

There were two cheese and herb omelets and warm bere bannocks. Signy found that she was ravenous and realized she hadn't eaten since yesterday's breakfast. She glanced at Ramsay, who seemed to enjoy breakfast food as much as she did.

She had a wistful thought of Gisela. If her sister hadn't died, she would be the one sharing meals with Ramsay. But the more time Signy spent with him, the more natural it felt. Gisela was the much-loved past. She'd always had a warm and generous heart, and Signy was sure that wherever her sister was, she didn't begrudge them this growing attraction.

If they had a daughter, they could name her Gisela. It was a thought too far in the future to be comfortable, so Signy applied herself to buttering a bannock. She would take her time with Ramsay day by day and enjoy it.

–

It was a fine morning to ride to Clanwick, and Thor seemed to be enjoying himself as much as Ramsay. He was a good-natured horse. Once Ramsay reached the town, he left Thor at the livery stable the family always used, then made his way to Olson's Bookshop.

He was greeted with pleasure by the owner, Gunnar Olson, who remembered how many books Ramsay had bought as a boy. Ramsay established a new account with the shop, then asked to see Greta, Gunnar's daughter, who was in charge of stationery and art supplies. A brisk and pleasant blonde, Greta said regretfully that she didn't have much on hand other than drawing paper, pencils, pens, and ink. More specialized items were available only by order. Additional materials were expected in the next shipment, but she wasn't sure when they would arrive.

Ramsay cleared the shop out of what they had and left the supplies at the livery stable. Now it was time for the difficult part of the day: Cousin Roald. Ramsay had stopped by his cousin's office when he arrived in town and set up an appointment for midday.

Roald kept him waiting for only a few minutes and gave him an effusive welcome when he was ushered into the lavish office. Roald was rich and wanted the world to know it, but it was hard to impress a man who had spent years around the palaces of Constantinople.

"Kai, my lad, good to see you!" Roald offered his hand. "How are you settling into your new position?"

"It's endlessly interesting," Ramsay said as he shook his cousin's hand, then took the seat indicated. "The visit to your kelp works was surprisingly exciting."

Roald grimaced. "I heard how you rescued one of my girls. Drummond told me of the safety precautions you suggested, and the rescue dinghies and life preservers are already in place. I don't want any tragic accidents in the future."

"I'm glad to hear that," Ramsay said, suppressing the cynical thought that Signy had voiced at the time. The rescue equipment was cheap and burnished Roald's reputation. The measure could easily have been put into effect years earlier if Roald really cared for his workers. It was being noticed by the new laird that had made him act now.

After a few more minutes of pleasantries, Ramsay said, "I'm here on business. I've been going through my grandfather's papers to find out what obligations I've inherited. I thought I'd found everything significant until I discovered my grandfather's daybook yesterday. One of the last items he wrote down was a reminder to talk to you about extended payment terms. You loaned money to him?"

"Yes, it was when the islands were suffering from the joint effects of the disease and the devil storm," Roald said. "Many people were suffering, and the laird wanted to help them out but didn't have much in the way of financial resources. No bank was willing to make a large loan when it was unclear whether the money could be repaid in a timely fashion."

This information was much the same as what Fergus Maclean, his grandfather's lawyer, had said. Needing the money, Duncan had borrowed from Roald and kept it secret even from his lawyer. "I've found no records of such a transaction, so I thought I should ask you directly if you have your copies of the loan documents. I need to learn how much was borrowed and when the loan is due."

Roald tilted back in his desk chair and frowned. "You couldn't find the documents? The old laird was always very careful with his records, but he was declining in his last years. He must have misplaced or accidentally destroyed the loan documents."

"Whatever the reason, I found no papers describing the loan," Ramsay said. "Are yours convenient?"

"Yes, give me a moment." Roald opened a lower drawer in his desk and swiftly pulled out a file. "Here it is."

Ramsay opened the file and found the loan document on top. One glance and his stomach sank. "I see it's dated almost two years ago."

"Yes, that's when the suffering was at its worst."

It was all there, including his grandfather's signature, and the document explained why there had been almost five thousand pounds in the laird's Bank of Scotland account. The original loan had been for twenty-five thousand pounds. Duncan had been using the money carefully because his people's needs were ongoing. But over twenty thousand pounds had been spent, and Ramsay would need to draw on the remaining five thousand pounds for estate expenses.

Feeling ill, Ramsay closed the file. "I'm surprised that you made a loan that might not be repaid."

Roald grimaced. "I'm a businessman, but I didn't want to see people dying of starvation in the streets. Besides, the loan was secured by Skellig House and the estate, and property always has value."

Ramsay looked into his cousin's cold, amused eyes and realized that the older man would like to see him default on the loan so the estate would come into his hands. The house, the lands, the horses.

Most of all, the status. Roald might not care to be laird, but he wanted to be the most important man in Thorsay, not merely the richest.

"Twenty-five thousand pounds is a considerable sum. When does the loan come due?" Ramsay flipped the next page and felt chilled. "September twenty-first of this year. The same day as the Thorsayian fire festival."

"It was an easy date to remember." Roald was watching him with a predatory gleam in his eyes. "Will that be a problem for you?"

"It will be difficult. My grandfather thought there was a chance that you might extend the loan. Is that a possibility?"

Roald leaned back in his chair, his brow furrowed. Ramsay had the sense that the older man was genuinely considering the question. To his surprise, Roald said, "With you so newly become the laird, it doesn't seem fair for you to have to deal with this so soon. Very well, I'll extend the loan for twelve months to September of next year."

Ramsay felt a rush of relief. "Many thanks! Do new papers need to be drawn up?"

"No need." Roald stood and offered his hand. "A gentleman's agreement that the loan comes due next year." He smiled. "Of course there will be more interest."

"Of course." Ramsay also stood and shook the other man's hand. "This will give me time to find the money for you. Now I'll be off. I've much to do."

Before he could leave, Roald's daughter, Annabel, entered the office. "Kai, I'm so glad to see you!" She extended a hand. Shimmering in silk and pouting prettily, she looked more like London than Thorsay. "I was hoping we'd be seeing more of you now that you've returned."

He smiled and took her hand. "Being new to my job, I've been very busy. But as always, it's a pleasure to see you. Good day."

Ramsay left Roald's office, hoping he'd received a genuine reprieve. The trouble was, he wasn't sure how far he could trust Roald.

Chapter 22

Once Ramsay was out on the pavement, he stood still for a moment, wondering what the hell he should do next. It was hard to imagine losing the land and home that were his birthright, but the dispassionate part of his mind recognized that it was a real possibility.

Since he was in Clanwick, he'd start by speaking to Fergus Maclean to tell him of the disastrous loan. Perhaps the lawyer would have useful suggestions, though Ramsay wasn't optimistic about that. But Fergus could complete the property transfer of Sea Cottage to Signy as soon as possible so that her ownership was secured no matter what happened to Skellig House and the estate.

He was about to head to the lawyer's home when a familiar voice called out, "Good day, Kai! How is your lairdship this fine sunny morning?"

Ramsay turned and saw Broc Mackenzie. His heart lifted. "Broc! It's good to see you. We still haven't sat down with a bottle of Callan's whisky to drink and talk. If you've some time, today would be a good chance to make a start."

Broc grinned. "It's a little early for whisky, so how about we go down to the harbor and pick up some mutton fritters and clapshot at Gordon's? Then we can sit and watch the harbor while we eat and exchange lies."

"That is the best idea I've heard today," Ramsay said. "As long as we don't forget the beer to wash it all down."

"Beer goes without saying." They fell into step together and made their way down the high street toward the harbor. His voice more serious, Broc continued, "When I was riding in this morning, I saw that Sea Cottage was wrecked in the storm. Is Signy all right?"

Ramsay repressed a shiver as he thought of that night. "She got out just in time, thanks to her dog Fiona, who came to me for help. They're staying at Skellig House until the cottage can be rebuilt."

Broc glanced at him askance. "It is safe to rebuild when the location is so vulnerable to storms?"

"There's some risk," Ramsay admitted, "but the cottage has been flooded occasionally in the past, though not usually so badly. My grandfather gave the cottage to Signy as a reward because of all she did for him and Thorsay over the years. She loves the place, so it needs to be repaired for her." Ramsay suddenly wondered if the laird had given her the cottage because he couldn't afford to leave her money.

Broc nodded with understanding. "In that case, rebuilding makes sense. This time with storm shutters."

"I had the same thought." Ramsay realized that despite the years that had passed they'd slid into the easy rapport they'd always had. This was just the sort of friend he needed today. "Do you know if Peter Swenson is still well and running his building business?"

"Yes, and he now has two strapping sons to help him. A fortnight back they were out to the farm to make some improvements to one of the barns where people are living now. They made short work of what needed to be done."

"Does he still live in that house on the western edge of Clanwick?"

"Yes, he and his lads have been expanding it when they're not busy elsewhere." Broc glanced at him. "By the way, has anyone shot at you again?"

Ramsay had almost forgotten that incident. "It only happened once, so it was probably a careless hunter." He hoped so, because he had enough other troubles without someone trying to kill him.

Gordon's was a cook shop on the harbor that served both the town's inhabitants and sailors. When Ramsay and Broc went inside, the ancient Mrs. Gordon glanced up and said, "Mutton fritters and clapshot and two bottles of beer?"

Both men laughed. "You have a fine memory, Mrs. Gordon," Ramsay said. "How many years has it been since Broc and I have been in here together?"

The old woman thought. "Fifteen years. About time you both came home."

She moved into the kitchen and called out their orders to another member of the Gordon family who was doing the cooking. It took only a few minutes to present the customers with a basket containing the food and drink.

When Ramsay reached for his wallet to pay, Mrs. Gordon said gruffly, "No charge just this once."

"Thank you," Broc said, looking as surprised as Ramsay felt. "That's very kind."

"It's good to see you two rascals home and safe," she said with even greater gruffness. "Now off with you. Don't forget to bring the basket and bottles back."

Meekly accepting their dismissal, Ramsay and Broc left the cook shop and by unspoken consent made their way around the harbor to the left. There were benches scattered along the waterfront, and one in particular had been "their" bench back in their school days, when they'd both attended the Clanwick grammar school.

When they'd settled, Broc investigated the basket. "It looks like we've been given double-sized orders."

"Because we've grown?" Ramsay pulled out a mutton fritter, which had just been fried up and smelled tantalizing. Gordon's also made the best clapshot in Clanwick. The dish was the Thorsayian version of what Scots farther south called neeps and tatties. Turnips and potatoes were mashed together with onions, butter, and a bit of salt and pepper, then served hot. Delicious, and very much the taste of home.

There was relaxed silence while they ate. After Broc finished his share, he said, "This certainly takes me back in time."

"We've both traveled long and winding roads since our school days," Ramsay said. He studied his friend's profile. Broc had the Celtic good looks of many Thorsayians, with dark hair and intense blue eyes. He was still Broc, who had been a friend since the nursery, but his features were harder and more wary than when they were boys. "Are you glad or sorry you went into the army? Your parents weren't keen on your going, but there was no holding you back."

Broc didn't shy away from the question. "Mostly glad. There was excitement and mud and danger and deep friendships, and in the end we defeated Napoleon. A miracle that I survived with only the odd scar here and there." He unconsciously touched the one on his cheek. "But after Waterloo, there was no point in staying on. Now it's time to figure out what I want to do with the rest of my life."

Ramsay asked, "How are you adjusting to being back in Thorsay?"

"You always were too curious," Broc said dryly. "But since you ask, it's a mixture of feelings. It's grand to see my family and to live by the sea again. I used to dream of the North Sea when baking on the plains of central Spain."

Ramsay gazed out at the harbor, where a trading ship was catching the tide to glide out into the open water. "I know what you mean. I've traveled widely, but I'm always happiest when near water."

"You wanted to study ancient times and places, and you've been able to do that for years." Broc tossed out a morsel of fritter. A seagull snapped it up before it hit the water. "Have you had your fill of travel, or do you feel trapped back here?"

"Now who's being curious?" Ramsay wiped grease from his fingers. "I came back with some reluctance, but I always knew I must return. I'm now learning to appreciate the many ancient ruins of Thorsay. They should keep me interested for the rest of my life."

He thought of mentioning Fiona Brae, but would save that for later. "How do you feel about becoming a farmer again?"

Broc grimaced. "Therein lies a tale."

Something in his friend's voice made Ramsay say, "If you want to talk, I'm still a pretty decent listener."

Broc sighed. "You always were, and I've got much to think about. I've never had a passion for farming, except maybe horse breeding, but with my father dead, coming back to Thorfield was the right thing to do. I was glad to be able to help my family, particularly my mother since she had so much to carry after my father died."

When Broc stopped speaking, Ramsay said, "I sense a 'but' coming."

Broc threw another scrap of food toward the harbor. This time two seagulls swooped in and fought over the scrap while a third one carried off the prize. "Right as always. When you had breakfast with us, remember that my mother said Thorfield has taken in people who've lost their homes because of the plague and the devil storm?"

Ramsay nodded. "Your mother has a very generous heart. Thorfield has enough barns and outbuildings to provide shelter for a fair number of people."

"Yes, and it's worked out well. People help each other out, and some work on the farm. With conditions improving, some have been able to move out."

"But?" Ramsay prompted.

"Remember Daniel Brown? Had a farm in the north-central part of Mainland."

Ramsay thought back. "Yes. A good fellow as I recall."

Broc nodded. "He lost his wife and his son to the plague, and eventually he lost his farm. He and his two little girls ended up at Thorfield. He's been a tremendous help. And as he and my mother worked together…" Broc stopped.

"Are they thinking of marriage?" Ramsay asked quietly. When Broc nodded, Ramsay continued, "Are you opposed to your mother remarrying?"

Broc tossed out another tidbit. "Not really. Daniel's a good and honest man. He and my mother laugh together. I like hearing her laugh again. But it's difficult to see him in my father's place. I no longer feel I'm needed."

Ramsay said wryly, "It's dire to make a sacrifice and then find it's no longer necessary."

Broc laughed. "That's it exactly! I didn't want to become a farmer, but it was my duty and I've always been good at duty. But it's not very rewarding to be doing work I don't want to do when there's someone else around who actually enjoys farming."

An idea began taking form in Ramsay's mind. "Would you like to take on a mission to London for me?"

"Yes," Broc said immediately.

Amused, Ramsay asked, "Without even knowing what it is?"

"It's bound to be more interesting than milking cows and tending sheep. What do you want me to do?"

"Several things. First, I want you to call on Captain Gabriel Hawkins Vance, once a sailor and now heir to a barony. I did a favor for him once, and I'm hoping he knows or can find a bank that would loan me a large amount of money on not much more than the strength of my word."

Broc gave a soft whistle. "Care to explain more about that?"

Ramsay found that he wanted to talk about his situation as much as Broc had wanted to talk about his. Succinctly he described his grandfather's loan and the reason for it, ending with his meeting earlier with Roald. "It was good of him to extend the loan for a year, but I'm not sure how much I trust him to keep his word. What do you think?"

Broc considered before answering. "Handshake agreements between gentlemen are all very well, but I'm not sure how much of a gentleman he is. If he finds a good reason to call the loan in before the year is over, he'll probably do it."

"My feeling exactly," Ramsay said, glad to have his doubts confirmed. "I'd much rather borrow from a traditional bank with more time to repay. I'm sure I can come up with the money eventually, but not in the next few weeks."

"Do you think this Vance person can find a bank that will lend to you?" Broc said a little doubtfully.

"He might be able to do it. He's very well connected."

"Do you have any friends who could afford to give you this kind of money as a personal loan?"

"Possibly." Ramsay frowned. "I'd really rather not do that to a friend. Though if I become desperate enough, I might try."

Broc nodded acceptance. "You said there would be several things you'd like me to do for you in London. What are the others?"

Ramsay grinned. "How do you feel about paintings and drawings?"

Chapter 23

"Paintings and drawings," Broc repeated, bemused. "I think of art as something one hangs on the walls and then forgets about. If you need an expert, I'm not your man."

"Luckily, your ignorance won't matter," Ramsay assured him. "Richard Maxwell has a London gallery that specializes in high-quality art. We've been friends ever since university. I'd like you to take some of Signy's pictures in to see if he'll carry them in the gallery. I think they're good enough."

Broc looked interested. "Didn't she do the watercolors of the island that hang in the front hall of Skellig House? I saw them when I called after your grandfather's death. They were lovely. Very evocative of Thorsay. She definitely has talent, though I don't know if her work will be to the taste of Londoners. Do you want me to give some of her work to Maxwell to sell?"

"No, I'm sending the pictures without Signy's knowledge. I want to find out if Richard is willing to sell them. If he is, I'll tell her of the opportunity. I believe that knowing her work is valued would please her greatly. If he's not interested, she doesn't need to know."

"Very well. That much art I should be able to manage," Broc said. "Do you have any other commissions for me while I'm in London?"

"Yes, though it may be impossible," Ramsay warned. "Signy really wants to study with an artist who can teach her more about painting. It may be some time before she can travel to London to do that, so I thought I'd bring an artist here for a couple of months of tutoring."

Broc stared. "Any particular artist, or should I just run an advertisement to find a starving artist desperate enough to come to the end of the world?"

Ramsay grinned. "An interesting idea, but there's a particular artist, Sophie Macleod, whose work Signy loves. I've seen Miss Macleod's paintings at Richard's gallery, and she's very good at capturing dramatic weather and the spirit of wild empty places. I'll pay to have her as a guest at Skellig House if she's willing to do some teaching. I thought it might help if you showed her pieces of Signy's work. If she agrees to come, you can escort her back to Thorsay."

"If Miss Macleod likes wild weather, she may leap at the opportunity to come to Thorsay." Broc gave Ramsay a long, level look. "This is well beyond rewarding Signy for what she did for your grandfather. Are you in love with her?"

Ramsay had a sudden desire to hide from that question. Instead he drew a deep breath and replied, "I rather think I am."

"Does she return your feelings?"

Ramsay grimaced. "She's somewhat wary, but I'm making progress."

Broc's smile was crooked. "Time to give up my dreams of courting her once I'm more sure of my future."

Ramsay tensed. "Are you in love with her?"

"No, but I've always been especially fond of her, ever since we played together as children. Remember the way she and Kendra fenced with each other when you were giving fencing lessons? The two of them were fierce little devils." He paused. "I haven't thought of Kendra in years. Do you know where she is and what she's doing these days?"

"She lives in England and has two children. Before her second marriage, she lived at Thorsay House." Ramsay grinned. "And she's still fencing. I saw her briefly when I came through London this last time."

"Perhaps I can call on her when I'm in the city. She's my cousin as well as yours."

"Thorsay isn't very large. Between the two of us, we're surely related to half the people in the islands." Ramsay's brow furrowed. "You were thinking seriously about courting Signy?"

Broc shrugged. "When I was on my way back home, I wondered if she was married. If not, I definitely wanted to renew our acquaintance to see what might happen, but so many years have passed that we'd be almost strangers. She's still a grand girl, though. Beautiful, intelligent, admirable."

"All true. And don't forget independent. She'll make her own choices, and marriage may not be one of them."

Feeling he'd said too much, Ramsay began packing the bottles in the basket. Finding a scrap of clapshot, he tossed it toward the water and several gulls materialized instantly.

"Time to go before we're swarmed on all sides by gulls." Broc rose. "When do you want me to leave, and do you have any special means of transportation in mind? It's a long way to London."

"Two or three days from now, if you can get away that soon. I own several small sailing vessels, so I'll find one that is available and can take you all the way to London and then wait for your return. You can stay at Thorsay House of course."

Ramsay realized that if his grandfather had mortgaged all his properties to Roald, that would likely include Thorsay House. It had long since been established as a place for traveling Thorsayians to stay, but Roald might turn it into a private residence for himself and his family.

Pushing the thought aside, Ramsay stood and lifted the basket. "I have a long list of things to do this afternoon." He offered his hand. "I'm glad we met up today. Thanks for listening, and for being willing to take on London on my behalf."

Broc smiled as they shook hands. "I think I benefited most from our meeting. London! Let me know when you have your ship arranged."

Ramsay wasn't sure how well any of his plans would work out, but at least he now had plans. That always made him feel better.

—

Signy behaved and spent the day in the laird's room, not even going downstairs to the kitchen. She hoped Ramsay had found more drawing paper for her, since she'd used a number of pages in the tablet he'd found for her. She did several general sketches of Fiona Brae but would have to return to the site for more detailed work.

Just for fun, she did a couple of sketches of the real Fiona and Odin, who were spending most of the day with her. Her favorite was of Odin lying on his back on the bed with his paws in the air as he snored gently.

She also made another attempt to draw Ramsay, but was again dissatisfied. His features were too regular, and the picture ended up showing him as blandly handsome without the intelligence and mischief in his eyes that made him interesting.

There was a knock at the door. "Tea service!" Ramsay called.

She hastily hid the drawing of him and called, "Enter, please!"

As he obeyed, she glanced out at the angle of the sun. "It's later than I realized," she said. "Are you just getting back from Clanwick?"

He nodded as he set the tea tray on the table. "I've had a very full day. I'll tell you about it over tea." He placed a package on the desk. "These are about all the materials the bookshop had. Greta apologized for not having much in stock, but more is on order."

Signy used her cane to walk to the desk and look at the materials he'd brought. "This will keep me busy for a while. Many thanks." She returned to the table and checked to see if the tea had steeped properly. Not quite yet. She sat down, realizing that she was more than ready for tea and conversation.

"You're walking more easily," Ramsay observed. "Your ankle is well on its way to healing?"

"Yes, in another day or two I'll be able to return to my normal routine." Thinking Ramsay looked tired, she asked, "Tell me more about your full day."

He grimaced. "The worst of it was calling on Roald and learning about the money the laird borrowed from him." Tersely he described the vast size of the loan and the terms.

Signy's eyes widened as she listened. When Ramsay finished, she said, "This is not good. I'd like to think that Roald will give you the full twelve months' extension, but he could easily change his mind and call the loan in at any time."

Ramsay nodded. "I'd have much preferred that he'd made the changes in writing, but I had a strong suspicion that if I insisted, he'd become insulted that I didn't trust his word and would stick to the original repayment date. This way there is at least hope that I'll have extra time."

"Do you have any ideas about how you might repay the loan?"

"Several." Ramsay took the chair opposite her. "I ran into Broc and we lunched by the harbor. I'm going to send him to London to talk to a friend of mine about finding a better bank. Broc will also be able to buy more materials for you. Make a list of what you'd like."

Visions of paint pots danced in Signy's head, but she'd make her list later. "Well done. What else did you accomplish?"

"I called on Fergus Maclean. The legal papers for transferring ownership of Sea Cottage will be finished and official by the end of the week, so your title to the property is secure no matter what Roald does."

"Thank you," Signy said quietly. "That makes me feel better even though the place is a wreck now."

"But not for long! I just engaged Peter Swenson and his sons to fix the cottage, and they can start right away. From the description I gave Peter, he thought that the roof could be repaired fairly quickly, though the interior and detail work will take longer."

"That's splendid!" Signy exclaimed. "How long does he think it will take to do the whole job?"

"He'll give you an estimate once he's been out there to evaluate the amount of work required," Ramsay replied. "Once the exterior repairs are done, one of his sons will bring in some laborers and they'll start cleaning up Fiona Brae."

"Good. I'll be able to do better drawings then." She poured more steaming tea and then helped herself to one of the ginger biscuits. "When will we return to your journeys around the islands?"

He eyed her a little warily. "I think you won't much like this. I know that I don't. But I'm going to visit the outer islands on my own. I think you should stay here and supervise the repairs on the cottage, and then the work on Fiona Brae. There isn't going to be any golden treasure there, but I don't want any of the workers to casually take home interesting bits and pieces like bones and bowls."

Her eyes narrowed. "Would you explain your reasons for traveling alone?"

"I greatly enjoyed traveling with you, and it was very helpful to have your background information and introductions," he said. "But more will be accomplished if we work separately, and there is much to be done."

"I suppose you're right," she said reluctantly. "But I've become accustomed to having you underfoot all the time. I'll miss your company."

"And I'll miss yours," he said bluntly. "But the more time we're together, the harder it is to keep my hands off you."

Startled, she said, "Is that a problem?"

"Yes." He stood and drew her up into his arms, then kissed her with shocking intensity.

After an instant of surprise, she wrapped her arms around his waist and kissed him back, feeling wildness rising inside her. His hands began roving over her body, bringing every place he touched to tingling life. When his hand covered her left breast, she pressed against him, wishing he were caressing her bare skin. She breathed, "I feel overdressed."

He broke the kiss and put a little space between them, then bent his head until his forehead was pressed into hers. "Which is why I need to travel on my own, my Nordic goddess. Being together all the time would be difficult. You know what I want, but it must be freely given, not stolen by seduction."

Jolted, she pulled her head back and looked into his gray eyes, which were stormy with emotion. "What exactly do you want?"

"You. All of you. Your hand in marriage and partnership, your lovely body in my bed." His smile was twisted. "Your tart tongue telling me when I'm wrong. Are you ready to agree to all that?"

She almost said yes, and that she was most certainly ready for the bed, but managed to tamp down her reactions enough to give reason a chance. All too aware of the bed only a few feet away, she stepped back so they were no longer touching. "That sounds lovely and romantic, but... you're right. I'm not ready for all that yet."

He gave her a twisted smile and retreated to his chair, removing Odin from the tea table in the process. "I was rather hoping I'd be wrong."

She seated herself again, pulling her way out of Ramsay's reach. "I think you know too much about women to be wrong." She hesitated, then asked, "Have there been many women, Kai?"

He shook his head. "I've always been much too busy to be a womanizer. There were occasional exceptions, but never love or a desire for something deeper. The only women I've cared for deeply have been Gisela and you."

"Is there some similarity between me and Gisela that draws you?" she asked, knowing it was a bad question but unable to stop herself from asking it.

He frowned as he sought words. "You both have traits that I've always admired," he said slowly. "Intelligence. Kindness. Curiosity. Charm. But other women have those traits also and I haven't been inspired to deeper feeling. Gisela was special, and so are you in a different way. You are yourself, not only Gisela's sister. She was my first love." He drew a deep breath. "I believe that you'll be my last."

His words were so powerful that she didn't know how to respond. Finally she said, "Love. Is that what we've been dancing around?"

He nodded. "Have you ever loved another man?"

"I've never thought about romantic love much, since I always felt that I was fated to be a spinster." She made a face. "I'm beginning to understand the lust part, though."

He laughed, his face lighting up. "That's progress of sorts. I think enough has been said for today. Except..." He hesitated before continuing. "If I lose everything to Roald and leave Thorsay because the only thing for me here is an empty title, would you lose whatever interest you might have in me?"

It was a serious question, so she thought about it seriously. He'd grown up with the prospect and now the reality of being the laird, and that inheritance had given him bone-deep confidence and an air of authority. He'd be a different man if he hadn't been raised with the knowledge of his position.

But confidence and authority were part of him now, and he'd have those qualities even if his inheritance was taken from him. She liked the man he was, and she was sure she'd like him still even if he was no longer the laird. "If you left Thorsay for a new life, would you take me with you?"

"Yes," he said without hesitation.

She gave him a slow smile. "I've always wanted to travel."

After several heartbeats of silence, he smiled back. "I think we understand each other, then." He rose to his feet. "And I'd better leave before I remember how close that bed is. Fiona, would you like to go for a walk?"

The dog bounced to her feet, ready and willing. Signy stood also, glad that her ankle didn't give more than a serious twinge. "I'll see you downstairs for dinner tonight," she said. "And I'll make lists of art materials for Broc, and the people you should call on in the outer islands."

"I find list-making a very attractive trait in a woman," he said with a touch of mischief in his voice. He stepped forward to brush a light kiss on her forehead, and then he was gone, Fiona dancing along at his heels.

Signy sat again and poured the last of the lukewarm tea. There had been no absolute declarations of love, nor a proposal or acceptance of marriage.

Yet she was quite sure that a mutual commitment had just been made.

Chapter 24

Broc liked London and had passed through often enough that he could generally make his way around. After stopping at Thorsay House to make sure they had space for him—they did—his first call was at the home of Captain and Lady Aurora Hawkins Vance.

A polite butler greeted him and said that the Vances were out of town but would be back soon and receiving visitors. Rather than pursue them to their country estate, Broc decided to leave a note saying he was an emissary from Ramsay. That should gain him entrance as soon as they returned. If they didn't come back to London in the next few days, he would follow them to the country.

Since it was late in the afternoon, he returned to Thorsay House, where he shared a fine dinner with the Browns, who ran the house on behalf of the laird. Mr. Brown was a native Thorsayian, and Broc knew some of his family. The couple enjoyed hearing the latest news from the islands.

Brown had retired from the army, met his wife in London, and they'd been here ever since. Broc wondered if the old laird had bought this house and created this position for the Browns. It was the sort of thing he'd do.

The next morning, Broc visited Richard Maxwell's gallery just off Bond Street. It was spacious and elegant and filled with an interesting assortment of objects and paintings. Since Maxwell was busy with another customer, Broc set the leather satchel of Signy's artwork on the gallery owner's desk. Then he browsed through the gallery, waiting for Maxwell to be free.

As he moved from piece to piece he noticed that many had classical themes, and scantily clad ladies in revealing draperies seemed very popular, but he was drawn to four paintings hung under the general title of "The Gathering Storm." The series began with a sunny mountain scene, then progressed through darkly ominous clouds, shattering winds, and lightning strikes, before the return of pale sunshine revealed flattened flowers and broken tree limbs. He was not surprised to see the signature "S. Macleod" in the corners of the paintings. An artist who excelled at painting weather. Just right for Signy.

A smooth voice said at his elbow, "They're striking paintings, aren't they?"

"Yes, they remind me of my home." Broc turned to see a well-dressed and highly polished gentleman who looked politely helpful. "Thorsay. I understand you're also Thorsayian?"

Maxwell's polished surface was replaced by a wide smile and Thorsayian informality. "Indeed I am." He offered a hand and switched to the Thorsayian Norn dialect. "I'm of Eastray. Which island are you from?"

"Mainland." Broc shook the other man's hand, also answering in Norn. "I'm Broc Mackenzie of Thorfield Farm, if you've ever heard of that."

"I have. Are you a friend of Kai Ramsay, the laird in waiting?"

"Yes, but he's now the laird. His grandfather died within a day of Kai's return."

"Not unexpected, but a loss. He was a grand old man." Maxwell ushered Broc back to the desk and switched to speaking standard English. "Are you the one responsible for that intriguing satchel? Dare I hope that Ramsay has sent me the work of some promising new artist?"

"You may dare." Broc also spoke English, which was a better language for business. "Actually, Ramsay has several favors to ask of you."

When they reached the desk, Maxwell spared a moment to ring for tea and wave Broc to a chair.

A tea tray was soon delivered from the back of the shop; pouring and fixing the tea took several minutes while the two continued their small talk. Broc had sometimes thought that even if Britons didn't really like tea, they'd keep serving it because it was socially so useful.

He took a sip. The tea was excellent. Nothing but the best for customers of the Maxwell Gallery.

At last, Maxwell turned to business. "Now, what can I do for you? And what favors has Ramsay to ask of me?"

"First of all, he has commissioned me to purchase some painting materials for a Thorsayian artist while I'm in London, since there isn't usually much available in Clanwick. Ramsay thought you would know the best places."

"No surprise there." Maxwell glanced down the list, then pulled a pencil from his desk and wrote an address at the bottom. "You should be able to get everything you need here. The shop caters mostly to serious artists, so the quality is good and the prices reasonable." He handed the list back. "What else?"

Broc opened the satchel he'd left on the desk. It contained several of Signy's drawings and watercolor paintings, which were carefully packed flat between sheets of heavier paper.

He laid them out across the desk. "These were done by a local artist. Ramsay thought they might be good enough to interest you for your gallery, but he hasn't told the artist that he sent the pictures with me, so they're not for sale. He just wanted to get your opinion."

Maxwell picked up the pictures one at a time, studying each carefully before moving on to the next. "The essence of Thorsay," he murmured. "They make me think it's time I paid a visit to the islands. It's been a long time since I left."

"Does that mean you're willing to carry this artist's work in the gallery?"

"Yes, I am, though I'd ask for exclusive rights at first. I like to have unique work when possible." His gaze lingered on a picture of the harbor at Clanwick. It was lovely, and the delicate lines of the ships and seagulls made Broc think of the meal he'd shared with Kai at the harbor that had started him on this journey.

"Is this work by the same artist who ordered the art supplies? He's very talented."

"She. Her name is Signy Matheson, and she was an assistant to the old laird. I believe she's hoping to have more time for painting now that he's gone."

"A worthy goal. I'll write a letter to her, telling her that I admire her work and the terms for selling through my gallery." Maxwell cocked his head to one side. "Any more requests?"

"One more. Signy saw a book of prints that included work by the artist Sophie Macleod and greatly admires her work. Ramsay had seen Miss Macleod's paintings here and assumed you'd be able to get in touch with her."

"Does Ramsay wish to buy a piece of Miss Macleod's, perhaps as a gift for Miss Matheson?" The glint in

Maxwell's eyes suggested he realized that Ramsay's interest in Signy was a great deal more than casual.

"I wouldn't presume to judge which painting to buy! If horses were involved, I'd have a solid opinion, but not art," Broc said firmly. "It's a different kind of request. Signy would like to study more advanced techniques such as oil painting. Because there is no such teacher in Thorsay, Ramsay hoped that Miss Macleod might be persuaded to visit Thorsay for a few weeks and spend some time tutoring Miss Matheson. She could stay at Skellig House and would have ample time for painting her own work. Do you think she might be interested? Transportation as well as housing would be provided, plus an honorarium for her time."

Bemused, Maxwell said, "I can't predict whether Miss Macleod would be interested. Like most artists, she's more than a little eccentric. But she might welcome the opportunity to get out of the city for a time."

"Plus she seems to like painting weather, and Thorsay has plenty of that." Both of the men laughed. Broc continued, "Would you be able to tell me how I might get in touch with her?"

"I won't give you her address, but day after tomorrow she'll come in during the morning to collect the money from the sale of one of her paintings. If you're here, I'll make the introductions and you can ask if she'd be interested in visiting Thorsay."

"Thank you!" Broc rose and offered his hand. "You've been very helpful. I'll come in two days to meet Miss Macleod." He began gathering Signy's pictures so he could safely pack them in the portfolio.

"You could leave those here to show Miss Macleod what her potential student is capable of," Maxwell suggested.

"These pictures are entrusted to me, so I'll take them with me and bring them back that morning."

"You're a cautious man," Maxwell said. "A good trait when dealing with art and artists."

As he left the gallery, Broc reflected that most of the paintings he'd seen there didn't interest him, but Miss Macleod's work did. There was power and mystery in her work. He hoped she would accept Ramsay's offer to travel to Thorsay with Broc. She'd make an interesting travel companion, even if she was eccentric. He smiled. Perhaps especially if she was eccentric.

Chapter 25

In the fortnight since Ramsay had left to tour the outer islands, Signy had fallen into a comfortable routine. After breakfast, she and Fiona headed to Sea Cottage to see how the repairs were going. Ramsay had been right about the efficiency of Peter Swenson and his sons. Once the fallen roof beam was raised and the back wall was repaired, she finally believed that her home could be reborn.

The inside work went more slowly. The floor needed replacement, and the Swensons were building cabinets for the kitchen and for her studio. She'd protested the cost, but Swenson said firmly that the laird had told them to make the cottage better than ever. The multiple panes of the large window would take time to replace, but in a few more weeks she'd be able to return to her home.

She had to admit that she was enjoying living in Skellig House, particularly since Ramsay wasn't there to tempt her. Though she might end up living in the hall with him, for now she yearned for the privacy of her own home.

After visiting Sea Cottage, Signy and Fiona continued up the coast path to Fiona Brae. Her ankle was mostly healed, but because it was still weak and subject to occasional twinges, she used the cane. Like the cottage, she'd soon be as good as new.

The Swensons had built a long sturdy ladder that reached from the bluff down to the level of the ancient stone homes. It felt safe and solid as Signy climbed down to the site. Fiona preferred skittering down the slope.

This morning was sunny, a good day for working outdoors. Andor, the older Swenson son, who was in charge of the Fiona Brae excavations, had set up a table and chairs under a wide awning to protect Signy from passing rain while she worked.

When she reached the bottom of the ladder, she called, "Andor, any interesting finds this morning?"

"Several tools stored in a side room, Miss Signy. Over here." He escorted her to the third house, which had the most soil to be cleared away. The tools seemed to be a shovel, an adze, a couple of awls, and a pair of crude stone knives.

"The owner was a carpenter, perhaps?" Signy pulled out her drawing pad and did a quick sketch of the tools and where they'd been found. Ramsay had left strict orders that all artifacts of any size should be drawn in location before they were moved.

When she was done, Andor would remove the items and they would be given numbers. Signy had done master drawings of the site, and she marked where each object was found. She wasn't sure what Ramsay would do with the information, but she presumed he had his reasons for proceeding in this manner.

She was also doing detailed drawings of each structure, and she'd done a site plan looking down on the connected buildings from the bluff. It was interesting to be part of the exploration of this ancient village, though she took occasional breaks to do watercolors of the sea and sky and gulls.

News of the find had become public once the excavation work started and sometimes curious islanders came by. Most looked from above, though a few climbed down the ladder. There wasn't anything valuable to steal, but visitors were watched by Andor and his crew. There had been no problems, other than gulls trying to fly off with food when the workers broke for lunch.

It was midday and Signy was feeling hungry, so she set her drawing pad aside and stood to stretch. Too much sitting knotted up her muscles. A voice from her left said, "Found any treasure yet, Miss Signy?"

"Ramsay! I didn't expect you back so soon." She whirled in delight, and there he was, tall and lean and strong, with that bone-deep confidence despite all the challenges he faced. She almost threw herself into his arms, remembering barely in time that they had an audience. Instead she caught his hands and beamed up at him.

He beamed back, and the sight they presented probably revealed almost as much as if they were kissing. Kissing would be a lovely idea if she could get him alone. Decorum won. She asked only, "How was your tour of the outer isles?"

"It went well. I called on the people you suggested, asked questions, and listened to the answers. Mostly people were glad to be heard, especially on the smallest islands." Reluctantly he released her hands. "How is the excavation work going?"

"Very well. Andor and his men have been careful, and I've been sketching the locations and details." She opened her portfolio and gave him the sketch pad.

He flipped through, nodding as he turned the pages. "Good work. When all these pieces are put together, we'll have some idea of how these people lived. Time to talk to Andor."

"First, I have a question. Since Sea Cottage was owned by the Thorsay estate when your grandfather borrowed the money from Roald, does that mean it goes to him if you have to default?" A fate almost too horrible to contemplate.

"No, you're safe," he said reassuringly. "On the way home this morning I stopped to see Fergus Maclean in Clanwick. He was able to get a copy of the loan documents from Roald's secretary. He tells me that if the loan had been a standard mortgage, your cottage probably would have been included, but since it was a personal loan, the listings weren't as detailed. Neither Sea Cottage nor Thorsay House in London were included." Ramsay paused thoughtfully. "I'm surprised Roald didn't want Thorsay House."

"Perhaps because he almost never goes to London?" Signy suggested, intensely relieved that Sea Cottage was still hers. Was it large enough for both her and Ramsay? Probably not, but God willing, matters wouldn't come to that.

"More likely he doesn't consider the place grand enough for him." Ramsay's eyes lit up. "Enough about legal matters. I want to see what you've found!"

Signy accompanied him to the middle structure, where Andor and one of his men were carefully removing the soil from another of the small side chambers. "Good day, Andor!" Ramsay called. "How does it feel to be advancing our knowledge of our ancient ancestors?"

Covered with dust and dirt, Andor emerged from the side room with a smile. "Interesting, though it's more satisfying to fix a roof so a family can have their dinner without being rained on."

"Hard to argue with that," Ramsay said. "What's the most interesting thing you've found here?"

"Miss Signy, you show him," Andor said.

Signy led Ramsay to the third building and gestured at the smaller bed. "A double handful of beads were found inside the stone frame. They're mostly packed up now, but I kept a few here to show you when you returned."

She pulled out a small folded fabric square and opened it to reveal half a dozen beads inside. "It took skill and a good tool to bore the holes for stringing. The beads are made from bone and the larger ones were carved, see?"

He inspected them carefully. "This certainly appears to be part of a necklace. Surely someone's treasure."

Signy laid a hand on the stone pillar at the end of the bed. "It's pure imagination on my part, but when we found these beads, I could see a woman jumping from her bed and running for higher ground when a warning was given. Maybe giant waves were pounding in, like the ones that uncovered these ruins. The string of her necklace broke as she was bolting from the house and the beads scattered across the bed. She surely wanted to come back and find them later, but she couldn't. Over the centuries, the mattress and furs disappeared, leaving only these beads."

"Something like that might well have happened," Ramsay said. "It's part of the fascination of places like this. In Italy, I visited the ruins of a Roman city called Pompeii. It was destroyed by a volcano, and many people were killed in their beds or as they went about their daily tasks." He looked around the stone interior. "I'd like to think that our people here all got out alive."

"Is it odd to care so much about people who have been gone for eons?" Signy asked.

"It's the reason for studying antiquity," Ramsay said quietly. "They were people just like us. The past is a mirror for the present."

She smiled up at him. "That's too philosophical for a fine sunny day. Would you like to explore the beach around the corner from the third house? Andor's crew cleared out some of the crumbly soil so there's enough space to walk around the point, but no one has bothered yet. I've wondered if there might be more houses like these. Probably not, but we might as well go look."

"If nothing else, we'll have more privacy," Ramsay murmured under his breath.

Signy smiled and led the way around the end of the third house, using her cane for stability on the slippery shingle. The edge of beach was narrow, and it curved to the left for some distance.

As soon as they were out of sight of Andor and his workers, she turned into Ramsay's embrace. His arms came around her hard, and their lips met in mutual hunger. She murmured, "I hadn't realized how much I missed you until I saw you again."

"I realized how much I missed you the moment I left Skellig House." His hands moved down to her hips to draw her tighter. She caught her breath, wondering just how uncomfortable it would be to lie on a damp shingle beach.

Very. Reluctantly she withdrew from his embrace. "Later."

He smiled wryly. "I occasionally wish you didn't have such good sense. Let's go see what, if anything, lies around this point of land."

She'd assumed that this sliver of beach would soon come to an end. She was surprised when it opened up wider just ahead of them.

She walked cautiously into the broader area of beach, then stopped and gasped. In the bluff to the left, a dragon-headed Viking ship was imbedded in the soil at the level of the beach.

She'd stopped so abruptly that Ramsay bumped into her. "What... ?"

He saw the ship and stopped dead, his hands locking onto Signy's shoulders. After a long awed silence, he breathed, "I think it's a Viking ship burial. Great kings and chieftains were buried in their ships with grave goods to provide comforts in the afterlife. At least that's the theory. I've read of such things but never seen one. Never anything like this."

Signy walked warily toward the ship, as if it were a soap bubble that might burst. "The bluff has been undercut by the waves, so I suppose this isn't visible from above. How old do you think it is? As old as Fiona Brae?"

"Fiona Brae is much older. I'd say this is more like a thousand years old. Perhaps from the time that Christianity came to these northern islands." Ramsay reached the partially exposed ship and touched the gunwale with amazement. "It's amazing that it's lasted this long and is still sound. There must be something unusual about the soil conditions here."

"You said this is a burial ship." Signy studied the length of the vessel, which was perhaps seven or eight yards. "There's a body buried in it? Or a number of bodies? Did Viking chiefs kill faithful servants and bury them together so the king would be able to order them around in the afterlife?"

"Not that I've ever heard of, though there are countries in the east where that was sometimes done." The deck of the ship was covered with sandy soil. He scooped up a handful. "There is probably a burial chamber in the middle with some grave goods inside and compartments for more such treasures around it."

"Treasures?" she asked. "Jewels and gold?"

"Perhaps." He shook his head as he studied the ship. "Weapons are more likely. Shields and a sword and perhaps a broken spear to symbolize a life lost in battle? The Vikings were masters of metalwork, but I don't know enough about them."

She gave him a mischievous smile. "After this ship is excavated, you'll have enough material to write a book about them."

A stunned male voice behind them said, "It's a ghost ship of the ancestors!"

They turned to see Andor Swenson emerging from the narrow passage around the point. Seeing their expressions, he explained, "You had been gone awhile, and I became curious about what might be back here."

"It's a Viking ship burial," Ramsay said, adding some of the explanations he'd given Signy but without any mention of possible treasure. "This also needs excavation, but it's far more fragile than the stone buildings of Fiona Brae. I intend to work on it myself. Do you have a couple of good men who could help me?"

Ramsay's gaze moved to the carved dragon figurehead, miraculously identifiable after so many years of burial. "I want this to remain a secret for the time being. Curious people aren't likely to do much damage to the stones of Fiona Brae, but it wouldn't take much carelessness to destroy this old ship. It's a wonderful scholarly find, and I don't want to see it damaged."

Looking properly impressed, Andor said, "I understand." He walked up to the ship and, like Ramsay, touched it with a wondering hand. "This feels much more like proper Thorsayian history than those old stone huts. And a grave as well! It deserves respect."

"Indeed it does," Signy said. Respect and protection. She had an uneasy feeling that while Fiona Brae was of interest for its history, this long-buried ship might attract a different and more dangerous kind of interest.

Chapter 26

Two days after his initial visit to the Maxwell Gallery, Broc returned in hopes of meeting Sophie Macleod. He arrived early so as not to miss meeting her. After a cup of Maxwell's excellent tea, he browsed through the gallery again, taking more time to study each item.

Following Waterloo, his regiment had been stationed in Paris to help keep the peace when the Allies who had defeated Napoleon gathered for a conference to work out the treaties that would deal with France's sins and the future of Europe. One of the more colorful disagreements had been about art. France had looted the treasures of every country it invaded, and now the original owners wanted their masterpieces back. Though he was no art connoisseur, he could understand their point of view. And he certainly could appreciate Signy's work. Her pictures were lovely, and they evoked his home.

He kept an eye on the customers who came and went, not wanting to miss his quarry. He had a mental image of Sophie Macleod as a tall iron-willed eccentric who might well brandish an umbrella when annoyed.

He was contemplating a statue of a nearly naked lady trying to avoid unnatural attentions from a swan when Maxwell called, "Major Mackenzie, Miss Macleod has arrived."

Broc made his way back to the main desk and was startled to find a petite redhead with a disturbingly sharp gaze. She was younger than he'd expected, probably under thirty.

Maxwell made the introductions, adding, "Sophie, Major Mackenzie has a proposition for you."

Her eyes narrowed. "I may be an artist," she said with a slight Scottish accent, "but I have no interest in propositions from debauched ex-officers."

As Maxwell watched with amusement, Broc said, startled, "Not *that* kind of proposition! I'm from Thorsay, and the laird asked me to see if I could persuade you to come north for a visit to tutor an amateur artist who is a great admirer of your work."

"I've had men say they were great admirers of my work as a first step toward behaving dishonorably toward me," she snapped.

Beginning to understand, Broc said, "Rather like the way some men assume that actresses are always women of loose morals?"

She glowered. "Exactly."

"I assure you that neither the Laird of Thorsay nor I have had any such thoughts. The artist who hopes to study with you is female," he assured her.

Before she could reply, Maxwell said, "Other customers are coming in, so perhaps you could continue this discussion in my back office."

"Very well." Sophie turned like an angry cat and made her way through the door that led to the back of the shop. Broc followed and was temporarily dazzled by the range of sculpture that was stored there. The largest was a nude Olympic athlete of startlingly male proportions.

The artist turned left into a private office that, unlike the desk outside, had stacks of papers held down by stone cherubs and bronze ornaments.

Sophie flounced down into the chair behind the desk. She still looked hostile, but at least she seemed willing to listen. "Tell me more about these people who want me to go to the end of the world."

"I believe that Shetland is the end of the world. Thorsay is next door to the end of the world," Broc said mildly. "You have a Scots accent. Are you by any chance an islander?"

Showing a hint of a smile, she replied, "Aye, I am. The Hebrides. Skye, to be exact. My island is cluttered with Macleods."

Though none like this one, Broc suspected. He removed a pile of books from the chair on the opposite side of the desk and sat down to answer her earlier question. "The old Laird of Thorsay, Duncan Ramsay, recently died at a great age and has been succeeded by his grandson, Kai Ramsay. For years Duncan was assisted by Signy Matheson, a very capable young woman and an amateur artist who rarely had enough time to paint.

"Now that Signy has fewer demanding duties, she wants to spend more time on her art work but has never had any formal training. She believes that working with a professional artist would be beneficial for her, and I know she'd like to paint with oils. Because of Signy's service to the old laird, his grandson hoped to persuade you to come to Thorsay for a few weeks and spend some time tutoring her."

"What about transportation and accommodations? Thorsay is not an easy place to reach."

"All of your expenses would be covered. The laird told me that it's impossible to judge the value of an artist's time, but there would also be an honorarium."

Sophie was beginning to look interested. "How does this Signy even know about me?"

"Apparently she found your work in a book of prints?"

Sophie nodded. "Maxwell paid for the publication of a book of prints with work by several young artists he considered promising, but the number printed was very small. I'm surprised a copy made it all the way to Thorsay."

"I have no idea how it did, but now that I've seen several of your paintings here, I can understand why Signy likes your work," Broc said honestly.

"'The Gathering Storm' series. Some of my better work." Sophie's eyes narrowed. They were green and rather catlike. "Is this Signy any good? Teaching an incompetent would-be artist is painful for both parties."

"Well, Kai and I like her work, and he's far more knowledgeable about art and antiquities than I. Here are some samples." Broc pulled out the watercolors he'd brought from his portfolio and laid them on the desk in front of Sophie.

She took her time studying each picture before laying it aside. Broc held his breath, unable to read Sophie's opinion from her expression.

When she was done, she squared the pictures carefully and looked up at Broc. "She's very talented. I see why my work appeals to her."

"You seem to be kindred spirits," Broc said. "You both like weather."

Sophie actually smiled. "That's reducing it to the basics. But yes, your Signy and I do have similar sensibilities, and it would be lovely to leave London for the islands again.

How much would the honorarium be, how and when would I travel there if I agree, and how will I return home again?"

Broc told her the amount of the honorarium, then continued, "If you decide to do this, I'll escort you to Clanwick on a Thorsayian ship. You'd stay in the laird's own residence, Skellig House, which is nearby Signy's home. It's no Blenheim Palace, but it's a sizable and pleasant house. We'll sail on one of the laird's own ships, and I guarantee that no man aboard will raise a hand to you."

He must have sounded rather fierce, because she gave a wider smile. "If a sailor does, you'll take that hand off?"

"I didn't mean to sound ferocious," he said with a touch of embarrassment. "A sailor wouldn't be much use with only one hand. But I assure you that I will stop any such behavior immediately."

"I'm sure one good military scowl would intimidate most common sailors." She looked down at her hands, folded on the desk. "I'm sorry I sounded so angry before. I've had... some bad experiences."

"The curse of being attractive, I assume," he said thoughtfully. "Some men are blinded by pretty faces."

"Exactly so." She gave him a genuine smile. "I accept, Major Mackenzie. It will take me at least a week and perhaps as much as a fortnight to collect the materials needed to teach your Signy and make arrangements for my departure. Is that satisfactory?"

He would have preferred to sail sooner, but he must work with her schedule. "Very well. Though she's not my Signy."

"Whose Signy is she?"

Broc was so surprised that he replied. "Kai Ramsay's, I think. The three of us were neighbors, and we grew up together. Friendship seems to be changing into something more for Kai and Signy, though I don't know for sure."

Sophie grinned and looked like a mischievous seventeen-year-old. "So I'm part of your lord's campaign to woo his lady?"

Broc grinned back. "That's my guess. But Signy is talented and would love to have a chance to work with you, and since you're an islander yourself, I think you'll find it an enjoyable holiday. We haven't the mountains of Skye, but there's a great deal of wild country and some-times very dramatic weather."

"Islands are special, aren't they?" she said, her expres-sion distant. "Each is unique, but all have a sense of being away from the mundane world."

"I've not thought about such things," he said. "Growing up on an island, I think of it much as a fish thinks about water. It was my world as a boy, and now it is again."

"And in between was Portugal and Spain?"

"Among other places." Since he'd been introduced as a major, it wasn't surprising that she guessed he'd been a soldier. But he had the impression her artist's eyes saw too much.

"You've an interesting face, Major," she said thought-fully. "I'd like to paint you."

He laughed. "I suggest you stick to landscape and weather." But as he collected Signy's work and returned it to the portfolio, he knew the voyage home would be more interesting than the trip south to London had been.

Chapter 27

Signy was pouring wine to accompany their dinner when Ramsay entered the laird's suite. The visit to Fiona Brae after the week's journey had made it a long day. If Signy hadn't dragged him away, he'd probably have spent the night excavating the Viking ship. But it had been there for centuries. It could wait a day longer.

After a blissful hot bath, he'd change into his loose, ankle-length black banyan. Signy also wore a long belted robe, blue in her case. For two unmarried people, such clothing would be an outrageous degree of informality anywhere in the South, but this was Thorsay and neither of them were children.

Signy handed him one of the glasses of wine. "I thought that your return and the day's discovery deserved some of the best wine from your grandfather's cellar."

He raised the glass in a toast. "To the old laird, whose wide knowledge extended to fine wines!"

Signy tasted the wine and relaxed into a smile. As she sat at the table by the window where the setting sun poured in golden light, she asked, "Did you get a chance to meet Ian Maclean in Stromburgh?"

"Yes, you were right to suggest him as a possible magistrate. I appointed him to the position immediately." After a satisfying swallow of wine, he opened his notebook and scanned the list of his visits.

He did want her thoughts and opinions on what he'd learned and what he'd been asked, but the real reason he'd suggested this private dinner was because he wanted to be alone with her. It felt so right and natural.

He was on his second page of notes when Odin arrived on his lap with a thump. "Are you hungry, my lad?" he asked as he petted the cat, who regarded him with his one piratical eye. "Is that why you're here this evening, because you missed your supper and are starving?"

Signy laughed. "He's probably here because he ate his supper in the kitchen and thought it was inadequate, so he's decided to try his starving kitten routine on you."

"He didn't get to be this size by skipping opportunities to eat." The cat's gray fur was sensuously soft, which made Ramsay think of Signy's magnificent hair, an invitation to sin.

Like Ramsay, Signy had also bathed and donned her long blue robe, tying her luxuriant red-gold hair back with a blue scarf. Though every lovely part of her but her hands and hair were covered, the boudoir intimacy was profoundly erotic. He thought again how in London, a scene so outrageously intimate between two unwed people would have meant a sudden march to the altar.

Which wasn't actually a bad idea…

"I don't want to talk about business this evening," he admitted. "The trip was valuable, and I've seen a great number of our islands and met many interesting and influential people, but I have nothing to ask you that can't wait until tomorrow."

She smiled. "You want to talk about your Viking ship, don't you? It's an extraordinary find. I can't wait to discover what is hidden under the sand and soil."

"Neither can I." He set Odin on the floor. "Go wash Fiona's face. You both seem to like it."

"They've been getting along well," Signy said, watching Ramsay uncertainly.

He stood and locked his gaze with hers. "As much as I want to excavate the ship, I want to explore you even more. A fortnight apart felt very long. Far too long."

He extended his hand. She clasped it and rose from her chair, her gaze on him. Wordlessly they embraced, just holding each other. She was a little tense at first, but soon she began to relax, her body warm and pliant. He loved how tall she was, how he could bury his face in her hair after he'd deftly untied the scarf that held the thick tresses back.

"At night when I was trying to fall asleep in a succession of strange beds, I thought of you," he murmured in her ear. "Which did not help my slumbers."

She gave a soft laugh. "At least I had Fiona and Odin sharing my bed. They're better than sleeping alone."

"When I stayed with the Jansens in Eastray, I was impressed by the pottery but even more by Chieftain, their gigantic lurcher hound who insisted on sharing my bed. I'm sure you've met him." He chuckled. "The beast was huge and smelled like a dog who lives a full life. He was no substitute for you."

"Chieftain is a very memorable dog, but I'm not sure whether I should be flattered," she said, her tone serious but her eyes amused.

"You definitely should be." His hands kneaded her supple body, enjoying her winsome curves and alluring strength. "What really kept me awake was remembering that I slept in your bed when I came to tell you that the old laird died, and nothing happened. Worse, I was so exhausted that I can't even remember what it was like!"

"If you'd tried to make something happen, I would have kicked you out of my bed," she said tartly.

"Would you do that now?" he asked, his voice soft. "Because I would dearly love to share that bed with you tonight and every other night." He bent his head into a tender kiss. Her lips were so soft, so quintessentially Signy...

Her mouth opened under his, and he blazed from tenderness into fierce longing. Passion was potent as it pulsed through his body, but even more than desire, he wanted to join with her so that they could share each other's essences. To be mated and stronger than either of them alone.

"You aren't very subtle," she said unevenly as the kiss ended.

He brushed her shining hair from her cheek. "I seem to be fresh out of subtlety today." He had an intense belief that now was the right time, coupled with an equally intense fear that what he was about to say would be disastrous. "You enjoy my kisses, and before I left, we seemed to have come to understand each other. What now?"

She slid her hand slowly down the front of his body. "I'm not entirely sure what comes next," she said hesitantly, "being inexperienced in such matters. Though I have a fair idea." Her moving hand stopped and gently clasped him through the heavy fabric of his robe. Mind-melting heat flared through him.

She squeezed very gently. "Perhaps... this is the night to become lovers." She kept her gaze down, her voice shy even as her hand became more bold.

Barely able to speak, he gasped, "Not lovers, my darling goddess." He lifted her chin with his hand and gazed into her golden hazel eyes. "I want more than that. I want you to share my bed as my wife. And we can make that happen right now, right here."

Her breath caught. "Do you mean a handfasting?"

He nodded. "We seem to be in the midst of antiquities today, and handfasting is a most ancient and honorable Scottish custom. Usually two people handfast with the intention of having a more formal marriage soon, an intention I most certainly have. I want to marry you in St. Magnus Cathedral with half of Thorsay watching and beaming with approval or envy. But tonight I want to make this private, personal pledge to you."

"Isn't a witness required?" she said uncertainly.

He gestured to where Fiona and Odin were curled in the corner. "We have our friends here. I suspect that Odin isn't entirely reliable, but I know that your Fiona is honorable and true."

Signy laughed. "A fair assessment." She pushed her hair back nervously. "Are we ready for this?"

"I am, and my deepest hope is that you are also." He caught her right hand in his as he captured her gaze. His voice deep, he said solemnly, "I, Kai Douglas Ramsay, take thee, Signy Anne Matheson, to be my wedded wife, forsaking all others until death us do part, and thereto I plight thee my troth."

Signy drew their joined hands up to her cheek. At first her voice was unsteady, but it became stronger as she spoke. "I, Signy Anne Matheson, take thee, Kai Douglas Ramsay, to be my wedded husband, forsaking all others until death us do part, and thereto I plight thee my troth."

He caught her other hand and drew her against him for another kiss, this one a pledge of eternity. Her mouth opened under his, sweet and welcoming. He felt a melting tenderness, a need to protect her against all others even though she was less in need of protection than any women he'd ever known.

"I think it's now time to consider the bed." She stepped back and untied the sash of her robe, letting the garment slide off her shoulders to pool around her feet. Underneath she wore only a pale, translucent shift.

He caught his breath, awed by the simplicity of her acceptance and the loveliness of her body. "You are magnificent," he breathed.

"And you are overdressed," she said with a mischievous smile as she tugged on his sash and his robe fell open.

And in that moment, he knew beyond a shadow of doubt that this was the right time and the right woman, forever and ever, amen.

In the sunset light, she saw that he was golden and naked under the robe. Naked, beautiful, and very ready.

Her eyes shot open. "I see that you were very confident."

"Not really," he said wryly. "But I had hopes."

"Obviously," she said, wrenching her gaze upward. "Of seduction?"

"As I said, I wanted more than that," he said in a steady voice. "And now we have more. Will you lie with me, my beautiful wife?"

"With delight and some trepidation," she said honestly.

"Let's start with the delight."

As the sun set, the bedroom was filling with shadows. He reverently pulled the shift over her head. Then he stepped forward and encircled her waist with his arms, drawing her against him so that they were skin to skin.

She could barely breathe as the sheer eroticism of that touching scorched through her, annihilating all her doubts and questions. She stepped backward, pulling him down with her as she tumbled onto the bed.

He followed her down gladly, kissing and stroking as he stimulated every fiber in her body. Intoxicated, she wondered how she'd gone from adoring him when a child to despising him when he left, to accepting first his presence, then his friendship, and finally the absolute rightness of this mating.

"My husband," she breathed into his ear as she moved to make it easier for him to touch her. He responded with his hot mouth and stroking fingers as he caressed, then probed, then found a hidden core of sensation that flared into shattering pleasure.

He held her close as she recovered. "You were indeed ready," he whispered with laughter in his voice. "We were made for each other, Signy. Meant to be together. And damned if my grandfather didn't know it!"

She laughed at that. "Despite all my resistance, he was right. We were meant to be mates." Her hand began creeping down his belly until she clasped him. He jerked and turned rigid. "And there is more mating yet to do, for this is mutual seduction, is it not?"

"As mutual as man and woman can be," he said raggedly as he moved between her legs, his deft fingers preparing her, then guiding himself into her as he watched her reactions intently.

They came together more easily than she expected. There was building pressure, then one short, sharp pang before he slid fully inside her. She was still for a moment, savoring the pulsing power and utter intimacy of their joining.

Then she began to move, exploring the dimensions of this mating. To her surprise, heat again began building inside her as they quickly found a rhythm that was intensely, mesmerizingly *right*.

With a groan near agony, he poured himself into her. She met him with her own release as they culminated their joyous dance of life. Annihilation and rebirth, their souls as truly mated as their bodies.

When his breathing returned to normal, he half rolled to his side and pulled her close. "Thank you, wife," he murmured before brushing a kiss on her temple.

"Thank you, husband," she murmured with a soft laugh. She burrowed her fingertips into his fair hair and stroked the back of his neck playfully. "I'm not entirely sure that I believe this has happened."

"Believe it, my love." They lay still together for long moments of contentment. His voice changed. "Someone in this bed has fur."

She raised her head. It was almost full dark, but she recognized the rounded shape. "Odin has curled up against your hip."

His hand fumbled behind him until he felt the cat's warm furry body, and got a swat for his pains. He rolled away and sat up. "At least Fiona isn't here too."

"She does take up more space." Signy sat up and put her feet to the floor. "It occurs to me that we have a dinner we didn't eat. I hope it tastes good cold." The evening air was cool, so she collected her robe and donned it again, then tossed Kai's robe to him.

By the time he had his robe on, she'd lit a lamp. She laughed as she regarded their dinner table. "How do you feel about sharing food?"

Odin had swiftly transferred his substantial self to the table and was enjoying a piece of fish. He returned her gaze without a shred of guilt, then swatted a piece of fish over the edge of the table to where Fiona was waiting to snatch it from the air.

"I'm glad to see that they've become such good friends," Ramsay observed as he slid his arm around Signy's waist.

"Since they were our witnesses, I think they're entitled to share the wedding feast," Signy said. "But since I'm hungry, how do you feel about our going downstairs to forage in the kitchen? It's late enough that I doubt anyone will notice us."

"A perfect way to end the night." He pulled her in closer for a kiss. Such kissable lips… "Because tonight, my dear love, everything is perfect."

Chapter 28

Several days had passed without word from the Vances, and Broc had decided that it was time to call at their London house again, and if necessary, travel to their country home. But the following morning, the Vances invaded the drawing room of Thorsay House without warning.

Broc had dined out the night before with an old army friend and enjoyed the luxury of sleeping late. He'd just finished his breakfast when Mrs. Brown entered the small dining room and announced, "Captain Gabriel and Lady Aurora Vance have called, and they're waiting for you in the drawing room."

"That's unexpected!" Broc rose. "Would you be able to supply tea and coffee for our visitors?"

"Of course." Mrs. Brown's voice dropped to a whisper. "That Lady Aurora is a real stunner!"

"I look forward to meeting her," Broc said mildly as he straightened his coat and headed for the drawing room.

"Major Mackenzie." Captain Vance was tall and brown haired and looked quietly, dangerously competent. He stood and offered his hand as he introduced himself and then his wife, who was indeed a stunner, though Broc guessed that was as much a matter of her bright manner as her golden good looks.

Vance said, "I'm sorry we're calling on you so early, but when we found Ramsay's message on our return to London, we became concerned."

Broc waved them to seats. "I'm not sure what he said in his letter. I gather that you're friends of many years?"

Vance smiled. "Not exactly. I've seen him only a couple of times, but in both cases, the circumstances were extraordinary."

"The sort of extraordinary that when he asks for our help, we reply 'Anything you want,'" Lady Aurora added.

"That sounds interesting," Broc said as he took a seat.

Vance chuckled. "I think that means you'd like to know the circumstance but are too polite to ask."

"Just barely too polite," Broc admitted. "Kai and I grew up together but went in different directions for many years, so I don't know what kind of trouble he's been getting into."

"Tell the major your story, Gabriel," Lady Aurora suggested.

Vance smiled at his wife. "Because there is nothing you love more than a good story, Rory."

She batted her lashes at him. "*Almost* nothing!"

They shared an intimate smile before Vance returned his gaze to Broc. "Very well. We met when we were imprisoned with three other men in a Portuguese cellar, accused of being British spies, all of us condemned to be shot at dawn. He was calling himself Chantry then for reasons unknown."

"It's a family name on his mother's side," Broc explained. "Though I don't know why he'd be using it. This isn't a chapter of his life I've heard about. Both of us are only recently returned to Thorsay, so we have a lot of history to share."

"The name isn't important. What matters is that the five of us worked together to escape from that prison. That creates a bond between men," Vance continued. "The next morning we went our separate ways after pledging that we would try to maintain a connection among us, and perhaps reunite after the war. If any of us survived."

"That would create a bond," Broc agreed, making a mental note to ask Kai about his adventure later.

"But there's more." Vance glanced at his wife. "Rory and her cousin Constance were captured by Barbary pirates and sent to live in the harem of a vile, powerful official in Constantinople. I went to the British embassy there to ask for help. They couldn't do anything for me officially, but I was handed over to Ramsay, who was in charge of special projects."

"I think that meant he was a spy of sorts," Lady Aurora said helpfully. "He certainly had some very interesting local connections!"

Vance nodded. "Because of those connections, we were able to rescue Rory and her cousin as well as a Frenchwoman who had been a captive in the harem for several years. If not for Ramsay..." Vance took a deep breath. "It doesn't bear thinking of."

"That is quite a story!" Broc said, forcing himself not to stare at Lady Aurora or wonder about harem life. "I can see why you are willing to offer whatever help you can. Just what did Kai ask you for?"

"He asked if I knew of a bank that would lend to him under less than ideal circumstances," Vance said. "It sounds as if he needs a rather substantial amount of money. Do you know enough of his situation to explain? He said explicitly that you were his oldest friend and could be trusted with anything."

Broc guessed that Vance would have moved heaven and earth to rescue his lady. These were indeed people who would do anything for Kai, who might need more than the name of a bank.

Succinctly, Broc explained about the hard times that had struck Thorsay, about the old laird's unfortunate but necessary loan from Roald Ramsay, and the possibly disastrous consequences if Roald broke his verbal agreement to extend the loan's due date by a year.

He finished, "Roald Ramsay is a shifty devil. Given half a reason, he's quite capable of calling in the loan at any time after the twenty-first of September. If he did that and Kai couldn't borrow enough money elsewhere to repay him, he would lose everything except the title of laird, which is essentially worthless if Kai doesn't have the resources needed to lead Thorsay."

Vance frowned. "Ramsay sent you all the way to London in the hope of learning the name of a friendly bank? That was surely a long shot. He has no friends who could lend him twenty-five thousand pounds under easier terms?"

"Even if he had a friend who was spectacularly wealthy and willing," Broc replied, "he's reluctant to borrow so much from a friend when he has no idea how long it will take to repay the money."

Vance nodded. "Most men would feel that way."

"He had another reason for sending me to London," Broc added. "His friend Signy Matheson was a great aid to Kai's grandfather, the old laird. She's also a talented artist who would love to come to London to study with a painter named Sophie Macleod, but it's unlikely that will be possible, so Kai sent me to persuade Miss Macleod to visit Thorsay."

"I've seen Miss Macleod's work at the Maxwell Gallery," Lady Aurora said with interest. "She's very good, with a unique way of viewing the world."

"Indeed, and I can see why Signy would love to study with her," Broc agreed. "I managed to persuade Miss Macleod to come to Thorsay for a few weeks so she can tutor Signy and get away from London. She's making arrangements and won't be able to leave for at least another week."

"How did you travel to London?" Vance asked. "It's usually a long and complicated journey from Thorsay, isn't it?"

"It certainly is!" Broc said with feeling. "But since time is crucial, Kai gave me the use of the *Freya*, one of the Ramsay-owned coastal vessels. The *Freya* brought me down and will take me and Miss Macleod back when she's ready." Broc grimaced. "The sailors are getting restless to return."

"I have an idea," Vance said slowly. "As I mentioned, the five of us cellar survivors vaguely planned to gather when peace arrived, and this may be a good time for us to sail up together. It will take a few days to organize the group, and by then I may have found a solution for Ramsay's financial problems."

"I know what you're thinking," Lady Aurora said softly.

"You usually do," Vance said. "And… ?"

"It's a good idea," she said decisively.

Wondering what the Vances had wordlessly decided, Broc concentrated on a different question. "How many people would be coming to Thorsay? The *Freya* isn't very large."

"If everyone can make it, there would be ten with the wives, who would certainly want to come. I certainly mean to!" Lady Aurora said thoughtfully. "Gabriel, do you think Kendra and Lucas would want to come also? He wasn't in that cellar, but she has fond memories of her summers in Thorsay."

"Is that Kendra Douglas?" Broc asked, surprised. "I knew her. She's a cousin to Kai Ramsay. A grand girl. I know he and Signy would love to see her if she can come. But how are you proposing we should make the journey? Are you thinking of hiring a larger ship?"

"I have a ship," Vance said, a glint in his eyes. "And I know how to sail it."

Chapter 29

Ramsay woke up the next morning as the rays of the rising sun lit up the room. He was lying on his side with Signy tucked against him, his arm around her waist, her glorious hair falling over her shoulder. Not wanting to wake her, he dropped a featherlight kiss on her temple.

Her eyes remained closed, but she murmured, "Good morning, husband."

"Good morning, wife." He released his breath in a sigh of complete contentment. "I've never been happier in my life. We should have married sooner."

"No, this was the right time." She rolled onto her back and looked up at him through sleepy golden hazel eyes. "I assume you've overcome your doubts about sleeping in your grandfather's rooms?"

He chuckled. "That was also a question of the right time, which this is." He hesitated, then said, "We haven't discussed possible children. Does that concern you because of Gisela?"

"I've thought of it, of course," Signy said seriously. "But I'm stronger and healthier than she was, and rather than concealing my pregnancy, I would make sure that the best midwife in Thorsay was looking after me." She gave him a slow smile. "I want to have children with you. And if we have a daughter, we must name her Gisela."

"Of course, my beautifully sane wife," he said, awed at how she'd simplified their complicated past. "Which reminds me…"

He swung from the bed and retrieved his black velvet robe from the floor, where he'd dropped it the night before. The subtle gold embroidery over the shoulders glinted in the sun. He felt in the right pocket and pulled out something else that glinted gold in the sun. Then he perched on the side of the bed and showed her the golden ring that was engraved with twining Norse patterns. "This belonged to my mother," he said quietly. "I meant to give it to you last night if you accepted me, but I became… distracted."

She laughed. "We both did!" She took the ring from his palm. "This is lovely. Was it her wedding ring?"

"No, she was buried with that. This was another ring my father gave her, one that my grandmother held for me to give to my bride." He retrieved the ring and lifted Signy's left hand. "With this ring, I thee wed, and I hope it fits!"

The golden circlet slid smoothly onto her third finger as if made for Signy's hand. She curved her fingers to admire it, then kissed the ring. "This is perfect," she said softly. "A gift from your mother and grandmother."

He smiled, feeling married in the best possible way. He started to put his robe on.

"You don't have to get dressed for my sake," Signy said in a sultry voice.

Laughing, he dropped the robe and returned to their bed to celebrate the first day of the rest of their lives.

–

Signy thought they were behaving with complete propriety when they dressed and descended to the kitchen for breakfast. They weren't touching, and there was a respectable amount of space between them.

Nonetheless, Mrs. Donovan greeted them with arched brows and a silent, scorching glance for Ramsay. Signy raised her left hand to show her wedding band. To emphasize the point, Ramsay put his arm around Signy's shoulders. "Handfasted until we have the time for a proper wedding at the cathedral, Mrs. Donovan."

The housekeeper gave them an approving nod. "That's all right, then, and about time! Your grandfather is very pleased. Now what would you like for your breakfasts?"

"Surprise us," Ramsay said as he escorted Signy into the kitchen. After they sat down and the cook went to work, he whispered to Signy, "Do you think she actually had a message from the spirit of the old laird? I've always suspected she has a touch of the sight."

Signy laughed, feeling as if today she could laugh at anything. "Better not to ask."

He laughed with her, his expression as joyous as hers must be. She said, "I'm trying to remember why I resisted this inevitability so strongly."

"You wanted to travel and see something other than Thorsay," he reminded her.

"Oh. That's true." She frowned, some of her glow fading.

"You forgot something." He laid his hand over hers in the middle of the table. "We can travel *together*. Which has some considerable advantages over traveling alone."

"I suppose it does." She turned her hand under his so she could clasp his fingers, realizing that she must have a wide daft smile on her face. "In fact, I'm sure it does."

He laughed and removed his hand, since the teapot and cups were arriving. If this is a honeymoon, Signy thought, I want it to last forever.

—

The next days were glorious. Even the weather cooperated and it only rained at night. Mornings started with lovemaking and laughter. After breakfast Signy would check the progress of the work on Sea Cottage. That was almost done, but she no longer thought of moving back in. She and Kai discussed the cottage and decided they would leave it as her studio and a private place for them to be alone. She supposed that if she and Kai had a fight, she could flounce to the cottage and spend the night there, but so far, they were amazingly disinclined to fight.

After visiting the cottage, she would continue up the cliff path to the excavations, where she made meticulous drawings of their finds as well as keeping a casual eye on the work.

Though she did everything required to record the antiquities at Fiona Brae, it was the Viking ship that enthralled her. The work crew had created another awning-covered space on that site for her to work in. She loved making the drawings, but she couldn't resist working on the ship itself, removing soil while, she admitted privately, hoping to find something rare and wonderful.

Feeling slightly foolish, she'd started bringing her dirk with her in the case that held her drawing supplies. There had been no thefts from the two sites yet, but word of the Viking ship had got out, and the possibility of finding some kind of treasure might bring out the greedy.

Ramsay would have worked on the ship full time if he could, but as the laird, there were demands on him to be somewhere else. Two laborers from the Swenson crew worked on the ship regularly, and sometimes Peter Swenson himself joined in. A long-buried Viking ship called to Thorsayian blood far more than stone huts did.

Signy found their first treasure one day when the workers were having lunch with their friends at the Fiona Brae site. Needing a good stretch, Signy had taken her trowel and brush to the ship.

To avoid pressure on the delicate old wood, the first step in the excavation had been to build a solid scaffolding a few inches away from the gunwales of the old galley. That made it unnecessary to step on the deck directly, since doing so would be dangerous to both the ship and anyone who stood on it.

The deck of the exposed half of the galley had now been cleared, and excitement was rising as they anticipated interesting finds. Today Signy concentrated on a spot amidships. The day before she'd sensed that the deck felt different in this place, so she cleared the area more thoroughly.

Aha! As she used her brush, fine lines appeared, proving to be a rectangle. She pulled out her pocketknife and drew the point along the faint lines until they were clear, then tried to delicately pry up the rectangular square of decking.

To her shock it lifted, revealing a cavity about a foot deep. A metal box sat in the middle with fine sand collected around it. Hands shaking, she lifted the box from its resting place.

"What have you there?" Ramsay's voice called as he came around the point from Fiona Brae.

"Come and see!" Signy said, so excited she thought her voice might squeak. She carried the heavy box to her worktable. It took the two of them prying together to open the box without causing damage.

At first Signy couldn't identify what was inside. Small objects were set in carved wooden niches, and a haze of colored dust was over everything. She picked up one of the larger objects and rubbed it against her shirtsleeve to clean off the thick dust. She found herself holding a squat, intricately carved figurine of a human about four inches tall.

Ramsay gasped. "It's a chess set!" He took out a different piece and brushed it off the same way she had. "You have one of the queens, I think. This is probably a king. Dear God, these are amazing! Each one is unique."

"They seem to be carved from bone or perhaps walrus ivory." Signy studied the chess pieces, which had been so lovingly created and secured centuries before. "If the grave goods reflect what the deceased wants in the afterlife, this man was clearly a chess player. Isn't it called the game of kings?"

Ramsay nodded. "Yes, and this is a set fit for a king." With a mischievous smile, he took the queen piece from Signy's hand. "I've captured the queen!"

Signy let her gaze travel down Ramsay's body, halting on his breeches. "And later I shall most thoroughly capture your king."

He laughed. "You are becoming delightfully improper, my lady. I like it." He set the chess pieces back in the box. "This needs to be moved to Skellig House immediately. Not only is it a historic treasure but it would be very valuable on the antiquities market."

"Exactly the sort of find we don't want people to know about," Signy agreed. "I have a canvas bag here that you can carry the set in." She'd brought the bag in case they found something that needed to be moved to the house and locked up safely. She replaced the pieces they'd taken out, put the lid back on the box, and packed it carefully in the bag. "On your way home now?"

"I'll drop the chess set off there, then I have to go into Clanwick. I stopped by here to see if you'd found anything interesting, and if you wanted a break." He waggled his eyebrows suggestively.

She laughed, loving this playful side of him. "Later. I'll see you at dinner."

"Till then." He gave her a thorough kiss that left them both breathless, then slung the bag over his shoulder and headed back along the beach with his long strides. He moved beautifully, and she would never tire of watching him.

Then he was out of sight, and the two excavators returned from lunch, chatting happily. She sat down to start a rough sketch of the chess set, letting her mind drift ahead to the time she'd spend with Kai later. And to how she would capture his king!

Chapter 30

Ramsay stopped at Skellig House and put the chess set in a storeroom with a large strong lock. He wished he could spend the rest of the afternoon cleaning up the chess pieces to reveal the stunning detail, preferably with Signy sitting across the table doing the same thing. He loved that she now shared his passion for antiquities.

Instead he rode on to Clanwick, making a mental list of all that must be done. The bank first, then Fergus to sign legal papers, then a stop at Olson's Bookshop to see if any of the art supplies on order had come in.

He'd taken care of the first two items on his list when he decided to make a short visit to the harbor. He never tired of watching the ships. If Broc were here, they could go sit on their bench. He wondered when Broc would be back, and whether he'd persuaded the lady artist to visit Thorsay. Enough time had passed that Broc could have made it to London and back.

As he approached the walkway that ran around the harbor, he was surprised to see two familiar figures ahead of him, standing still as they watched the harbor. Cousins Axel and Annabel were talking in low, intense voices.

He was too close to pretend not to have seen them, so he called, "Good day, Cousins! It's a fine day for watching boats."

They both started before turning to greet him. Annabel looked fashionable but upset, as if she'd been crying, and Axel looked even more sullen than usual.

"Good day, Kai," Annabel said politely. "I'm sorry we've seen so little of you since your return."

"I've been traveling around the islands and reacquainting myself with the places and people," he explained. "Soon I'll be in Clanwick more often."

"I heard you've also been finding buried treasure in a long-lost Viking village," Axel said, his eyes sharp.

Ramsay laughed. "I see that the rumor mill is alive and well. Yes, that last great storm washed away a piece of coastline and revealed several very old stone huts. No treasure to be found there, unless one likes studying the past, which I do."

"Is it from Viking times?" Axel asked.

Ramsay disliked lying, and since the rumors were out there, he should take this chance to clarify what they were studying. "The stone huts are much, much older than that. I can't even guess how old. We also found what seems to be the wreckage of a Viking ship. It was uncovered by the same storm, but it's so fragile that a cross word might make it collapse into splinters."

"Do other parts of the world have as many ancient ruins as Thorsay?" Annabel asked with apparent interest.

"Not that I've seen, though there are places in Asia Minor that come close," Ramsay said. His gaze was caught by the sight of a ship slowly entering the harbor. "Excuse me, my ship *Freya* is coming up to the docks. I've been wondering when she'd return."

"How many ships does your estate own?" Axel asked with interest.

"Three. Two are fishing boats," Ramsay replied. "The *Freya* mostly carries freight around Scotland and northern England."

"She's a sweet little yawl," Axel said with critical appreciation.

Ramsay was surprised that Axel paid that much attention to boats. He didn't seem interested in much of anything else.

Ramsay was about to move away when Annabel said with an edge to her voice, "I've heard that Signy Matheson is wearing a wedding ring now. Is that another rumor?"

Ramsay caught her gaze and said in a firm voice, "No, it's quite true. We're handfasted and will have a proper wedding in the cathedral soon. Sometime in the early autumn, I imagine."

"So Signy has won the prize," Annabel said, annoyance in her blue eyes.

Ramsay had to laugh at that. "If you think I'm a prize, you don't know me very well. Luckily, Signy is tolerant of my eccentricities. If you'll excuse me, I must go to meet my ship."

As he moved away toward the pier where the yawl would dock, he thought of what an unhappy pair his cousins were. Being the wealthiest young people on Thorsay obviously wasn't enough for them.

He waited impatiently for the *Freya* to dock, wondering why Broc wasn't on the deck waiting to come ashore. When the ship was safely moored, the captain, Alan Innes, emerged from the wheelhouse and waved to Ramsay as he saw him waiting.

Ramsay impatiently swung onto the ship, saying, "I hope you had a good trip, Alan. Is Broc Mackenzie with you? I can't believe he's seasick belowdecks."

"No, he's well and healthy and likely still in London. He had to wait to take care of the business you'd sent him on, so he suggested we leave and run some cargo up to Edinburgh on the way. My boys were getting restless about being too long at anchor."

Ramsay frowned and wondered what the devil Broc was up to. This didn't seem like him. "Did he send some sort of message?"

"Aye, so he did." The captain reached into his coat and pulled out a letter wrapped in oil cloth, then moved aft to talk to some of his men.

Frowning, Ramsay ripped the letter open immediately and scanned the lines.

Kai—

Sorry not to be in Clanwick in person yet. Briefly, I located Sophie Macleod and persuaded her to come to Thorsay, but she said it would take a fortnight for her to make arrangements and buy the art materials needed. I think she and Signy will get on well.

I also had to wait to meet with your friend Captain Vance, since he was out of London. When they returned, he and his wife called at Thorsay House and explained the interesting circumstances of your acquaintanceship.

They both want to help you survive Roald's uncertain behavior. Vance thought he could work out a way of securing the financing you need, though he was vague about it.

He also said that you survivors of the Portuguese cellar (there's a story I want to hear more of!) decided to call yourselves Rogues

*Redeemed and had vague plans to gather after the
wars to celebrate your continued survival.*

Ramsay paused, realizing that he hadn't thought of that
possible gathering in quite some time. He'd been too
damned busy since returning home. But it would be
interesting to meet the other survivors again. When he'd
traveled through London on the way home, he'd read the
letters they'd all sent to Hatchard's as a way of keeping in
touch, as well as dining with Vance and Lady Aurora.

The cellar survivors had all done interesting things,
and had all married, as he recalled. Well, he had his own
magnificent wife to show off. He returned to the letter.

> *So Vance has decided to gather as many of your
> cellar mates (and their wives) as he can and bring
> them up to Clanwick, along with Miss Macleod
> and me. Apparently he's the owner of several
> sailing ships, and as a former blockade runner, he
> likes his ships to be fast.*
>
> *His latest ship, the* Lady Constance*, has been
> designed to carry a mix of cargo and passengers, so
> it has several good-sized cabins. As soon as he's
> collected as many of your Irredeemable Rogues as
> are willing and able to come, we'll be on our way.
> We should arrive home before the Fire Festival. If
> we do, that will be quite an experience for these
> Southerners!*
>
> *How many guest rooms does Skellig House
> have?*
>
> *Broc, bemused*

Ramsay lowered the letter, equally bemused. He hoped to
God that Vance had found a suitable bank to refinance the

loan, because he had an uneasy feeling about what Roald might do. It was also good news that Broc had persuaded the artist to come to Thorsay. She'd be a sort of wedding present for Signy.

But a dozen or so visitors? How many guest rooms *did* Skellig House have? He started mentally counting as he jumped to the dock, stopped in at Olson's, and then headed to the livery stable for Thor so he could ride home to tell Signy about all this.

—

Signy blinked with astonishment at Ramsay's recital. "We're being invaded by the English?"

He laughed. "I'm sure they'll all retreat to the south rather than face a Thorsay winter. Do we have enough space for everyone?"

Signy thought. "Yes, but only if they aren't the kind of aristocrats who find it unacceptable to share rooms with their spouses."

"Why would a husband and wife not want to share a bed?" he asked. "It's the best reason to get married!"

"Especially in the cold north," Signy said with a smile. "I'll talk to Mrs. Donovan and make sure that all the rooms are ready."

"And between now and the time they all arrive, we can return to exploring our Viking ship," Ramsay said. "I wonder what other treasures we'll find?"

—

The next treasure was discovered the following day. It was an exquisitely made golden cross about three inches high with cloisonné enamel on the arms. Set in the middle was a golden coin that made Ramsay gasp when Signy had cleaned the cross well enough to make out the detail.

"Good God!" he exclaimed. "That's an ancient Byzantine coin! I have a couple like it in my collection. How on earth do you think it came to be here at the end of the world?"

Signy shook her head. "I can't really guess, though the Romans were a great lot of travelers. For that matter, so were the Vikings."

The two men who had been working on the excavation crowded around to see what had been found. The older man, Edmund, breathed, "It's beautiful! May I hold it?"

"Of course." Signy passed it over.

Edmund crossed himself reverently as he studied it. "So our dead king was a Christian."

"He must have been," Ramsay agreed.

Edmund passed the cross to his coworker, who was equally awed, though his question was, "How much is this worth?"

"It's hard to say." Ramsay accepted the cross back and studied it again. "The ship is on my land, so legally what we find is mine, but this kind of history belongs to all Thorsayians."

"Perhaps you can establish a museum in Clanwick someday," Signy said. "Not just for the dramatic items like this, but for the everyday stone objects from Fiona Brae. They're all part of our shared history."

"That's an excellent idea." If he someday had the money to take on such a project.

Thinking about money, Ramsay caught the attention of the two workers. "It's best not to talk about our finds," he said. "We don't want people coming at night to plunder our ship and probably destroy it in the process."

Both of the men nodded agreement, but Ramsay was still uneasy. Though he believed the workers were honest, treasure in a long-buried ship was too good a story not to share. He'd have to think if there was a good way to protect the site when no one was working here.

He and Signy discussed the issue that night, but the site was a difficult one to safeguard, particularly since it could be approached from the sea in a small boat.

Finally Signy said, "I think guards will have to be hired if we can afford them. How much money do you have available?"

He sighed. "Not a lot, but you're right. We don't want looters to destroy the ship before we even have it uncovered. We need not only money but guards who can be trusted."

"Maybe some of the people who have taken refuge at the Mackenzie farm?" Signy suggested. "I'm sure that by this time Flora Mackenzie has a good idea of who can be trusted."

"That's a good idea. I'll talk to Broc when he returns, which should be any day now." Ramsay certainly hoped so. The equinox and Fire Festival were approaching fast.

Chapter 31

The next night, Ramsay achieved his dream of sitting on the opposite side of a table from Signy, both of them cleaning newfound Viking artifacts. While Ramsay worked on a rusted sword, Signy polished up a massive bronze cooking pot designed to hang on a chain over a fire. She asked, "Do you think this could be used in the kitchen at Skellig House when we have a lot of company?"

Ramsay laughed. "It may never have been used. It's probably part of the grave goods as a symbol that the king could afford to feed a large war band of his followers."

Amused, she said, "I'm glad to see something domestic. Even in the afterlife, people must want to eat."

"Symbolically it makes sense," Ramsay said. He held up the sword they'd found. "I wonder if this was a weapon the king used personally? I'm guessing not. When we find and open the casket, his shield, helmet, and personal sword will probably be on his body."

"I'm not sure I want to be there when the casket is opened. It seems... undignified."

"We antiquarians wrestle with the conflict between respect for our ancestors and the lust for knowledge," he admitted.

"I imagine the lust for knowledge usually wins." She gave a final polish to the cooking kettle. "But I do understand the fascination with learning more about the past."

"I like your idea of building a museum to display Thorsayian antiquities. People should be able to go in and appreciate our history." He raised the sword to see where more cleaning was needed. "At least our king would still be here in Thorsay, the site chosen for his final resting place."

"I hope a museum will be possible." Signy started a drawing of the cooking pot, which had interesting enameled plaques on the side. "For now, your storeroom is our museum."

When they'd both finished their cleaning work, they placed the artifacts in storage, then went down to the kitchen for a late supper. After they'd eaten, Signy moved to the window and gazed out at the night. "It's a full moon tonight. Do you want to go for a walk? I'd like to see our ship by moonlight."

"What a splendid idea. We'll need to wrap up warmly, though. This close to the equinox, the nights are chilly." He didn't like thinking about how late it was in September. Broc and the rest of the guests still hadn't arrived, and the official due date of the loan was almost upon him. All he could do was pray that Roald would make good on his promise to extend the loan.

They both bundled up with the skill of Northerners. He raised his brows when Signy slung her drawing bag across her shoulder and chest. "I might want to draw the ship by moonlight." She gave him a mischievous smile. "And I have a small bottle of Callan's best whisky as well."

He laughed. "I love how well you look ahead." Then he took her hand and they set off together.

It was indeed a splendid night for a walk. The eternally moving waves were silvered by moonlight, and the hills had an unworldly sheen that made him think of fairyland.

There was no need to speak as they traveled the familiar cliff walk. They descended the ladder to Fiona Brae, which looked like an ancient dream, then kept walking on the narrow beach path around the point. Ramsay was beginning to wonder if there would be a bit of beach smooth enough for making love.

They rounded the corner to the wider area that held the Viking ship and Ramsay stopped dead. A sailing dinghy was beached in the middle of the curving shore, and breaking sounds came from the Viking ship.

Signy whispered in horror, "Someone is looting the ship!"

Outraged, Ramsay swept across the stretch of beach, shouting, "Damn you, get down from there, you thieves!"

Furious cursing was followed by two dark figures stepping onto the scaffolding. They looked unintimidated and ready to fight.

—

Ramsay had charged forward too quickly for Signy to stop him. Didn't he realize that tomb robbers might be armed?

Her fears were confirmed when both of the robbers produced pistols and aimed them at Ramsay. And—dear God, it was his cousins Axel and Annabel! Dressed plainly for once, Annabel held her pistol in both hands, eyes narrowed and determined. She looked like a dangerous criminal instead of a light-minded flirt.

"*You!*" Axel growled. "Why the devil did you come tonight? I probably shouldn't kill you, but I will if you make it necessary."

Signy realized that they hadn't seen her in the shadows. Silently she opened her art bag and drew out her dirk.

She hadn't fenced with it for years, but she kept the blade sharp.

Leaping on the scaffolding and challenging Annabel and Axel to a duel wouldn't be wise when they had pistols. But what if she got under the scaffolding? There was enough space below to move underneath, and the sound of the waves should cover any noise she made. The shadows cast by the bluff would hide her until she reached the open end of the scaffolding. Dirk in hand, she moved silently through the darkness and under the wooden framework.

Naturally Ramsay was talking, his voice calm and interested. "Why are you stealing old Viking bits and pieces when you're two of the richest people on Thorsay? Do you need to steal because your father doesn't give you enough money?"

"He doesn't give us any money!" Annabel said resentfully. "He'll buy us things, but he won't give us what we want most: the freedom to leave Thorsay and live the lives we want!"

"Does he keep you prisoners here?" Ramsay asked.

"Close enough," Annabel snapped. "Even if we could escape, we'd be penniless."

"He makes me spend time at the kelp works, which I loathe," Axel spat out. "And when I'm at the works and Annabel is home alone with him, she has to lock the door of her bedroom when he's been drinking!"

Axel's words were chilling. Signy knew such things happened, but she wouldn't have suspected Roald. It was clear why his children wanted to escape him.

But living in a gilded cage didn't give Annabel and Axel the right to damage and steal from a priceless ancient ship, or to kill Ramsay. Signy crept along under the scaffolding until she was below the Ramsay cousins. Through the narrow gaps between the boards, she could easily see the bottoms of the tomb robbers' feet.

Who should she go after first? Axel was probably a better shot. He seemed to be wearing shoes, not boots. Good.

She lifted her dirk and slid the blade up through the slats, then slashed the dirk across the soles of his shoes with all her strength.

He shrieked with surprise and pain, then scrambled away from her dirk while she shouted, "Ramsay, dodge out of his aim."

Then she swung around and slashed the bottoms of Annabel's feet.

Annabel screamed and stumbled away. Signy guessed that her shoes had thinner soles. Losing her balance, Annabel fell from the scaffolding onto the shingle beach, knocking herself breathless.

She made it just too easy. Signy dived out from under the scaffolding and pinned the younger woman down, then wrenched the pistol from her grip. "Sit up and put your hands on top of your head," she ordered. "I have your pistol and my dirk, and either will do for you if you make me angry enough."

Weeping, Annabel did as she was told, her head bowed under her hands.

Above them, the fight between the two men was raging. Ramsay had taken advantage of Signy's intervention to vault onto the scaffolding and grapple with Axel. They teetered back and forth until Ramsay yanked Axel off the scaffolding. They rolled across the pebbles until Ramsay was able to wrest Axel's pistol away.

Axel was swearing and trying to claw his opponent's eyes out when Ramsay rolled onto the younger man, pinning him with his greater weight. He cocked the pistol and jammed it against his cousin's temple. Axel froze in terror.

Annabel screamed, "*No!*"

More calmly, Signy said, "Best not to kill your cousin, Kai. It hardly seems fair when he's not half the man you are. Besides, I'm thinking that the pair of them are more to be pitied than despised."

After several ragged breaths, Ramsay sat back on his heels and uncocked the weapon, though he kept it pointed at Axel. "Very well, my dear. What do we do next with these two budding criminals?"

"Not very competent criminals," Signy said. "Just what did you hope to accomplish? Artifacts stolen from the ship have value, but only if you know where and who to sell them to, and Thorsay hasn't got those kinds of buyers."

Annabel's weeping had stopped and she stared down at her lap. "We hoped we'd find gold coins, like the one that was in the center of the cross you found."

One of the workers had obviously been talking about the excavations. "That's not much of an escape plan," Ramsay said, unimpressed. "Axel, are you sure you want to give up being heir to a substantial business empire?"

"I don't want any part of my father's damned empire!" Axel snapped. "I wouldn't mind having the money, but my father isn't that old and could easily live another thirty years. I'd rather drown myself than live as his captive for that long!"

The words were melodramatic but had the ring of truth. "What would you do if you had the freedom to choose?" Signy asked.

Axel looked startled, as if he'd never been asked that. "I'd like to be the captain of my own ship. I love the sea. My father thinks it's a fool's ambition."

"There are many fools who choose the sea over all else," Ramsay said. "Are you sure that is what you want to do with your life?"

"Yes! But I couldn't leave Annabel alone here with him."

Signy's turn. "Annabel, what do you want to do?"

"Go to London and be presented and flirt with handsome men at balls," Annabel said. "Then choose a nice gentleman who treats me well and marry him."

"London is a difficult place if you don't have friends or family to launch you into society," Ramsay observed. "It would take a great deal of money and influence, and you'd be starting with nothing."

"London isn't the only possibility," Signy said. "Wasn't your mother from Dublin? Do you have family there who might take you in?"

"My aunt has offered to sponsor me several times," Annabel admitted. "But I don't know how I'd get there, because my father would never let me go." She pouted. "And I want *London*!"

"Sometimes we have to accept what is possible rather than break our hearts yearning for the impossible," Signy said crisply. "I hear that Dublin is a lovely city, and if I recall correctly, your mother came from a well-established family. I'm sure you'd be able to attend balls and meet handsome gentlemen there. You're beautiful, so you should be able to find a desirable husband. This is an achievable future. Does it sound so bad?"

Annabel bit her lip, her tears dried. "No. No, it doesn't."

Ramsay turned his attention to Axel. "How much sailing experience do you have?"

Axel gestured toward the sailing dinghy. "I sail here whenever I have a chance. I also go out with friends who need crew for larger boats."

"It's a beginning." Ramsay frowned. "If you really want a sailor's life, I'll ask Alan Innes to take you on as a kind of apprentice and train you to be a ship's master. It will take time and a lot of hard work, and if you act like an arrogant young lordling, he may toss you overboard to the sharks, and I wouldn't blame him."

He looked seriously into Axel's eyes. "But if and when you learn to be a ship's captain, I'll give you the *Freya* or a similar ship."

"A... a ship of my own?" Axel stammered, his eyes widening. "I'd like that more than anything!"

"You'll earn it, but if it's the life you want, it can be yours and you'll be free of your father." Ramsay was very much in his laird mode. "Are you both satisfied with these prospects? You need to decide right away. Just now, your father is over at the kelp works, but he'll be home before the Fire Festival."

The siblings looked at each other. Annabel gulped. "Yes. Axel?"

Her brother took a deep breath. "You'll be safe and be able to meet eligible men, and I'm not likely to get a better opportunity than this one." He raised his gaze to Ramsay. "Yes. Yes, we both accept."

"Then you need to return to Thorsay and pack," Signy said. "Annabel, you may arrive at your aunt's penniless, but you have quite a good wardrobe, I believe."

"Yes, I do." She got to her feet. "But these shoes are ruined."

"Serves you right for stealing and threatening people with firearms," Signy said dryly. "Kai, when should they be off in the morning?"

"I have to talk to Alan Innes, but I believe the tide turns late morning, so by then." Ramsay offered Axel a hand to help him up.

The younger man lurched a little but made it to his feet. "Thank you, sir," he said seriously. "Thank you both for listening and giving us the chance to make our own lives."

Signy chuckled. "I won't miss seeing the two of you swanning around Clanwick pouting and looking ill-used."

Annabel started to protest, but her brother caught her arm and steered her toward the dinghy they'd come in. "She's not wrong, Bel. You're getting a new beginning and so am I. Let's be grateful."

"One last thing," Ramsay said. "Did you take anything from the ship?"

Axel shook his head. "We'd just started."

"I hope you didn't do too much damage," Ramsay said. "Now off with you!"

Signy went to his side and slid an arm around his waist while he hugged her shoulders. Silently they watched as the young Ramsays departed, sliding into the moonlight until a breeze caught the sail and the boat turned south toward Clanwick.

"Ill met by moonlight," Signy murmured. "Do you think they'll find the lives they want?"

"There a reasonable chance of it," Ramsay said. "They want to escape their father's control, and they've apparently always been each other's best friend." He glanced down into Signy's face, subtly lovely in the moonlight. "When we arrived here, I was wondering if I might be able to seduce you on the beach, but I'm ready to go home."

"So am I." Her voice dropped into deliberate provocation. "We can discuss the issue of seduction when we get to Skellig House."

He laughed and swung her around, and they started their moonlit trail home.

Chapter 32

Later that night as they lay in each other's arms after making love, Signy asked softly, "Have you thought much about what you'll do if Roald demands repayment of the loan and you haven't enough funds?"

Ramsay sighed. "I've thought about it a lot, mostly going in circles. I'll still be the laird even without Skellig House, but I don't know how much I'll be able to achieve. Fergus tells me that the three ships aren't included in the collateral for the loan, so at least I'll be able to fulfill my promise to Axel if he earns it. But I'll miss Skellig House, and what if Roald tries to take our horses?"

"We could send Odin after him. He's a first-class rat catcher, and Roald is one large rat."

When Ramsay chuckled, Signy shifted so that her head was on his shoulder. "I've been thinking too. I have a very pleasant cottage, but it might be a bit tight for two tall people. We'd be on top of each other."

He kissed her forehead. "I wouldn't mind that! We can take turns being on top."

She smiled into the darkness. "It's too small for entertaining, but it could still be your official residence. By this time you've met people all across Thorsay. They know and like and respect you. You're still the laird with all the legal powers and responsibilities that go with it."

"You're right," he said slowly. "I believe I can make it work as long as you're beside me."

"Where else would I be?" She lifted herself up enough to kiss him. "And now to sleep, my bonny laird. Tomorrow will be a busy day."

As she drifted off to sleep on his shoulder, he spared a moment for a prayer of thanks that they had found each other. Now that she had pledged herself to him, she was sharing her intelligence and warmth completely.

How had he become so lucky?

–

Ramsay was up early the next morning to go into Clanwick to talk to Alan Innes, captain of the *Freya*. It was surprisingly easy to persuade him to take Axel on as an apprentice. "He's often around the harbor," Innes said. "I talk with him sometimes. I think he has a sailor's soul."

"I hope you're right," Ramsay said, a little surprised to learn that Axel really had been showing interest in a sailor's life for years. But Ramsay had been away for so long, it wasn't surprising that he didn't know his cousins well. He liked the idea of helping them escape from their father's crushing control.

But Roald wasn't going to like it one damned bit.

–

The truth of Ramsay's realization was demonstrated that night when he and Signy were about to dine. Roald stormed into Skellig House, slamming doors and shouting threats. "Damn you, boy, I'll tear you into pieces of fish bait!"

"The laird is in the dining room, sir," Mrs. Donovan said calmly before she wisely got out of his way. Signy was telling Ramsay of a new find at the ship, this time a box containing two small gold coins. It was a spectacular discovery, and Ramsay was grateful that his cousins hadn't seen it. They had done some damage to the old ship, but it could have been much worse.

When Roald crashed in, Signy said in her best hostess voice, "Good evening, Roald. Would you like to join us for dinner? Or perhaps a glass of wine?"

Ignoring her, he bellowed, "You stole my children from me!"

"No, I just gave them a chance to live their own lives," Ramsay said coolly. "They both wanted desperately to escape your control. If you'd been a better father, they wouldn't have wanted so much to get away."

"I gave them everything!" Roald roared. "Annabel was the best-dressed girl in Thorsay, and Axel was going to inherit the largest industrial operations. But that wasn't enough for the ungrateful brats. Traitors!"

Ramsay managed not to say that if Roald weren't so obsessed with his own self-interest and listened to what his children said, they wouldn't have run away.

His cousin spat out, "Annabel left me a note saying that they were both leaving. She didn't say where they were going or how they'd get there. Just gone. Gone! And it's all your fault!"

"Signy and I just opened some doors, and they both rushed out." Ramsay rose to his feet. He was several inches taller than Roald. "If you won't join us, it's time for you to leave."

"You'll pay for this," his cousin said through gritted teeth. "I'm calling in the loan. If you don't pay me by the end of the business day on the twenty-first, everything your grandfather pledged as security will be mine. This house, the estate, whatever small businesses that were listed. Mine. *Mine!* You can starve in the streets of Clanwick for all I care!"

"But I'll still be the laird, and Signy will still be my wife." He glanced at Signy, needing the reassurance in her steady gaze. "I hope you won't feel too offended if you're not invited to the official wedding celebration."

"I'd rather burn in hell than attend!" Roald snarled.

He was turning to leave when a thought struck Ramsay. "Several weeks back, someone fired a rifle at me when I was riding in the hills up island. Was that you?"

Roald's scowl darkened. "I took the shot on impulse. I didn't mean to kill you, but I wish now I had. I'll see you at the Bank of Clanwick at five o'clock in the afternoon. Be prepared to sign over everything you own to me. If you don't, I'll hire men to take everything." He left the dining room with a door slam that rattled the crockery.

Ramsay sank back into his seat, shaking. He'd expected some scene like this, but the reality was uglier than he'd imagined.

Signy reached across the table and took his hand. "You knew this would happen."

"Yes, but the reality of dealing with Roald is worse than I thought." He squeezed her hand. "Even if Broc and the rest of them should show up tomorrow with the name of the most generous bank in Britain, it will be too late to arrange a loan. We'll lose all this, Signy." He released her hand and made a gesture that indicated the house, the land, and all the people who worked for the estate.

She shrugged. "I've lived with much less my whole life." She smiled. "If my cottage is too crowded, we can live in one of the Thorfield Farm barns. I hear that Flora Mackenzie has made them quite comfortable."

He relaxed and caught her hand again. "We'll manage." He raised her hand and kissed the back of her fingers. "As long as we're together."

The next day was a quiet one. It rained, so Signy stayed in and worked on her drawings and Ramsay rode into Clanwick to give Fergus the bad news. The lawyer confirmed that Ramsay would have to move out of Skellig House immediately if Roald called in the loan.

Fiona Brae and the Viking ship were on estate land. He couldn't bear to think of them falling into Roald's uncaring hands. Perhaps Fergus could think of some legal delaying tactic? The lawyer wasn't optimistic about that.

After leaving Fergus, Ramsay walked down to the harbor and bought himself mutton fritters and clapshot and beer at Gordon's. The essence of Thorsayian food.

The rain had stopped for the time being, so Ramsay sat on a bench to eat and watch the ships. None of his were in port, and the *Freya* was well on her way to Dublin with Annabelle and Axel on board.

There was no sign of Broc or the Rogues Redeemed and whatever possible salvation they might bring with them. They'd be traveling on one of Vance's ships, which would be larger than most of the vessels that called in at Clanwick.

When he'd eaten, he brushed off his hands and returned the basket and bottle to Mrs. Gordon. Then home to Signy, the one part of his life he was completely sure of. They'd both sit in the library and work on anything that might distract them from the Sword of Damocles hanging over their heads.

Chapter 33

The next morning dawned with pale sunshine. Unusually, Ramsay didn't want to make love when they woke up. Understanding that there was no room for joy in him today, Signy simply held him as the sun rose.

After breakfast, she moved all of her artwork to Sea Cottage as well as her personal possessions and the bedding and cookware they'd need. Technically those things belonged to Skellig House, but she doubted that Roald would be counting sheets.

All the household staff knew what was about to happen, but only Mrs. Donovan commented, "It won't be the same, Miss Signy."

"No, but for better or worse, change happens." She gave a shaky smile. "Roald would be a fool to discharge you and your husband. You're much too good at what you do." Privately she feared that Roald was vindictive enough to sack servants who had been loyal to the old laird, but she prayed she was wrong.

After their last lunch, Signy and Ramsay rode into Clanwick. As they stabled Thor and Loki, he said, "I keep looking at the harbor to see if a larger-than-usual ship is sailing in." He gave her a twisted smile. "Obviously I believe in miracles."

She took his hand. "We have other miracles in our lives even if there isn't a financial one."

He kissed her, murmuring, "You're my miracle, my darling girl."

"And you're mine, but don't we sound like a pair of chirping seventeen-year-old sweethearts?" she said playfully.

He laughed. "Indeed we do, but that's not a bad thing."

Hand in hand, they headed down the high street to the bank, which was situated by the harbor. The bank president escorted them to the upper floor, where there was a spacious gathering room with a splendid view of the harbor through a wide window. "Very impressive," she remarked.

"Businesses might fail, but banks seldom do," Ramsay said dryly.

Fergus joined them, and the two men sat down and spread the table with documents. Signy didn't have anything to do but watch the harbor, which was fine with her. She could watch the water indefinitely.

As a large graceful sailing ship glided into the harbor, she felt a shock of excitement. Hoping to high heaven this was Broc and the Rogues Redeemed, she said, "I'm going out for a short walk. I'll be back before the fatal hour strikes."

Ramsay glanced up with a nod of acknowledgment before returning to the documents. Signy knew Fergus was trying to retain everything he could for Ramsay.

As soon as Signy left the room, she raced down the steps at a most unladylike speed and crossed swiftly to the harbor, where the ship was docking. It was the *Lady Constance* out of London.

Heart hammering, she stood on the dock and waited for the gangway to be let down. Above her she saw Broc in the midst of a crowd of well-dressed people. He waved, his manner buoyant.

As soon as the gangway was in place, he raced down. "Sorry we were delayed. There were sharp squalls in the Channel and some damage to the sails. But we're in time, aren't we?"

"Barely." She saw his travel companions streaming down after him. "And our guests may have to sleep on the ship since Skellig House will not be available."

"They all need to come with us." He waved a "follow me" arm and set off toward the bank at a fast pace. "First, I've brought Sophie Macleod to spend some time tutoring you. You are going to like each other a great deal."

Startled, Signy looked over her shoulder and saw a petite redhead a few steps behind. "I've brought all sorts of paints," the young woman called. "For later!"

Broc gave Sophie a fond look, then turned his gaze toward the bank. "Let me explain…"

-

Roald swaggered into the bank's gathering room, a predator moving in for the kill. "I see you have your paperwork. And I have mine." He dropped a folder of documents on the table. "Shall we begin?"

"It's not five o'clock yet," Fergus said firmly.

Roald shrugged and sat down in one of the chairs, snapping his fingers to summon a young bank attendant. "I sent a bottle of champagne over earlier. Bring it to me. Only one glass will be needed because I'm the only one who will be celebrating."

The attendant gave him the respectful bow owed the richest man in Thorsay before going off in search of the champagne.

Ramsay glanced around. Where was Signy? She said she'd be back, and she wasn't one to avoid unpleasant scenes.

He heard a thumping sound and after a moment identified it as the sound of people coming up the stairs. Quite a number of people.

The door opened and Broc and Signy entered, followed by a dozen or so others. He recognized all but one of the men, and each man had an attractive female moving in tandem with him. The wives of the Rogues Redeemed, plus his cousin Kendra.

He stood and stared, not sure what was going on. Signy moved to his side, her eyes dancing. Under her breath, she said, "The redhead on the right watching the rest of us is Sophie. Thank you so much for bringing her here!"

"She was the best wedding present I could think of," he said simply as he nodded at the artist. He owed Broc a bonus.

Captain Gabriel Hawkins Vance stepped to the front of the group. "It's good to see you again, Ramsay, who used to be Chantry."

Ramsay had to smile. "It made sense at the time." His gaze went to the others. Tall and broad Will Masterson, who had turned out to be an army major, standing with a magnificent Amazon as tall as Signy.

Beside the Mastersons was the blond and clever Gordon Audley. The bright-eyed lady on his arm had red-gold hair that was a close match to Signy's.

Vance was there, of course, with his Lady Rory on his arm, looking much more presentable than on the memorable night he'd met her in Constantinople.

Then Duval, another army officer who had turned out to be more English than French. Ramsay recognized his wife, the lovely French Suzanne, whom he'd also met that night in Constantinople.

Then his cousin Kendra, who stepped forward from her handsome husband's arm to give Ramsay a kiss and Signy a hug. "I'm so glad to be in Thorsay again!"

Roald barked, "Dammit, who are all these people? They have no business here!"

"On the contrary." Once more Vance was the spokesman. Looking at Roald with contempt, he said, "Kai Ramsay performed a service beyond price for several of us, and we've come to repay our debt."

He laid a bulging purse on the table. "Ramsay, you saved my Rory's life. Here is five thousand pounds, though she is worth infinitely more."

He smiled at his wife, who stepped forward and laid another fat purse next to his. "This is for my cousin Constance, dearer to me than my own sisters. She lives in America now, so I'm contributing five thousand pounds on her behalf."

Ramsay was so stunned that all he could do was stare. The next to step forward was Simon Duval. "You rescued my Suzanne, a gift beyond imagining." He gave a swift smile. "And a bargain at the price!"

There was a ripple of laughter. Then Suzanne said softly, "I was surviving as a piecework seamstress when Simon found me. Rather to my surprise, we later found that I am something of an heiress, so I think it only fair that I pay belatedly for my own ticket to a new life. Five thousand pounds for Mr. Ramsay, the man with the most useful connections in Constantinople." She laid her purse next to the others, then stepped back.

Kendra Douglas, who presumably had another married name now, stepped forward. "Kai, you and I are blood kin." She shot a disdainful glance at Roald. "Fortunately on our mothers' sides, so I'm not related to *him*." Her gaze moved to Ramsay and Signy. "Some of the happiest times of my life were the summers I spent here in Thorsay playing with you and Broc and the others. Those days shaped me.

"And since I happen to be an heiress also"—she produced a fat purse and laid it with the others—"I want to contribute this in honor of your grandparents and because you will keep Thorsay the special place it has always been."

Roald had turned a furious red and looked on the verge of explosion. Fergus stood and said, "Mr. Ramsay, let's take your payment into the smaller room next door. I expect you'll want to confirm that you've received your full twenty-five thousand pounds in a timely manner."

The wall clock began to chime. Five o'clock. Fergus swept Roald and the young attendant away, leaving Ramsay with the men he'd bonded with in that damp cellar so many years and miles away. He swallowed hard. "I... I don't know what to say."

"Thank you will suffice," Vance said as he shook Ramsay's hand, then moved away so the other Rogues Redeemed could approach to greet him.

Duval mused, "It's a miracle we all survived. Have each of you redeemed yourselves as we discussed that night while passing around bottles of bad brandy?"

"I think I have, rather belatedly." Ramsay pulled Signy against him. "Signy had much to do with my redemption."

Masterson put an arm around his splendid Amazon. "A remarkable woman like my Athena does so much to bring out the good in a man."

"And a good man can bring out the best of a woman," his wife said sweetly. "Though sometimes even the best of men need a bit of training."

After the laughter, Gordon asked, "What's this Fire Festival we've heard about?"

"It's quite jolly," Signy explained. "Groups of men carry torches through the streets singing a very old song in the Norn dialect. If you don't know the words, you can just hum along with the tune. The groups meet at the harbor and an effigy of a Viking is burned in a grand bonfire. Food and drink are involved. Everyone for miles around attends."

She smiled at the other women. "We frail females stay inside where it's warm and get to know one another better until the bonfire is lit."

Ramsay added, "Since it's the fall equinox and we're moving into the cold, wintry time of year, the fire symbolizes the light and warmth that will lead us through the dark toward spring."

"Good symbolism accompanied by a bonfire, food, and drink. What more do we need?" Gordon asked rhetorically as he caught his wife's hand. "Callie and I will thoroughly enjoy it!"

"We have another grand entertainment coming up." Ramsay clasped Signy's hands and looked into her warm golden eyes. "Signy and I are handfasted now. Sometime in the next few days, we'll have a grand formal wedding in St. Magnus Cathedral, and you're all invited!"

He leaned into Signy for a kiss, murmuring, "For once and always, my dear love."

She moved in so closely that she could feel the beat of his heart. "I love you, my laird but not my master." Then she kissed him back with an intensity that caused their friends to applaud.

The laird and his lady, together for always.

Author's Note

The Truth About Thorsay

Several years ago after speaking at the RNA conference in Leeds, England, I had the great pleasure of visiting Orkney and Shetland with my writer friend Patricia Rice and our husbands, the Mayhem Consultant and the IT Guy. Both island groups are wonderful places to visit, but Orkney in particular spoke to me and inspired the setting for this book.

Thorsay is a fictional archipelago that I placed between the real Orkney and Shetland in roughly the location of the real Fair Isle. Orkney has its own history and customs and laws, and creating my version of the islands gave me a great deal of freedom to combine different elements. Kelp burning was a real and profitable industry at the time this book is set, though a few years later the market collapsed when other materials were found for use in soaps and glass.

Orkney has the most extensive Neolithic ruins in Northern Europe, and amazing sites can be seen everywhere. Fiona Brae was inspired by the real Skara Brae, a collection of eight linked stone houses that were uncovered by the waves of a great storm in 1850. It's considered the most complete Neolithic village in Europe and is a UNESCO World Heritage Site, older than Stonehenge or the Egyptian pyramids.

Ship burials are scattered throughout Scandinavia and northern Britain. For the ship burial in this book, I borrowed freely from the Sutton Hoo ship burial in Suffolk, England. It was discovered in the early 20th century and is remarkable because it was never plundered, so it contained an amazing trove of objects.

Modern Orkney has many talented artists and jewelers, and Signy's painting was inspired by the wonderful tapestries, drawings, and paintings of the mother and daughter artists Leila Thomson and Jo Thomson. Their work is on display and for sale at the Hoxa Tapestry Gallery (https://www.hoxatapestrygallery.co.uk/).

Their stunning creations reflect the sea and sky and marvelous landscapes of Orkney, and I left with a number of prints of their work. I highly recommend a visit to the Hoxa Gallery if you're fortunate enough to visit Orkney.

I brought home some lovely silver Orkney jewelry as well! If you like such work, take a look at https://www.olagoriejewellery.com/. Ola Gorie's designs combine Celtic, Scottish, Viking, and contemporary elements, and more.

Another wonderful jeweler is Sheila Fleet (https://sheilafleet.com/), who happens to be the sister of Leila Thomson. They're a talented family, and all say they are inspired by the unique land they call home.

Acknowledgments

I want to give special thanks to our Orkney guide, Lorna Brown of See Orkney. A native of the islands, she did a warm and wonderful job of showing us the history and natural wonders of her amazing homeland.